To Gil:
With all my best,
affectionately,
Joe Ricapito

FRATELLI

a novel by

JOSEPH V. RICAPITO

Bloomington, IN Milton Keynes, UK

authorHOUSE®

AuthorHouse™
1663 Liberty Drive, Suite 200
Bloomington, IN 47403
www.authorhouse.com
Phone: 1-800-839-8640

AuthorHouse™ UK Ltd.
500 Avebury Boulevard
Central Milton Keynes, MK9 2BE
www.authorhouse.co.uk
Phone: 08001974150

First published by AuthorHouse 12/5/2007

ISBN: 978-1-4343-0310-3 (sc)

Library of Congress Control Number: 2007902125

Printed in the United States of America
Bloomington, Indiana

This book is printed on acid-free paper.

This book is dedicated to my grandfathers, Giuseppe Ricapito and Paolo Cervone; my father, Francesco Ricapito; and my uncles Giuseppe Cervone, Vito Cervone and Giovanni Mancini, all granite cutters.

PART I

She woke when a small stone bounced off the half-opened window of her room. With the sunlight streaming into the room, she slipped off the bed and went to the window. Below in the patio her father had been working for several hours. Filomena watched him as he circled the large granite block, his chisel in one hand, and the mallet in the other.

Mastro Paolo measured everything with his eyes, squinting to ward off the flying chips of stone. His hair and full, flowing moustache were thick with stone dust, and flecks of shiny rock glistened there. He moved slowly, his feet always knew where to be as he hit the stone. His chisel hand was strong and his grip had strengthened over the years. He never spoke when he worked and everyone knew not to bother him. At ten in the morning his sister, Maria, brought him a small cup of coffee which she placed near him and disappeared back into the house.

Filomena, still in her nightgown, watched until her Aunt Maria came in and shooed her away from the window. Since Filomena's mother died last year her aunt took care of her. The rough contours of a lion's head had begun to emerge from the stone. This lion would someday grace the entrance to a palace or a museum. As she dressed, Filomena could hear the blows of the hammer. Her day would be different from her father's or brothers'. At ten she would go to a neighbor's house where she would be taught to embroider and sew. After lunch she would go to Signora Gori's house for her mandolin lesson. She could hear the tap, tapping and the chips flying and hitting the windows, walls and the floor, as the lion emerged head first from the stone.

PART II

Gambalunga made sure everyone understood that things would begin on time. Mastro Paolo would sit on one side of the room and Signora Marta on the other. This was the first meeting of the prospective couple.

Gambalunga devoted herself to arranging marriages, among other things. She was considered the best at this of all her occupations. She did births, prepared bodies for burial and offered cures for sterility and impotence. She also carried secret messages between lovers. Gambalunga could be trusted to keep secrets, such as an unmarried daughter who became pregnant. She could even make the problem disappear, if it came to that. Her mouth was shut tight as a clamshell. Most important, she knew the best and the worst of human experience. She could look at a person and map the whole geography of that soul.

Gambalunga was a nickname but no one ever referred to her any other way. Her name meant long leg because in the course of a day she covered so much ground around town. She scurried from one task to another. When a priest walked through town carrying the communion wafer to a sick person, everyone knew his mission. When Gambalunga passed, a familiar silhouette in black dress and black kerchief, everyone knew that those swirling skirts were also on a special mission.

Calling upon Gambalunga was out of keeping for Mastro Paolo. He looked down on her and her activities. He was well-known for his probity, and, for this reason, people confided in him. Dealing with someone like Gambalunga meant that he lowered himself.

When he decided to turn to her, he sent his son Silvio with his request. Having someone of Mastro Paolo's stature request her services

3

lifted Gambalunga to a more respectable category. She chuckled to herself, her uneven, yellow teeth showing; she was no longer among the poor fisherman or the peasants who only came to town on special occasions and were easily identified by their country dress. Gambalunga was being summoned by one of the most respected citizens of the town, Giovinazzo, near Bari, and so she walked down the street with her grey, wispy knot of hair held high. She had no greetings for anyone.

At the door of Mastro Paolo's house she assumed the stooped posture of a weak person. Whatever he commanded, she would agree to with humility. Let him lead the way, she thought.

"You know my wife died more than a year ago." Mastro Paolo began once they sat down. "I have a family that needs the presence of a woman. Although my boys are grown, a woman is needed, especially for my daughter Filomena. She needs the hand of a woman, a woman who perhaps may be in a position similar to mine. Think about it and recommend somebody who would fit this situation without any great problems."

Gambalunga listened with understanding. She knew his situation. His daughter Filomena was young but soon she would be at the age when the juices flowed and the head could become confused. How easily a girl could go astray.

Mastro Paolo's wife, Adriana, had been a wonderful person. If Paolo was held in great respect it was due in some measure to his wife. When she was a child her parents came from Taranto to Giovinazzo. They were cloth merchants who knew it would take some time to be accepted in the town. They were careful not to disturb petty power structures. The townspeople had to know if her father could be trusted. Was his word to be taken seriously? And her mother, was she *seria* not a *pagliaccia*, empty headed, the potential disturber of family tranquility, the agent of passionate crime?

As Adriana grew up she made her way easily into the society that her parents occupied. She was counseled by Don Maggi, the parish priest and Sor Margherita, a nun whose knowledge of human life was well hidden under her wimple. Adriana received her religious direction from Don Maggi, but the practical advice came from Sor Margherita. Adriana was lucky to have such care.

Adriana was known by her teacher and her friends as something special. At fourteen, plans were being made for her future by everyone in their class. Without Adriana's knowledge, calculations were even being made about her potential dowry. An only child in a family of merchants should have houses and property.

One of those who planned was Mastro Paolo. He was the eldest son of a family of stone merchants. He would inherit the family business and his brothers would have to find their own way or work for him. One brother, Giuseppe, did not relish this prospect, and his mind became intoxicated with thoughts of going to South America, *l'America grande*, as they called it. One day he left for Argentina, and was never heard from again. It was as if he had disappeared into the jungle or fallen into the sea. Mastro Paolo became the anchor of the family. He could not fail. Too much depended upon him. A good match was a must so that all his work and sacrifice would not go to waste. Adriana became the focus of Paolo's parents' attention, and it was necessary to begin the process that could culminate in a marriage.

Adriana's mother died after suffering from strange fevers, which the doctors could not explain. It was one of those illnesses that resisted the cure of either mountain or seaside air. After a year she expired. Her father contacted Mastro Paolo's father about carving a monument for his wife. Mastro Paolo's father, Don Silvio, suggested that he send his son to Adriana's house with some plans for a monument. On such a task, Paolo certainly could not go dressed in his usual overalls. He dressed, shaved, and made himself appear very serious. During this visit, in which Paolo was in a nervous panic, Adriana was nowhere to be seen. Paolo laid out the monument designs for her father. In his grief, the father viewed them absent mindedly. Paolo at the end asked that Adriana look at them also, since, it was hinted tactfully, she would be around when both her mother and father were gone. Her father made no response, only nodding mechanically. Paolo said that he would return again to pick up his drawings and see if they had arrived at a choice of one. A short time later, he had made some changes in the original design and before doing the work he wanted her father to approve them. Paolo used the visit to announce to Adriana's father that he would be the one to do this job personally, out of respect for him and his family. The father nodded, but Adriana did not appear.

On one more visit to approve the final plans and designs, Paolo, desperate, insisted that Adriana also see the designs. Whether or not her father was aware of Paolo's intentions, he would never know. But with a certain amount of reluctance, which had more to do with his pride and authority—after all, he was going to decide, not Adriana—the father called her in. She came into the room, a sixteen-year-old beauty, fresh, modest, carefully guarded from life's ugliness. Fair and blonde, she was a clear descendent of the Normans who had come to occupy Puglia and left their mark in green or blue eyes and fair, pink complexions.

Their glances crossed. Paolo may have been the first man to get this close to her, since she lived in the protected atmosphere of the convent school. But his glance stuck like a seed in the ground.

After this, they noticed each other a few times. During the annual saint's day festival, the *Madonna di Corsignana*, the well-to-do townspeople got to carry the statue of the saint on their shoulders. The best-looking of their children, Adriana among them, formed a parade dressed as nuns who walked in the procession holding candles.

Paolo was afraid that Don Maggi and Sor Margherita had filled her head with so much religion that she seriously considered taking holy orders. That was a possibility but her glance told him that there could be a bond, if however tenuous. They were of the same social standing, so a marriage was possible. The first step, a casual meeting, was taken and now the matter would have to be carefully handled.

The gravestone was made and placed, leading to other casual meetings. The fathers, each individually, sensed that something was happening with the young people. But there was still a long way before it could become official.

In time the fathers sat down to discuss such a union. Paolo was considered a serious, purposeful man with a skilled trade—an artisan, the future owner of the family stone cutting business. Financially and economically the marriage was sound. Paolo seemed to have no particularly bad habits. He did not drink too much. He smoked only occasionally, as everyone else did. During the annual fair he met prostitutes that came from Egypt, but he did not make a habit of it. In view of his strong virtues, his vices were few.

Over time, the unspoken agreement of the fathers went into force. Finally, all of them met and officially declared that the two youths would marry. Paolo was overjoyed, and Adriana was also happy but began feeling nervous. She knew that in time she would become a mother and because of the modest manner in which she had been raised, that made her curious and uncomfortable. Sor Margherita would now have to prepare her for wifely and motherly duties. The news of their marriage agreement was greeted with general approval in the town.

———————

In time they married and had four children, three boys and a girl, Filomena. It was a modest family by most standards, and the voyage of life, as Don Maggi put it, had begun. Paolo ran the family stone cutting business which prospered modestly.

Some time later, Adriana began having fevers. These would trouble her for many years. Finally, after a bad spell she died leaving Paolo alone with their children. After a time he felt that he needed a companion, not only to warm his bed, but to be his friend and confidant. His children were hard workers and a tremendous source of pride, but he needed someone to whom he could open his heart. For that reason, he had asked Gambalunga to look into it. She knew immediately who was right for him.

Marta was the only daughter of a spice merchant. It was a profitable business, and he developed it wisely, making decisions such as the timely importation of spices. Business was such that it enabled him to employ his brothers. The merchant enjoyed the financial advantages that his enterprise brought him until one day he fell ill. It was a stroke, and he never woke again. His wife did not understand the ways of the business and depended upon her brothers-in-law. She hoped that she would continue to receive the profits from the business and she never thought it would be otherwise.

The brothers resented the fact that the business was owned by their oldest brother, and they did not share in the profits; they were merely employees of their brother. It's true that it was a job for them, but their wives envied *"La Signora,"* as people called her. Her daughter, Marta, dressed well, attended the best school, and accompanied her father and mother when they went abroad on business. She had been to Alexandria and London and had planned to go to Paris. Her aunts were green with envy.

The dead man's brothers got together and decided that they would do the unthinkable. A little at a time, *La Signora* saw profits dwindle. It was not like before where her every wish was satisfied—she had bought furniture from abroad and had the best cloth for her dresses. The brothers told her that business was bad. "How could it be?" *La Signora* asked. But matters worsened. In time she had to sell the house and the properties because she could not meet the bills for her way of life. She had gone from being in a position of relative wealth to being a person who had to watch her expenses carefully. Gone were the grand tours, the pretty dresses, the gold jewelry. She and her daughter had become impecunious. They were now regarded in the town as the fallen rich.

Her situation was saved by Mauro, a purveyor of food products, who proposed marriage to Marta. *La Signora* saw that although Mauro was not on Marta's level socially and in most other ways, he was economically stable. Mauro had accounts up and down the Adriatic. He seemed honest, sincere, hard working and was not bad looking. Marta and her mother were not concerned with love. They were worrying about where the next meal would come from. Marta and Mauro married and moved closer to Brindisi, and in time *La signora* heard that the brothers had the business flourishing. They lived in bigger and better houses. Their wives became *Le Signore* and hounded the poor domestics. The brothers had bought their sister-in-law off at a miserable price.

Marta and Mauro had a son and called him Giovanni, a lively, bright boy, full of imagination and energy. In those years something called Spanish influenza ravaged Europe. Mauro, who traveled a great deal, returned from a trip to Foggia and quickly died from this dreaded disease. The fact that people were dying by the thousands all over Europe was little consolation.

A relative of Mauro, who knew the business of food purveying, wanted to buy the business. The price he suggested seemed fair. At least, Marta thought, she would not be reduced to the kind of humiliation her mother had known.

Marta knew widows who spent the rest of their lives dressed in black and went through life alone. Marta, in spite of the bad luck she had, still felt young. Mauro had unlocked the desires of her heart. The thought that she would now be placed in a corner to watch time crawl by was not a happy one. This was the state of Marta's feelings when one day Gambalunga came to visit. Gambalunga had been there once before, to assist in Giovanni's birth. When Marta opened the door, she sensed what the old woman had in mind.

Gambalunga's proposal was not without its problems for Marta. Remarrying would not be easy, but she knew what lay in store for her, the dwindling of her money, the slow decline in status and various humiliations. However, what if there was another person who had the same experience as she, who felt that he still had a life to live? Gambalunga looked at her and said that she was still a young, attractive woman. She could provide a man with much comfort, give him another home and she would not spend the rest of her life drying up in a corner, never leaving the house. Everybody knew, she said, that Marta had a small nest egg but that wouldn't last forever.

Marta listened carefully and wondered who the man was. Gambalunga got up to leave and looked for a sign. "If you are interested," she said, "let me know. Send that fine boy down to my house if you think that you would like to consider the matter. Remember, there's a lid for every pot. Your friend Gambalunga will not let you down. Don't you think that your husband, may he rest in peace, would be happy knowing that you were not in need?"

Marta's only problem was trying to figure out who was the prospective suitor. There were several good possibilities and a few bad ones and some she would never consider. There were people so below her level that she preferred to die a widow rather than be tied to some *cafone*. Better to rot away in a black dress then to spend her life with the likes of some of them.

She had to admit that while she loved Mauro after a fashion and wished to be faithful to his memory, she recognized that her choice had been arranged and dictated by her mother. He had been good to Marta and his ambition and business acumen truly saved her and her mother's life. But she wanted more. Of course, Giovanni, her son, was her life now and would always be. She would always believe that he would be her support, but she still wanted a life. Marta spent many nights turning the matter over in her mind. Just as Mauro had saved her life once, perhaps another could do it again.

Giovanni had known the town his whole life and there wasn't a corner of it he didn't know. But still, going to Gambalunga's house, about which he had heard many stories, held a certain excitement. Marta gave him the message that she would consider the matter but without any commitments. She was to be free to drop the matter if she wished. Her reputation came first, she insisted that was most important. Giovanni rehearsed the message to himself as he walked through archways and down cobblestone streets and took a short cut through the cathedral. He arrived at Gambalunga's house, at the end of a very small alley near the harbor, known as "*dret a purt*," behind the port. It had an entrance of no particular distinction and the bricks were dark from the salty, moist air.

When Gambalunga answered the door, she stared at Giovanni, wondering who he was. Then she broke into a slow smile, showing her bad teeth. "Ah, from Marta. Come in, *ragazzo*, come in."

Giovanni looked around the dark room. Religious icons hung on the walls. There were figures of arms, fingers, and a leg all made of tin pinned to pictures of saints.. The house smelled stale, like something left cooking too long. He realized that perhaps it was Gambalunga herself who smelled.

"Yes, yes, Marta's boy." Giovanni stood straight and delivered his message, all in one breath.

"*Sì, sì*," she said nodding her head, "All right. I shall talk to your mother in a few days, maybe earlier. "Good." Giovanni sensed it was over, thanked her and left. He wanted to get away, get that acrid smell out of his nose. He ran down to the harbor to breathe the salt air and clean out his lungs.

Several days later Gambalunga came by and said that she, Marta and Mastro Paolo would meet in Marta's house. Everyone else, children, relatives and any other interested parties, were excluded.

When she heard his name, Marta was relieved. Mastro Paolo was a handsome man, solid in physique. Yes, she had known his dead wife, not well, but remembered her and her illness. He certainly was among those that she would consider.

As the day of the meeting drew near, Marta felt confused. She had no idea what she should do and how she should act. She didn't know what was expected of her. Why hadn't Gambalunga told her? All she knew was that she now had to be ready in her own house, for what she wasn't sure.

At the appointed time, Gambalunga came with Mastro Paolo. Once in the room, Gambalunga took the lead. She pointed to Marta and told her to sit in a certain chair. Mastro Paolo, who also seemed ill at ease, was directed to another chair. Silence. Gambalunga talked, looking straight ahead as if talking to no one in particular.

"We are here to talk about two fine people— *brava gente*. God's will has put a stop to some lives. Their consorts now live without the comfort of the spouse. Their lives have an emptiness and God will fill it. Let the parties speak of their lives." She paused and lowered her head piously. She was not praying. She thought for a moment about the money she would receive and that the fact that she was dealing with two good, socially respected people who would pay without complaint.

Mastro Paolo spoke first, noting how his wife's death had affected him and how in the aftermath he had not been able to reorder his life. He said he needed an anchor to which he could attach himself and his family. He wanted a woman who was serious and sensible, who would treat her child as his own and hoped she would open her heart to his children. As he spoke, she looked at his firm square forehead, the line of his hair, its fullness, his brush moustache. As he spoke, he gestured with his hand. She noticed he was still wearing his wedding band. Marta was not displeased by him. It was now her time to speak. She straightened up in her chair, and spoke slowly.

"I too have been shocked by my husband's death. It left me alone with my son, but as a person I am alone. I thought that if I found the right person I would try to have a new life. I hoped to find a person like my husband, someone balanced, serious, and hard-working. Yes, I could even see myself starting another family," and she added, "but for the right person. I have a thousand *lire* from the sale of my husband's business that I would bring to the marriage." She finished, sighed, and sat back.

Gambalunga stood up clasped her gnarled hands together prayerfully and spoke,

"It is now in the hands of God. Let Him show us the way." She remained a moment looking up in silence, bowed to them both, and then she and Mastro Paolo left.

Marta felt lighter. Mastro Paolo could be the right one. He had all the traits she was looking for: well respected in the town, industrious and thought of as a good provider. Yes, he could be the one.

A week later, after both parties had thought the matter over, they communicated their further interest to Gambalunga. Of course, she had a feeling and thought that all would be favorable between them. However, in the second stage the meeting would be different. The second time it was important to have the children of both parties present and that was what she ordered.

Marta's house was not that big, but she managed to drag some chairs from the basement and arranged one set on one side of the room and the other opposite it. In the middle sat tall, bony Gambalunga mediating the proceedings.

For Marta, her son Giovanni was a gift of God. He looked across the room. There staring at him were Silvio, Francesco, Paolo, and Filomena. Giovanni was about the same age as Paolo, and Filomena was their younger sister.

For Mastro Paolo, his children were a source of support, physical and otherwise. Mastro Paolo's sister, Maria, had carried a big part of the load of looking after the children. Although Filomena was still a child, she did whatever she could to help, but she was still going to elementary school.

Mastro Paolo was dressed in solemn black. It was the suit he wore at his wife's funeral, and he never stopped wearing that formal attire for any social appearance.

In spite of her feelings of loyalty to the memory of her husband, Marta could look at Mastro Paolo and see in him the man, the entrepreneur, the father, and she sensed in yet another way, the lover. His handsome face gave off a look of strength but with a touch of sensitivity. She could, yes, she would accept him as husband and lover and for a fleeting instant imagined the joining of their bodies. Yes, it had been a long time since she had felt passion. Marta had fought off such feelings as a widow in the name of wifely loyalty. She could be his spouse in spirit and flesh.

While Gambalunga spoke about the importance of family, Mastro Paolo's children looked at Giovanni. He was fourteen and lean. Silvio was the oldest of Mastro Paolo's sons. He was strong with large hands already molded by work. He wondered where Giovanni would fit into the family stone cutting business. Most probably he could be a granite cutter like everybody else.

Francesco, who was Mastro Paolo's second son, was neutral about Giovanni, but Paolo took an instant dislike to Giovanni. To Paolo he seemed like a *figlio di mamma,* a mamma's boy. Paolo had not had that luxury. Paolo tended to be overlooked in the family though in the workshop he felt he could hold his own with anyone.

Gambalunga finished her musings on the importance of marriage and the importance of closeness and even the greater importance of bringing different threads together in unity. Eventually all the strands would make a single rope. She enjoyed preaching to the gathering. She preened as she urged that the interested parties think the matter over well, look into their hearts and understand the stirrings they found there. They should consider all sides, but basically weigh the cost of loneliness. She stood up and strode around the room. She stood still a few seconds before she whispered "loneliness."

"Gambalunga," Mastro Paolo began, "you have been a part of the lives of most of our townspeople from birth to death. There is not a person that has not in some way passed through your hands. You have served us well and you have opened new thoughts to Signora Marta and me, about our lives and our futures, without ever forgetting the ones that God has chosen to take into His bosom. If Marta is willing, I accept her to share what is left of my life. I am convinced of her seriousness and her devotion. I accept her son as my own." Young Paolo felt a stab in his heart at these words. "And I will love him as if he were my own, just as I hope Marta will take my children to her heart and be the mother they no longer have."

Marta listened carefully to every word, sensing the sincerity behind each one. She felt some vague fears and in agreeing to a second meeting she could feel the noose of involvement grow tighter around her. But she heard nothing foolish nor did she perceive any insincerity or duplicity behind what he was saying. As Paolo spoke, the memory of her husband, all that he was and was not, faded. She could take Mastro Paolo to her heart. She could see herself talking to his children in a true motherly fashion. She nodded agreement to Gambalunga who, satisfied as a human being ever could be, looked up with her twisted smile and said,

"God himself could not be more pleased by what we have concluded today."

Paolo and Giovanni put down their tools in the quarry when Silvio signaled that lunch time had arrived. Paolo shook off the small stone chips that were on his overalls, and all the other stone cutters did the same. A fine powder covered their faces and hair, and tiny pieces of stone were caught in the matted webbing of moustaches and beards.

Giovanni went to the horse-drawn wagon that would take them back home. Further down the road, they would pick up Francesco. On the wagon they spoke very little, especially today when they had to discuss some important things with their father. The wagon bounced along the dirt road and birds went scattering out of the brush as they passed. The squeaky wheels churned out a tune. Outside town giant fig trees spread their branches like wings. The dryness that gave them life had contorted them into desiccated, twisting shapes. In the early spring, blooming almond trees bore white puffs like snow on their branches but that time had passed and dust and grass accumulated at the foot of the trees. Further beyond, olives loaded the tree branches. At maturity, they would fall to the ground and machines would make of them, thick, smoke-colored oil. God had been good to Giovinazzo but a little more rain might have made a better gift. Coming into town, the wagon swept past street corners to let off workers here and there. At Via Piano 42, the brothers jumped out. Filomena was at the door to give each of them a damp cloth to wipe their faces and hands

After he cleaned up, Giovanni walked in the patio, kicking aside pieces of granite that had not been swept up from his father's morning work. Giovanni ran his hand over the sharp edges of a horse his father was carving. It would be Giovanni's job later to smooth them, just as it was his job to do the letters on monuments and tombstones and to use his skill on fine details such as decorative cornices.

When Mastro Paolo finally emerged from cleaning up after work, everyone came to the table. Marta, his wife, ladled out thick soup. The wine they drank was squeezed from the grapes that grew on the hillside. The bread they had baked was sliced thickly, long spears of hard crusted bread.

After dinner, Silvio made a sign to his *fratelli*, and they disappeared into the parlor. Mastro Paolo sat at the table waiting for the soft torpor to come over him, from the combination of the morning's vigorous work and the deep red wine, so he could close his eyes for a few minutes before going back to his task of carving the horse.

"Pappa, could we talk for a few minutes?" Silvio asked.

"You can talk. There is no law against talking in this house."

"Pappa, let's go inside the living room and talk."

"Why can't you talk here at the table?"

When Silvio did not answer, Mastro Paolo realized this was something important. This kind of gathering usually meant bad news. The parlor was used for serious talks and wakes for the dead. He held his breath for a moment and rose up slowly, hitching his belt in his fingers. He strode to the parlor.

Francesco, Paolo and Giovanni sat in the room, their strong, calloused hands folded in their laps. Their stern faces were washed and their bristly hair was parted and combed instead of matted down by a work hat.

"All right," Mastro Paolo said gruffly, "What's this all about?"

Silence for a minute. Then Silvio spoke up.

"Pappa, since the end of the war we seem to be working harder and making less money. Stone work goes elsewhere, but here we keep high prices, and the stones and blocks are piling up. Who is going to buy our work?"

Mastro Paolo said nothing. Silvio was merely reciting back to his father all that he heard his father say so many times after meals. When Mastro Paolo was young, his work, stone cutting and stone carving, came from consignments that he received. These consignments sat on a table in Mastro Paolo's room, held down by a paper weight of a bronze tiger, tense and ready to spring. Orders for work had come from Liverpool, Alexandria, Budapest, Zagreb, and when finished they were shipped out in large crates from the ports of Bari, Monopoli and Brindisi.

"You don't say anything, but if the orders don't come in, how do we eat? You think I don't know that you keep taking money from the bank? You hope that the lions, stones, blocks of granite you keep in the warehouse will be sold, and once again we will have money. You are making the Banker Maldoni rich with the interest you pay on the loans. You even sold that piece of beautiful land outside town, rich with vines and olive trees. That was to be Filomena's dowry. Now what has she got?"

He hoped Filomena did not hear, but she did. She had learned very early that there were momentous decisions made in that room and being in the kitchen nearby you could hear what went on.

"You want us to stay, Mastro Paolo, I know, because you feel strong with all of us here together. But now we are too many, too many arms that may have nothing to do and too many mouths with nothing to eat."

Mastro Paolo still said nothing. He could not imagine himself without his sons.   Whenever a problem came up it was Silvio or Francesco who were dispatched to take care of it and Mastro Paolo knew that matters were in good hands. Silvio helped take the weight of many cares off his shoulders. After Silvio, he took his other sons, first Francesco, then Paolo, then Giovanni, and to each one he taught the gift of a special skill: Silvio, the careful cutting of stone; Francesco, delicate and complicated cornices; Paolo, the decorated capitals of pillars; Giovanni, the art of making letters, well-proportioned and exact, the turns and corners of each number, the curl of a rose petal.

Neither Silvio nor Mastro Paolo wished to say what both were thinking: that his sons would have to leave Giovinazzo and go out into the world to earn money and send some of it back. From Liverpool he received letters saying that stone cutters in England and Germany were closer and therefore less costly. He viewed every newly arrived letter from abroad with alarm. The pile of orders, correspondence, became less and less, fewer and fewer, and the bronze, tensed tiger paper weight became heavier and heavier with nothing under it. Soon he feared the bronze tiger would sleep on the slick lacquered table.

Silence. A long pause. Throughout all of this, Francesco, Paolo and Giovanni said nothing; Silvio was the spokesman.

In the other room, Marta, Mastro Paolo's wife and Filomena sat quietly in the kitchen where they could hear everything. They said nothing. When Filomena's nervous fingers made noise with the noon dinner's table service, her mother threw her an angry glance. Soon they would be without the men, she was thinking. Filomena would be without Giovanni who was the only brother who played games of hide and go seek with her. Although Filomena was younger than Giovanni, she felt a special kinship with him, thanks to his warmth and kindness. With Silvio, Paolo and Francesco there was a more formal kind of affection. They acknowledged her, they tweaked her nose on occasion but rarely more than that. It was Giovanni who showed her the stars and told her a story about each one.

"I'm afraid there is no choice, Pappa," Silvio broke the silence. Mastro Paolo remembered how the Widow Magdalena used to speak of her husband who had gone to San Francisco in America only to die there, leaving his body to foreign worms; or the Widow Teresa, whose husband went to Australia and was never heard from again. Mastro Paolo had been to other parts of Europe, Albania and Greece when he needed to. But unlike some of his townsmen who went to America he always came back to find his house clean and neat and filled with honor.

His title "Mastro" came from the fact that he was an acknowledged master stone cutter, but also because he had earned enough money to be comfortable, not needing any longer to travel abroad. In the town everybody knew that he was well off, and this conferred a kind of honor.

Now his sons would go. Without saying anything, Mastro Paolo merely nodded, then got up and walked out.

One by one the brothers walked into the kitchen, stood around and then one by one they prepared to return to the quarries to work. As Giovanni came out of the room, his face grave and beautiful, Filomena ran to him and gave him some fruit which he put in his shirt. He leaned down and hugged and kissed her. He wondered what new story he would make up for her to remember before he left.

Silvio and his brothers waited for the cart to come by, and when it did they jumped on, and Giovanni looked back to Filomena who was standing at her window recalling a story he told her about gypsies that came and kidnapped children, he said, "Look out for the gypsies, Filomena, look out."

PART III

Slowly, Bari became smaller and smaller in the distance as the boat chugged out of the harbor. Silvio, Francesco, Paolo, and Giovanni, all dressed in austere black suits, leaned against the railing, watching the shore until Mastro Paolo and the women disappeared from sight. Then all that was left was the water, as the ship steered south, headed for the open sea.

On the ship, swabbies mopped up the water that rose over the sides. The sea was like a blue carpet that rose and fell. Giovanni knew that if the sea wanted, it could swallow them whole, boat and all, and no one would ever see them again. Then he felt a sick lurch inside and vomited until it felt as though there was nothing left inside of him. Francesco and Paolo laughed as Giovanni doubled up in paroxysms of gagging.

And that is how the trip went until they arrived in Alexandria, Egypt, a city that was alive with activity. Each street was crowded with shops; not even shops, they were holes in the wall from which each entrepreneur haggled and bedeviled customers and prospective customers. The wares flowed out the front of each shop: rugs, furniture, pottery, bird cages, copper and brass.

Rather than streets there were warrens of alleys, one disappearing into another. Men in caftans walked the streets. Occasionally, a person with a veiled face would walk by. Some men wore business suits, but the cut of the cloth was foreign.

Mules plodded along the streets dropping their manure in piles which people avoided. The mules carried everything. Atop their backs objects rose up in a pyramid. A man walked along, snapping at a train of mules with a whip to keep them going. People turned and twisted to avoid being brushed by the mules. Some mules carried leather hides on their backs either going to or returning from the tannery. The noises rose and fell. Voices rose in anger and were punctuated by gestures and stamped feet. The brothers looked on in amazement. Everything was a marvel to them. In one stall a man sat with his legs bent. He etched an arabesque on a large brass tray, holding it in place with both his big toes. His hands moved swiftly over the brass face of the tray and where his fingers passed lines appeared, tortuously twisting and turning in a series that never ended.

In another stall a stone cutter carved Arabic letters on stone. The brothers understood nothing of the letters. Giovanni, who was the expert letterist, watched him carefully the way one watches a competitor. He saw how he chose his scalpel, then struck with the mallet and deftly brushed away the chips and powder with his scalpel hand. He looked up at Giovanni who looked intently back at him. Giovanni's fingers itched as he watched. Francesco and Paolo listened to the voices all around them speaking a language they did not understand. Fresh off the boat, they were excited by the atmosphere and activity.

They finally wrenched Giovanni away from the stone cutter and continued trying to find the address of the employment agent. In and out of alleys, up some streets, down others, they followed a rough map a policeman had drawn for them. They went to the building that was indicated to them. In the office they asked for Attilio Perrini, *agente*. The clerk was sleepy-eyed and indolent. Francesco spoke Italian to him but was not sure if the clerk, swarthy and short with heavy-lidded eyes, understood him. He looked for a long time at the slip of paper with the name "Perrini, Attilio" written in bold letters. He nodded, turned and disappeared behind a cloth curtain. They seemed to be thinking, what if after all the time, trouble and money, there was no job, or worse, no Perrini? They waited. Then the curtain whipped open and a short, fat man with curly hair, a trimmed moustache and a pince-nez appeared. He said in a clipped Italian, "Perrini, Attilio. At your service." Francesco knew immediately that he was not from the south, in fact, his accent seemed not to be from any particular place. Giovanni and Paolo had also picked up on this.

"My brothers and I were told that you need stone cutters here in Alexandria. We've come all the way from Bari, Italy."

"Yes, yes," he nodded but then looked up with a sigh of desperation. "So many come but they do not really want to work. They fight and bicker. Their work is not always good."

He shook his head. The moustache was perfumed and Perrini's hands were soft and pudgy. Paolo rubbed his own calloused fingers together.

"We have always worked. We are skilled stone cutters, and my brother Giovanni is a skilled carver. I can assure you that there have never been any complaints about our work."

Francesco didn't tell him that they worked for their father and that the family business had all but failed. Perrini waited, his pudgy hands clasped together on his vest. He reminded Giovanni of a woman. In a wig, he would have passed perfectly for a middle-aged woman.

"There is work, you see. They are building here, large, stone buildings. You have to know what you are doing."

"How much do you pay?" Francesco asked. "Twenty drachmas an hour," Perrini curtly answered. "How much is that in *lire*?" Perrini turned his face and gestured from side to side: "A *lira*, maybe two an hour." How could they send money home with those wages Francesco thought. That was barely enough to live on here, and Francesco told him so. "What can I do?" Perrini said, looking up plaintively. "That's what they pay," and his voice trailed. "Of course there is the agent's fee." The phrase seemed to slide from his lips, disappearing quickly in the air. "An agent's fee?" Francesco asked, "How much?"

"Three lire per week per worker."

"Damn! You pay wages that we would only pay slaves in Italy and on top of that you want a fee?"

Perrini's fingers drummed a tune on his vest. "Those are the conditions," he said. Francesco motioned to his brothers, and they stepped aside to speak. They had heard that wages were higher than those in Bari. But what else could they do? There was nothing else to do but accept, at least for the moment, until something else came up.

"Tell us where we are to go, and we'll be there," Francesco said.

"The National Palace, behind the Ministry of Justice. Be there at 6:30 in the morning," he said. "And gentlemen," he smiled in a squinting way, "the agent's fee is payable in advance or...or...there is no work." Paolo wanted to step behind the counter and give him a hard kick. He wanted to do something to that round ball of fat, so oily and cunning. Francesco paid but not without a very long and hard look as the lire fell into Perrini's fat hand one by one. Francesco was sure he was not Italian. What could he be? As they turned Perrini called out: "Where are you staying? Do you have a hotel? I have a good friend who has a boarding house for workers. It's reasonable."

He passed Francesco a card with the name *Pensione Montalba*, Prop. Enrico Ragni. Francesco shook his head. Another person with an Italian name but where did these people come from? "We'll look into it," he said, and they filed out the door.

"Caspito! If we had stayed at home we could probably be ahead." Francesco said. "We don't know anybody, nobody knows us. We can't even understand the fellow kicking the mule that just passed by. At this rate, it will take years to send enough money home to do any good. But we are here. Let's see what we can do to work and start saving money. The first thing we have to do is find a place to stay." Francesco feared that they would be exploited again.

The Ragni boarding house was a modest house. They would all occupy the same room, which was not particularly big. The proprietor claimed that the food was the best to be found in all of Alexandria. The brothers found the price to be reasonable. There were rules: No noise, night or day. No gatherings of any kind—you know, *paesani* that get together to play cards and talk. "No women" said Ragni very sternly. "My wife and daughter live here too." There was to be no lack of decorum. This was his home and it would be regarded as such. Food was served promptly at 6:00 A.M., 2:00 P.M. and 8:30 P.M. "Even if you come a minute after, you don't get served. No guests for meals unless I am advised ahead of time and the price is to be paid in advance." One by one, Ragni read these rules to them. After a while Paolo stopped listening. "To hell with it," he thought. "I no longer care what he thinks. I'll do as I please."

Their life was work, work, and work. Leave the boarding house, go to work, return for dinner, back to work, return for supper, back to work and return at night. In the evenings they walked the streets, looking at rugs they would never buy, fingering cloth, trays, and slippers. They came to know the streets by heart and the shopkeepers as well. In one café, they treated themselves to a coffee and that was their only luxury.

Every cent after their expenses was to be sent home. There were no luxuries.

After they were there several weeks, someone spoke of the *Circolo Italiano d'Allessandria*. Like everything else in Alexandria the title gave them a picture of something lavish. It was in reality a large, dirty room in an old building. Chairs were arranged against the walls and the floor was full of cigarette butts. Francesco wondered when it last had been swept. On that particular night they were the first to arrive. They waited, no one saying anything and then one by one people started filing in. This one from Naples, a carpenter, another one from Palermo a cook, this one from Salerno, a mason, another from Rome, a civil servant. They sat around, without a particular agenda, just talking about whatever came up. Francesco and his brothers said that they were stone cutters from Bari looking for work so they could send money home to their family.

They each spoke about home and what they missed most. Now was the time for the olive harvest; or today there was a feast day in their town. They spoke of sick relatives in Italy dying or maybe already dead. They could not know because of the distance. Now the figs would be at their ripest. Paolo smiled as a man spoke about black figs, his hands turning around in the air. They also spoke about Alexandria, the power of the French, the power of the English. The Italians had a colony but they had no real power. The city was filled with men like the Perrinis and Ragnis, all living like parasites off the immigrant laborers. There was no real power in Italian hands.

The door opened and a large man dressed in a white suit came in. Someone pushed forward a chair. He took off his hat, wiped his brow, greeted all and noticed Silvio and his brothers.

"New ones?" he asked between huffs and puffs.

"From Bari," Francesco answered.

"Where are you working?"

"We are stone cutters working on the National Palace."

"Ah yes, the National Palace. Who sent you there, that pig, Perrini?"

"Perrini was the agent, yes."

"That pig, Perrini, sends them to these jobs like sheep. Perrini gets rich while we all break our asses."

He used the word pig so many times that Francesco started counting them. The fellow was Giovanni Cicogni, a teller in a bank, a man of political ideas. Politics was something that never entered the mind of Silvio and his brothers. For them politics were made in Rome, their life was back in Bari and that life revolved around cutting stone. Cicogni's eyes glistened when he spoke about politics. He knew the politics of Rome and worked for an Italian bank branch in Alexandria. He knew everyone in Alexandria or at least knew something about the most important people of the city. Through his hands passed, he said, all the business affairs of the city. That is why he knew so much about Perrini. Cicogni handled all of Perrini's dealings personally with the president of the bank.

There were two groups of Italians in Alexandria. First, the workers like Francesco, his brothers and Cicogni who came there hoping to find a way of surviving. The second was a colony of Italians whose forebears came there decades ago. They intermarried with more powerful families and groups, and in this way they established businesses. This is how Perrini became established. He was the third generation in Alexandria. He went back to Italy on his honeymoon years ago and that was the closest tie he had with Italy. Thanks to powerful friends close to the Egyptian king, Perrini got the lucrative job of obtaining workers for building projects. He kept an office with connections to Milan, Rome, Naples, and Palermo and he paid the agents in Italy a small fee from the money he took locally every week.

Cicogni spoke well and glibly about politics. He spoke of strikes, organization, labor, capital, management, and the corporate state. It all seemed incomprehensible to Silvio and his brothers. Cicogni wanted to see the workers banded together to get higher wages, and if the owners did not yield, then they would shut down the building projects. Only the Italians, he argued, were prepared to do the special work on the buildings. The Egyptians that worked on these projects did the manual labor. The Italians could halt work on these jobs in a day. His dream was to strike, then drag Perrini down there and cut off his balls. Perrini was Cicogni's constant obsession. Cicogni spoke about his friends in Rome who were Socialists, and at that point he pulled out a page from a newspaper that was folded in his pocket. It had become greasy with handling but he opened it and pointed to a writer's name. They had gone to school together. A big man, he said, a very big man.

The truth was that most workers in Alexandria did not understand anything about politics. There was Rome and then there were the priests, and the priests had their own politics. All the workers wanted to do was work, save money, send it home, and to hell with all the rest. Cicogni could talk until he was blue in the face about labor and capital; as long as they worked, that was all that counted. It was talk; that's all it was. Most of them figured that if Cicogni had any real brains he would get his foot in the door somewhere like Perrini and make a lot of money. Perrini was hated because he made a lot of money and turned his back on the workers he exploited.

There were many, many nights that Silvio and his brothers went to the Circolo; there were few other distractions. Occasionally they saw street performers. One man charmed a snake, another broke chains around his chest and one did imitations. When the hat was passed to them, they turned away.

Giovanni wondered about the women of Alexandria, particularly Ragni's daughter who never said anything to him or any other boarder. She ignored them completely. Ragni's wife was matronly and haughty, maintaining a reserve toward the boarders as if they were unwanted outsiders. She felt that keeping a *pensione* was beneath her dignity. Like Perrini, the Ragnis were descendants of earlier Italian immigrants who had lost all real contact with Italy. Both Ragni and his wife jealously guarded their daughter, Anna. She had dark hair, brown eyes and moved lightly with an elegance her mother had drummed into her. At night Giovanni would imagine Anna asleep in her room which was at the far end of the *pensione*—to be sure, the farthest room of the *pensione*. He imagined her lying in bed with her breasts spilling out of the nightgown. He thought and thought about it—if not the daughter, then the mother who was attractive in a buxom way.

There were prostitutes in Alexandria, all kinds and all colors. Cicogni told him of a whorehouse run by a French Madame where the girls were young and the price reasonable. Cicogni had a French favorite named "La Belle," and every payday he visited her. When he talked about it his eyes lit up. Giovanni wanted to go but that cost money and the brothers had promised themselves that every *lira* earned would be sent home.

Francesco warned him that Anna wasn't interested in anyone like Giovanni. They would never consent to her having interest in an immigrant worker so he had better forget about it, Francesco said.

Ragni ruled over the *pensione,* noting who entered and who left and when. He knew at all times where his wife and daughter were. If a boarder went to the bathroom which was in the corridor that eventually led to Ragni's own rooms, Ragni would peer out of his room and take careful notice that the boarder went back to his room. Ever vigilant as he was over the virtue of his daughter and the honor of his wife, Ragni hovered, guarded, and took careful note of everything that went on in the house. This only piqued Giovanni's curiosity. There were times when Giovanni crossed the daughter's path in the narrow corridor, sometimes feeling her brush against his shirt.

Giovanni knew that the daughter stepped out occasionally during the day. One Saturday he followed her down to the market place She had some bundles and waited impatiently for the errand boy to carry these back to the boarding house. Giovanni walked by and stopped as if surprised to see her standing there. In a courteous manner he asked if she needed help. She tried to dismiss him with an indifferent look, but it was the first time she ever really looked at Giovanni's face with its sensitive lines, almost feminine, his blue eyes and dark blond hair. His eyes swept quickly over her lovely bosom. As they neared the boarding house, her father stepped forward, his jowls shaking, and took the packages from Giovanni. He muttered, "I can take that. Where's the boy I sent to help you?" His daughter shrugged indifferently. Giovanni repeated this for a few Saturdays. Then came the time when they paused a moment before turning the last corner into their street. She mentioned that at night before going to sleep she liked to step out to the balcony and look at the stars.

The next night Giovanni climbed to the roof of the house next door, and jumped the short distance between the buildings. It was dark but the moon and a street light helped him find his way around the rooftop toward the balcony. A gutter led down the corner of the wall. Giovanni clung to it as he shinnied down the drain.

The terrace had been built by Ragni so he and his family could eat there on cool days. In the middle of the terrace was a table with four chairs and along the two walls were numerous plants. Giovanni stood behind a large plant, covered completely by its foliage. About ten o'clock a door squeaked open, and a figure in a nightshirt with long flowing hair peered out into the night.

Giovanni waited. He could hear her humming a tune. He glided, catlike, from behind the plant and whispered, *"Mia cara*, it is me, Giovanni." The nightshirted figure jumped and screamed. It was the mother. Giovanni froze in fear. The mother stood rooted to the floor, still screaming. Lights from nearby homes flashed on. Giovanni leaped out onto the drainpipe to escape, and it ripped from the wall. He clung to it as it crashed down on the table, scattering the chairs helter-skelter. The woman kept screaming. Ragni rushed out in a nightshirt. He carried a broomstick and his porcine face was flushed. He saw the overturned table, the body lying by it. He began to beat Giovanni furiously. Giovanni rolled himself into a ball trying to protect his head. A crowd formed below in the street and high-pitched whistles sounded as the police arrived. Ragni whipped Giovanni as the shrill cries of his wife continued. When the police came and rescued him, Giovanni was cut and bleeding. Ragni saw that it was one of his boarders and screamed "Thief, burglar, rapist. You'll pay dearly for this." Ragni's daughter, in her nightshirt, cowered in a corner as they hustled Giovanni off to jail. Francesco watched, unable to help. He could only follow the police who dragged his younger brother along.

Ragni used his influence to see to it that the rule that food could be brought from outside to prisoners was cancelled for Giovanni. He would have to subsist on bread and water. Francesco devised a plot by which food would be raised up to Giovanni through his barred window. He enlisted the help of Varola, the Piedmontese, who was nicknamed St. Christopher because of his great height. Paolo stood on Varola's shoulders like a trapeze artist and Francesco passed up the food. The bread slid through the bars easily enough as did the wine, so did the veal kabobs. The spaghetti was another thing. Paolo gingerly picked it up with his fingers and passed it carefully through the bars to Giovanni who collected it as best he could, transferring it to a plate. Strands fell, some on Varola's shiny black hair, one strand draped over his fine, aquiline beak. When the guards caught on to this trick, Giovanni was transferred to an inner cell.

On the day of the hearing, Marcello the lawyer, an Italian originally from Genoa, said, without any true conviction in his voice, that Giovanni had heard steps on the roof. Thinking that it was a thief, the hero had decided to take the law into his own hands and pursued him. How sad and ironic it was, Marcello concluded, that this Good Samaritan was beaten and jailed.

The judge listened to both sides. and ruled that it was not conclusive that Giovanni was there to steal. Was there perhaps a romantic interest, a young lady boarder in the house? Ragni's face flushed a deep crimson. "My daughter," he screamed out. The judge hit his gavel to maintain order. Ragni sat fuming. The judge considered the situation—a young man, a beautiful young girl. He decided that Giovanni was not guilty of attempted robbery, but certainly guilty of trespassing beyond the part of the house that was rented to him. He would be fined and turned over to the immigration people since he was a foreign worker. The immigration official, an old friend of Ragni, urged that he be deported as an undesirable. The judge agreed, but Ragni was not completely satisfied. He would rather the young lout had been flogged and then hung. The lawyer Marcello stared grimly at Giovanni and his brothers, the fear of not being able to collect his fee etched on his face.

Once the lawyer's fee was paid, Francesco bought passage for the three of them back to Giovinazzo. They had little money to show for their Oriental journey.

PART IV

Most men in Giovinazzo who had nothing else to do just stood around at the café, if not there, in front of the church of Sant'Agostino. People talked about what had happened yesterday, last year and in the last decade. What might happen tomorrow was not a topic because the future looked bleak and uncertain.

One man was called the Undertaker because he was always dressed up. The Undertaker exuded an air of importance and when he walked, he waddled. He was a factotum in City Hall. If you needed a birth certificate or had to pay a tax, you saw The Undertaker. He carried a row of pens in his jacket pocket. They were in all colors and looked like a rainbow. One day, Paolo reached to borrow one and found out that it was only the top of the pen.

The Corpse, named for his pale, gaunt look talked with several *paesani* gathered around him. He told about Gaetano, the son of Pietro, the ditch digger, who had come back from America. Gaetano came back wearing a dapper dark suit, he had his hair plastered down and had grown a moustache. He had worked on a big building cutting stone and made enough money to come back home, this time to get married and bring a wife back to America.

Listening to these stories made the men wonder. Alexandria was the farthest away most of them had been. They talked as though they had seen everything, but in their hearts when they listened to Gaetano who had been to America, they marveled. They heard about the big buildings in New York City, the port as wide was the ocean itself and the strange people Gaetano had seen. Jews! Where had they ever seen Jews? Not even in church did they talk about Jews. If they ever did, they would call them Christ Killers. According to Gaetano, the Jews were vendors, who traveled about with their wares on their backs. They had long beards and looked like pictures of the Patriarchs. There were also Turks there who would carry a tank of lemonade on their backs, selling it for a penny a cup. Americans seemed to bark, not talk; at least, that was the way it seemed to Gaetano. but "America, America," he said, *"Com'è bella l'America!* How beautiful America is."

Mastro Paolo did not react when the brothers told him that they thought it might be a good idea to go to America and try to make some money. Again, Silvio spoke for all the brothers, giving further reasons why it would be good to go: the family business kept going down; the requests for cut stone, for buildings or for decoration, became fewer and fewer. "Lucky for us," he said, "the house and the property are all paid for, the stone cutting equipment also. If the business goes to hell, all we would have to do is send money home for you and the others to live on."

As he spoke, a cloud of sadness came over their father's face. He looked at his hands which had carved figures and cornices for churches the world over and tombstones for his friends, their parents, and even their children. What would he do with these hands?

Silvio was convincing. The other brothers sat stone-faced waiting to hear Mastro Paolo's response. Marta was ready to cry. Her sons with their strength and energy had made their parents feel strong. Thank God, her husband had been a good provider but her sons, her beautiful sons, with their bronzed faces and their feet moving surely around the stone yard; they were necessary for her very life.

The next day Mastro Paolo went to see the Banker Maldoni. He was, after all, talking about buying four tickets to America, sailing from Naples. He could afford to pay for it all but the Banker Maldoni advised against it. He suggested that Master Paolo pay for one ticket and borrow the money for the other three, this way he did not have to dip into his capital. Mastro Paolo realized that the Banker Maldoni would make his money on the interest. Mastro Paolo was no fool and besides he didn't want the banker to think that he couldn't afford to spend the money, so he laid it out for the four tickets. The banker handed them over in a big envelope.

Leaving the family in tears, the brothers said goodbye one more time. Giovanni was especially tender with his sister. He knew he would miss Filomena a lot.

———————————

The train rattled along towards Naples, where they would embark on the boat to New York. There they would be met by Gaetano's brother who would help them get settled. Paolo was smart enough to have brought along a deck of cards. Out came the coins as they played games of *scopa*, *briscola* and *tresette*. But even that became boring and they just sat looking out the windows at the green landscape of Puglia.

They arrived at night. Their father had warned them to beware of Neapolitans. They would steal the shirt off your back if you gave them the opportunity, he said, so they walked along the street carrying their belongings. Four workers together, they went down the Via Roma hearing the Neapolitans make cracks about immigrants with their baggage tied up with cord. But the Neapolitans were not going anywhere; they watched others leave their misery behind them as they crowded onto ships, rushing for fear of being left behind. The Neapolitans felt a certain sorrow mixed with envy watching them climb the gangplank. The children gripped onto their mothers' skirts, their faces full of wonderment and surprise. The fact that they were peasants was made obvious by their humble clothing and by how thriftily they traveled.

The toot of the ship's whistle told the brothers that they were about to begin a new life, that they were never going to be the same again. Even if they came back with their tails between their legs, they would at least have seen a new world.

There was an unexpected problem—Giovanni was not able to get on the boat, he got no further than the immigration building on the dock. There a health official examined him, declared that he had tuberculosis, and denied him an exit document. In spite of this, the other brothers decided to continue on to America. Giovanni would have to return home alone.

PART V

Coming off the boat in New York City, the three brothers were wide-eyed, trying to take everything in with one sweeping look. The confusion was incredible: children screamed, people waved at relatives, small trucks honked and manoeuvered in the crowd, sailors loaded coal, tugboats passed dragging boats and carters hammered at dockside ignoring the people who embraced and cried.

There were many scenes of wives reunited with their husbands. The women had feared that when their men went to America they would forget their Italian families and start new lives with pink-faced American wives who couldn't cook. Their tears were of relief. They had pictured themselves arriving and finding no one to meet them.

Gaetano's brother was there as arranged. He had borrowed a horse drawn cart. The baggage was loaded on, strapped down with rope, and they all piled in and rattled off on cobblestone streets. Large wagons hogged the road, so small carts like theirs couldn't go very fast. Everywhere the brothers saw giant buildings and electric activity. Twisting and turning like an ant in its burrow, the cart finally came to rest at an old building. The address was 80 Mulberry Street. All around were stores with signs in Italian. The brothers almost felt as though they hadn't left Italy at all. Everywhere they turned they saw people who looked Italian. In the stores giant, waxy *provoloni* hung like chandeliers alongside the mortadelle, salami, capocolli and all the rest. They heard two women having a noisy argument. At least, Francesco thought, we can understand the language, remembering their misadventures in Alexandria.

Gaetano's brother brought them to an apartment that was dark and not very clean. It cost a dollar fifty a week per person, he said. The best deal you can get. The brothers looked around at the beds, which were really cots with blankets on them. There was nothing on the walls, no paintings, certainly no sculptures like there were at home. Gaetano's brother sensed that the house was a disappointment.

He shrugged—"Look, what do you want from me? My brother told me to look after you, to try to have something here waiting for you. You want something more deluxe? Later when you start making more money you can move."

"No, no," Francesco said. "It will do for now, and we thank you for the trouble." Gaetano's brother seemed pacified. The next day the brothers lugged out their tools and with yet another *paesano* this time, Gennaro, the son of Mastro Gabriele who had left Giovinazzo two years earlier, they took the subway for the first time. Paolo marveled at the tile walls, decorated cornices and trains that came thundering into the station. Out to the Bronx they went, none of them was used to traveling so far to get to work. In Giovinazzo and Alexandria they lived right by the stone yard. Gennaro explained that it was not likely to have a stone yard right in the middle of the city. Stone yards in New York City were to be found next to cemeteries, and the cemeteries were outside the city in Queens or the Bronx.

On the long trip they had short snoozes. Francesco picked up a newspaper that someone had left behind. He looked at the strange letters and tried to pronounce them. They made no sense to him. He ran letters and sounds together. It sounded like the unsure steps of a skater sliding from one side to the other. He shook his head. He never did learn Arabic or French when he was in Alexandria and probably wouldn't learn English either. At the far end of the car were two men having a long and complicated conversation in Italian. He looked at their hands which were large and strong. *Muratori*, plasterers, he thought, with clothes always speckled by cement and plaster. They had the rubicund complexion of those, who, like the brothers, worked outside in sun, cold, and wind. Italians seemed to be everywhere but there were others on the train, Chinese, he thought, with high cheek bones and narrow eyes.

At the stone yard the brothers were introduced by Gennaro to the foreman. He was not Italian but he seemed to understand what Gennaro told him. He told the brothers, "The wage is daily, you don't come to work, you don't get paid. You miss two days in a row, you lose your job. No sneaking breaks. You don't go behind the stones to snatch a bite to eat. Lunchtime is a half hour. You don't have to join the union if you don't want to. Any questions?" They looked at each other and nodded their heads and they agreed to the terms. The foreman took each one to a work place and told him to start working on a job, Silvio, a large block of granite, Francesco got a granite tombstone, Paolo some cornices. There wasn't anything there they had not done before.

And so it began. Each day the long trek to the Bronx and home, day in and day out. At night they stopped by a store to pick up some food which was hastily made on a small stove in their room. There was always spaghetti and then some meat or fish. The first of the month they pooled their savings and sent a bank draft home.

On weekends they loafed, being too tired to do anything else. Saturdays, the streets were alive with shoppers. In the store windows octopuses wriggled, purple and grey, or huge provoloni hung. When the cheeses were cut, they usually needed two or three persons to hold on to them, because they were so big, and oil dribbled out from the center. Pushcarts of fruits and vegetables lined the street and the gutters were littered with the rotting discards. Each vendor had his own particular chant. Francesco had the feeling that half of Italy was in those streets selling wares.

Each Saturday was long. Since Francesco had been in New York he had not had any contact with women but he saw them everywhere. He could smell them close to him on the subway and feel the crush of their bodies against him. He saw their faces, some lined, some old and some very young. Thoughts about them ran through his mind as he watched them walk through the streets.

Saturday night there was usually a dance sponsored by the local church. During the evening men put on their best suits, awkwardly-fitting garments worn rarely—perhaps for a birth, a baptism or a funeral. The band was a few pieces that played without any feeling, just a rat-a-tat-tat of a waltz or a Neapolitan ballad.

Those who danced were mostly married couples. The unmarried girls sat closely watched by older brothers or sisters. It was unseemly for an unmarried woman to dance with a stranger. If a girl danced at all, it might be with a brother or a cousin. Francesco walked around the hall looking at all the women there.

Francesco wondered if he could ask an unmarried woman to dance without first asking a father or brother for permission. There were groups of young men clustered, laughing, telling stories and the young women sat at tables.

The dancing continued with a Neapolitan master of ceremonies asking people to dance, please, please, dance. Francesco decided to chance it. He went near a table where he saw some good-looking women. To judge from the way their hair was done and the strong resemblance between them, they were all sisters. He motioned to one with his fingers twisting, imitating the act of dancing. She blushed and shook her head. Her sisters started teasing her. She blushed more while he impatiently asked her again. By now the sisters were practically pushing her into his arms. He took it all in good humor and hoped she would too. He helped the process along by taking her arm and leading her to the dance floor. By now her sisters were giggling and watching the two of them. Once again, Francesco felt the soft press of flesh and saw close up her hands, her light olive complexion, and the little hairs along the side of her arm. She moved stiffly like someone who was not accustomed to dancing. Francesco tried to make conversation with her. Dora was her name, and she was from Calabria and worked as a dressmaker in a factory. He guessed she was eighteen or nineteen. She had two brothers and two sisters. They were all at the table. They were having a grand time joking with each other. She avoided his glance and pretended disinterest, although she noticed how handsome he was. At the end of the dance he led her back to the table where the sisters kept silent until he left and then broke out into comments.

Silvio and Paolo admired Francesco for his daring. They knew he could do things better than they could and socializing with the opposite sex was one of them. Francesco stood around looking very pleased. Later, he went to the same table and chose a different sister to dance with. Paolo followed suit. Francesco went back then and got Dora and danced. By that time the band had broken into a *tarantella*, and they were twirling around the floor becoming a bit lightheaded from the music and the twirling. The whole night went that way until one by one people started to depart and the tables emptied out. The brothers asked the sisters permission to accompany them home. They looked, blushing, at each other. They consulted their brothers, who agreed. But not to their house, they said, just to the nearest corner. Francesco kept trying to wheedle their address out of them but none would budge or tell where they worked. There would be other dances, they said, and perhaps other times to meet. The sisters were careful not to seem encouraging. Finally, Francesco gave up trying. When they reached the stopping point, they shook hands all around and said goodbye.

It was still not late. Francesco was excited from the dancing, the closeness with the girl and seeing other couples walk on the street, arm in arm.

"You know," he slyly suggested, "Gennaro said there were girls in an apartment on Hester Street. Two dollars."

Silvio frowned. "We are supposed to be trying to save money to send home."

"Look, two measly dollars. What are they going to do back home with two dollars? Will it buy property?" Paolo said.

Silvio wasn't convinced, but they continued walking in that direction, crisscrossing through streets and alleys until they arrived in front of the apartment. The doorway was large and dark. A curtain on the door prevented people from looking in. Was it the right place? What if it turned out to be someone's house? "Well, we would say that there was a mistake," Francesco said.

They walked up the stairs all three abreast and rang the bell. No answer. They rang again. A figure came down the steps on the inside. A portion of the curtain was pushed aside to see who it was. The door was opened a crack.

"Yes?"

"Is this where the dance is?" Francesco asked.

"There is no dance here. Who do you want to see?"

"We were told that there were some ladies here to dance with." They all hovered around the door.

"Let me see," she paused. "Who sent you?"

Not knowing what to say Francesco said "Gennaro."

"We don't know any Gennaro here."

"That's his name. He said there were some women here that liked to dance."

Another pause. Then she opened the door and had the brothers slip in, one by one. She was a tall, dark woman who spoke Italian with an accent they could not identify. Looking at her dress Paolo thought she looked Turkish. She led them up the stairs to a corridor from which individual rooms branched off. She opened a door and motioned Francesco in with a very efficient gesture, military almost. He went in. The room was clean but sparse.

In the middle was a bed. A woman got up and walked toward him. "Sit down," she said, unbuttoning his jacket. He immediately felt his blood chill and then a rush of heat went down his stomach. Her fingers moved slowly and dexterously, with her hand grazing his chest and stomach. By now, Francesco could feel warmth all over and he put his hand under the shift she wore and found the crisp, moist hairs. A rush of contentedness came over him as he raked his fingers across her. She led him by the hand to the bed where she lowered the top of her shift to reveal her breasts, small but young and firm. Francesco undid his belt and fly and moved against her until he came and all of him seemed to drain into her. With a slight smile she indicated that time was up, although he would have liked to stay longer. Off he went, as she went to fix herself by the washbowl. After he stepped out of the room the Turkish-looking woman asked him for three dollars. "Two," he said. "Three," she said, "for the first visit, then two for all others." Somewhat reluctantly but happily he shelled out the three dollars.

Two other doors opened and the three brothers were ushered out the front door. Once in the street they were all excitedly describing their women, their bodies, their charms, their smells. They waved their arms, stopping occasionally in the street to stress some point. No one thought about Mastro Paolo and the family back home.

One of the workers in the stone yard was a big Irishman named Murphy. He was taller than anyone else on the job. He was also powerful. He wasn't a trained stone cutter like the brothers, he was a manual laborer. Murphy was hired by the old Jewish owner because he was strong and could be counted on to move heavy objects around the yard. When he first started out, he mixed cement if it was needed or carried bricks if bricks were a part of a job. Any time people needed help they would yell out "Murphy," and he would come and help move or lift something, and so Murphy made a place for himself in the yard.

The owner kept Murphy for still another reason. As time moved on Murphy started acting like a boss. The owner did not discourage Murphy because he noticed that whenever Murphy shouted an order to any of the other workers, they quickly obeyed. He was not to be confused with the foreman who was a trained stone cutter and therefore had an important say in the work plans. Murphy's size caused him to be taken very seriously by the stone cutters, almost all of whom were Italian and almost all of whom spoke little or no English. That was the key to success in America, knowing English. Murphy could stand up and say stupid things but he said them in English and in English that flowed and never faltered. All the sounds were there, every letter, every word. The other workers confused their grammar and turned he's into she's. Murphy—and at times the owner—complained that they could not understand the Italians. Occasionally and secretly, Murphy complained that he couldn't always understand the Jewish owner's English. The workers often talked about Murphy behind his back, in Italian, of course. They watched him every day, day in and day out and formed a picture of him. They pretty well knew what his moods were like. They knew when to deal with him and how and when to avoid him. The Italians kept silent most of the time but their eyes took it all in.

Murphy took particular pleasure in teasing and criticizing the Italians. For him, they were always wops, the wops this, and the wops that. Even the Italians got so used to it they never said anything in protest. For lunch the Italians usually brought lunch pails with sandwiches and pieces of provolone or stuffed meat, *brasciola,* wrapped in a napkin to eat alongside the sandwiches. Inside crisp, crackling bread, their wives had packed stuffed peppers or artichoke omeletes. Some even brought bowls of spaghetti and ate them cold. Nothing could send Murphy into greater spasms of laughter than to see an Italian stone cutter eating spaghetti from a dish that had been carefully and lovingly wrapped to prevent the spaghetti from falling out. He always managed to say something like "Hey, Luigi, don't forget to leave some spaghetti for the dog!"

The workers' appetites were sharpened by the fact that they had been up for quite a few hours. Just coming to the stone yard might mean two hours travel on the subway and then they worked hard. The lunch whistle was a sweet sound.

Since Francesco seemed to be the most gifted cook of the brothers, he did the shopping for supper and for lunches. Some times he made a little extra for supper so that what was left over could be used for lunches. Paolo had once said that eating a piece of cold lasagna, no matter how large, was no particular pleasure, but he said no more.

For lunch Murphy usually went to a bar a few blocks away that had a lunch counter. No one had heard of what he ate. He spoke of dishes such as: "Corn beef and cabbage." More often than not whatever Murphy had for lunch was washed down with beer. Those that worked close to him could detect the acrid smell of beer on his breath. After returning from lunch he often belched as he talked or moved about. Occasionally, Murphy had more than just one beer to wash down his corned beef and cabbage. He would return a few minutes later than the others, swaggering as if the time didn't mean anything. He was, after all, a kind of underboss. When he came back his face, always red, was even more flushed, and he was more verbally abusive. Occasionally, he would grab someone's collar or sleeve, which made the victim back down and beat a hasty retreat cowed by Murphy's size and temper, both of which were large. The workers quickly learned to avoid him when he was in such a state. If the owner left the yard, Murphy would find an empty tool shed and nap for an hour or two in the afternoon, while the others were working. Even the foreman would not tell the owner that Murphy had a bit too much to drink at lunch and had a snooze. They were, after all, paid by the hour. In the shed, Murphy dozed, his red face pointed up, his mouth open, snoring. The foreman figured, better to leave him alone. When he woke, he usually wasted more time, not feeling like he wanted to work very much, and managed to find something to do that resembled work.

At the end of the day, most of the workers grabbed their lunch pails and made for the subway for the long ride home. The humming sound of the engine and the light tossing of the subway car as it sped from station to station often lulled them into a nap which they enjoyed and felt they deserved.

Murphy loved to tease and torment the workers. Once he had the foreman call Gigi the Calabrese to look at some stones. When Gigi came back and reached for his mallet he found it nailed to a board. Murphy watched from a short distance for Gigi's reaction and then exploded in laughter.

Another gimmick of Murphy's was to stand close to someone and press his size thirteen shoe on the foot of the victim. He would then glare down at his victim and push his finger into his chest. Sometimes he pushed very hard so that the victim almost fell over backwards. This too would send him into gales of laughter and he walked around the shop with his face red and lit up. "Did you see that guinea?" he would say.

Francesco was not particularly big but he was wiry and muscular. Under his coveralls he gave the impression of being smaller than he was. Murphy gave him the foot treatment a few times and Francesco didn't like it. Like most victims he didn't say anything but walked away hearing Murphy's laughter ringing in his ears. Nailing somebody's mallet to a board may have been funny for Murphy but for Gigi or Francesco it meant having to buy another handle. While it wasn't particularly expensive, when you were sending money back home each month it meant you sent less.

On Friday afternoon at about four thirty, the owner got the payroll ready to be distributed at five o'clock. Around three thirty on Fridays Murphy began to come alive, chattering more than usual, telling the "wops" that on the weekend they were going to eat lots of spaghetti and meatballs and they would be humping mamma and making lots of bambinos. When he said this he accompanied it with a pumping gesture of the arm and hand. He said this in mock, broken English. "You gonna a-make-a lots of bambinos," pump, pump.

At five, the owner went from bench to bench distributing the pay envelopes. The brothers enjoyed the solidness of the pay envelope, the folded bills and the change that had fallen to the bottom. Francesco placed his in the most secure pocket. Then he tapped through the pocket to make sure it was there and stayed there. Murphy ripped open the envelope and dumped the contents into his hand. Once the bills were counted, he pushed them into his pocket. "All right you guinea bastards, go-a-make-a bambinos," and he would go off without taking the time to wash up or change his work clothes. He ended up in the Trip-in Bar two blocks away, the same one that said in small gilded letters in one corner of the window, "Ladies Invited. Use the ladies entrance." There Murphy stayed until God knows what hour.

It was not uncommon to see him on a Monday morning, morose and mean, his eyes bleary. Sometimes he didn't show up on Monday. When that happened, the Italians kidded about Murphy, "*ubbriacone*," drunk, they said with relish. Gigi said Murphy couldn't make any bambinos because he had probably passed out. No one knew about Murphy's family, that is, if he had one. He never spoke about a wife or children.

Murphy's behavior toward Italians bothered Francesco but no one wanted to stand up to him, partly because the old owner was a bit afraid of him too. Francesco tried to avoid Murphy as much as he could but sometimes that wasn't possible. Murphy had made a habit of standing on Francesco's foot and pushing him until he fell too many times. Francesco decided to get back at Murphy in little ways and give himself some satisfaction.

Sometimes when Murphy took his post-luncheon snooze due to the abundance of beer he drank, he took his large shoes off. One time, when Francesco was sure that Murphy was asleep he gingerly carried two of the yard dog's turds in a piece of newspaper and placed them in Murphy's shoes and then lifted the shoes lightly by the heels so the cargo slid to the toe. He put the shoes back in their place and sneaked out of the shed. Some time later Murphy got up, put his shoes on and walked around the yard in his usual post-luncheon sour mood. Francesco smiled to himself watching a puzzled look come over Murphy's face. He'll have a surprise when he gets home, Francesco thought.

After a week in which Murphy was very abusive to Francesco and the others, Francesco racked his brain to see what other damage he could do to Murphy. Since Murphy didn't use tools, Francesco couldn't nail his mallet to the bench the way Murphy had done. On Friday night Francesco had to stay late in the yard because he wanted to finish a particularly delicate piece of work. On his way home toward the subway, walking by the Trip-in Bar he noticed that Murphy was staggering along the street as drunk as can be. So that's where Murphy's pay envelope ended up, he thought. Murphy staggered along bumping into fences and hydrants and mumbling to himself, greeting people who weren't there. At the end of the block, he sat down on the stoop of one of the tenements.

The next week Francesco decided to take advantage of Murphy's drunkenness. One day he brought to work a large paper bag, the kind that was strong, heavy and double ply.

Once again, Francesco came back after quitting time and waited, the poultry bag folded under his arm. True to form, about seven thirty Murphy, completely drunk, staggered out of the bar and started his walk down the street. Francesco watched him. When he got to the house with the stoop, Murphy climbed the stairs on all fours and sat down. Francesco slipped across the street and scampered up the stairs of the adjacent house all the way to the roof. He ran to the edge of the roof and saw Murphy sitting below him carrying on a long, blubbering conversation with himself. Francesco looked for a water faucet. When he found one he opened the poultry bag, which was almost four feet long when fully open. Francesco started filling it with the water, knowing he had to work fast before the paper absorbed the water and broke. When it was two-thirds full he closed the opening and lifted it as best he could. He carried it to the edge of the roof. Murphy was still in a stupor. Giovanni went as close to the edge of the tenement roof as safety would allow and let the water-filled bag go. Falling, it looked like a rectangular box and hit Murphy squarely on the head, then broke open, dousing him completely. Murphy was knocked out on the edge of the stoop. Monday morning Francesco watched Murphy when he came in, and he was more dour than usual.

One day the boss wanted a wall whitewashed. Murphy sent Francesco and the Calabrese to do it. A scaffold was set up. They made their whitewash and brought it up the scaffold and started painting. Francesco wasn't happy about being chosen to do this. He was a skilled stone cutter. While Francesco painted, his mind went back to the many mallet handles that Murphy ruined, to the many times Murphy pushed and taunted him. He continued to paint without saying anything. The Calabrese nattered on. Francesco was not listening or talking.

43

The wall was high so they progressed slowly, painting, then lowering the scaffold. Murphy walked by occasionally and Francesco watched him out of the corner of his eye.

Around four in the afternoon, they were about twelve feet up on the wall. Earlier Francesco had his lunch and told his brothers how much Murphy bothered him. He bothered everybody, they answered, stay out of his way.

Up on the scaffold Francesco kept painting. Murphy had walked by a few times barking commands all around. There he was, his hat placed cockily on his head, yelling you wops this and you wops that. Francesco put down his brush, took the bucket of whitewash and turned it over. Whitewash splashed down on Murphy in one gush. Everyone in the yard was stunned.

Francesco looked down on Murphy, dripping from head to foot in whitewash, wiping his face with his sleeve, his hat on the ground. Murphy looked up. "You dirty little wop. I'm going to kill you." Francesco scampered down the scaffold, falling to the ground and getting up. He rubbed the dirt off his hands. Murphy came at him bellowing. The other workers and Francesco's brothers came close. Moving toward Francesco, Murphy looked like a man swimming, opening the air with his hands. Francesco did not take his eyes off Murphy and carefully manoeuvered away from him. He had never fought this way. His instinct was to avoid Murphy without running away. He had seen pictures of boxers and assumed an awkward stance in imitation of a prize fighter. Murphy connected with a punch and Francesco tasted his own blood, bitter in his mouth. He started fighting back; Murphy loomed over him looking as tall as a spire. Francesco reached up and hit Murphy, feeling the soft flesh of his face under his fist. Francesco circled him swinging and avoiding being hit by Murphy. He rushed and butted Murphy hard in his big belly. He could hear Murphy groan. By now, his brothers and the other workers were cheering as the little man outfought the big one. Even the boss was smiling a bit. Murphy lunged at Francesco who slipped away and managed to get in a hit. Francesco's lungs were burning and he could still taste the blood on his lips.

Unexpectedly, Murphy dropped his fists to his side. "All right," he panted, unable to get his words out. "I'll let you go this time, but you're fired." Everybody got quiet. Both fighters stood by, wary still of each other.

"You're fired." The words rang in everybody's ears. Francesco turned to the owner, who shook his head. "No, he's not fired, and neither are you, Murphy. It's Friday, get your pay envelopes and go home. Monday morning you come and you work. No craziness, no fighting. You, Francesco, you don't paint. You, Murphy, you leave him alone."

On the way to the subway, Francesco smiled, even though his face hurt. When they passed the stoop where Murphy got the poultry bag treatment, Francesco smiled as he described to his brothers what had happened. From then on that spot was known as "*il bagno di* Murphy," Murphy's bath.

Attilio Chiari was from Torino, and this gave him a certain cachet with many of the Southern Italian workers. He spoke an Italian that others often found difficult to understand. In fact it was almost like another language. He dressed like a dandy, used a walking stick, wore a vest, gold chain and watch and his fedora had a snap brim. Some called him "*Avvocato*," lawyer, others "*Ragioniere*," notary. It was obvious that he did not work with his hands. Chiari came to the stone yards and construction sites and talked to the workers. When he talked he would pull out pamphlets and broadsides and point to statistics dealing with workers. Everyone thought he was a "*rivoluzionario*" a revolutionary, but Chiari's dress and demeanor tended to discount that possibility. However, he was always talking about "*la lotta dei lavoratori*," the war of the workers, "*l'impegno e la responsibilità*," the involvement and responsibility of all workers. From his mouth flowed full fledged "*discorsi*" about salaries, health, and dangers on the job.

When he came by at lunchtime some people offered him things from their lunch pails which he would accept politely, sometimes asking if the fruit was washed. When he finished, he pulled out a handkerchief and delicately wiped his lips and hands, saying "*cari ragazzi, cari ragazzi*," dear fellows.

Chiari had no regular time that he came by, but usually came by to explain the principles of a strike, or a contract or sometimes he collected money for a strike fund. It was never very much that he collected, but people felt rather sorry for him. At the end of his visit, Chiari jingled the change in his hand, "So long, *fratelli*, see you soon." And off he went, no one really knew where but probably to another stone yard or construction site.

One afternoon Chiari showed up at lunch time, cadged a few things to eat then took out papers and pamphlets and passed them around. On the cover in block letters "Sacco e Vanzetti – *Ingiustizia*," Sacco and Vanzetti, Injustice. Giovanni recognized the picture of those two *paesani* standing in their long black coats, one of them with a dark droopy moustache, the other clean shaven, with a challenging look and a wide forehead.

"Sacco e Vanzetti - *Ingiustizia*," Chiari declaimed as he passed the papers around. "*Ragazzi*, they are from our people. The great machine wants to eat them up and spit them out in bits. Why? Because we are slaves, their dagos and wops. These boys understood '*la lotta*,' the battle, and so they want to destroy them. If you see through the dirty game, *ragazzi*, look out. They'll find something they can pin on you." The listeners nodded and mumbled. Paolo thought Chiari was a "*rivoluzionario*" and didn't trust him. He rarely gave him any money. Francesco liked the way he stood up and spoke, punctuating everything with his fingers and hands and at the end would pull out a sheaf of papers and read relevant passages from it.

"*Ragazzi*," he said, "do you know why they are trying to kill Sacco and Vanzetti?" Silence. "Because they are anarchists, that's why. We are raising money for their defense, *ragazzi*. So reach into your pockets, deep, find those nickels and quarters. We must save Sacco and Vanzetti from the evil machine." Silvio thought that if you were to put a cassock on Chiari he would be very much at home as a priest. "Deep into the pockets, *ragazzi*, don't be afraid to reach in there. They are killing our flesh and blood," he said. Very few of the workers really understood the facts of the case. It seemed so complicated, but Sacco and Vanzetti didn't look like killers at all.

One night Francesco had a dream. He was walking along Mott Street where the sidewalks were lined with pushcarts. One of the peddlers, a man with a droopy moustache, yelled out "Fish, fresh fish," but there was a sad look in his eyes. In his hands eels writhed as he hit them against the sidewalk to stun them and then he skinned them. When he woke, Francesco felt an overwhelming, sad feeling. Chiari's words echoed in his ears. "*Ragazzi*, they are trying to kill us all."

After one of his usual visits, Chiari, motioning with his head, took Francesco aside. They stepped behind a large stone that Francesco was carving. Chiari had sensed Francesco's interest.

"You want to help our good *paesani*, don't you?" Francesco nodded. "Francesco, I need someone I can trust. I want you to be a representative here at the stone yard for the defense fund. You know what the defense fund is?" Francesco nodded. He wasn't sure, but he didn't want to look dumb either. "Each Friday," Chiari continued, "I want you to approach all of the workers, here and the other stone yards in the area. You go every Friday afternoon. They'll know what you are there for. Ask them to empty their pay envelopes of the change and give it to you. After a few days, you come by my room and turn it over to me, *capisci*, 'understand'?" As he spoke, he made the motion of squeezing open the envelope and turning it over. Francesco got the picture.

Every Friday, Francesco went from workbench to workbench, asking for the workers' change. Then he went to other stone yards, and one after the other they squeezed open the envelope and dumped the change into Francesco's open hand. At night when he came home, he felt the change in his pocket bouncing against his leg. "Sacco e Vanzetti - *Ingiustizia*," he said to himself. And on the weekend he went to Chiari's house, a sullen, drab room in Little Italy. When he got there Francesco dumped the money into a chest that Chiari kept locked under the bed. To Francesco's eyes it seemed like a silver fortune, glimmering change that must have added up to many dollars. Before he left, Chiari told him, "Francesco, don't forget Sunday night at Webster Hall. There's a big fund raiser. I'll be there with some pretty important people. Real *pesci grossi*, big shots. Remember, we are going to save our *paesani*."

That night Francesco and his brothers went to the dance at the church. At a corner table he saw the sisters. They remembered the brothers and smiled at them.

It didn't take long for Francesco to go over and sit with them. He liked the sister, Dora, with the dark hair and the dark eyes, and she knew he liked her. She thought Francesco was cute, with hair that was almost blond and green eyes. She hoped he would ask her to dance, and yes, he did. For the rest of the evening they did waltzes and *taranatelle* feeling closer and closer all the time.

"Sunday night they are having a big fund drive for Sacco and Vanzetti. I'm invited."

"Sacco and Vanzetti? You mean the two *rivoluzionari*'? Are you a Bolshevik?" she asked.

Francesco laughed. "No, I'm helping to raise money for them."

"I was told to look out for them," she said. "They hate the church." She made a sign of the cross and then a shuddering gesture.

"Look," he said, "Why don't you and your sisters come with me? Do you know Attilio Chiari? You don't know Attilio Chiari? He invited me personally. He's *un pesce grosso*," Francesco said shaking his head impressively. "There will be opera singers, and maybe even a dance. What do you say?" She would decide, she said. They danced and each spoke of their families. On the way home, they held hands in a hidden way so her sisters wouldn't see it. Yes, Dora decided they would go, they would meet outside Webster Hall at seven.

After the brothers walked them home, they made a special visit to the Turkish whorehouse.

Out of sheer nerves Francesco and his brothers got to Webster Hall early. People filed in slowly, and Francesco kept looking down the street hoping to see Dora. He looked at the people, hoping to identify them by their nationalities. So far, all he saw were *Americani*. Occasionally, he saw a Jew with a black frock coat and long beard. Francesco and Paolo had been to Webster Hall to hear opera, one of their great loves. A long sleek car came and more *Americani* got out. Still no Dora. Francesco wondered if she had had trouble getting out of the house. It was certain that she would not be able to come without her sisters as chaperones. This meant that he would have to pay for all their entrance tickets, which also meant that he would have less to give to the defense fund.

Coming down the street wearing a large *Borsalino* hat and holding a small briefcase was Attilio Chiari. He nodded greetings and tipped his hat to all he knew with his easy, self-assured manner. Pamphlets bulged from his pockets. As he walked in, he noticed Francesco and merely nodded. Francesco had expected a bigger hello from Chiari. Francesco had worked hard collecting the money, and Chiari had given him the feeling that they were a team. Francesco's mind was still on Dora as more and more people walked through the doors. He spied her and her two sisters coming down the street, arm in arm. Francesco waited for them to get closer. He could see in Dora's face the same apprehension that he had on his own. Then he stepped forward out of the people congregating at the entrance. When she saw him she gave a slight jump and then broke into a slow smile. Francesco shook hands with her and her sisters. "Shall we go in?" he said. "There's a big crowd already."

Inside on a stage, musicians sat on rickety folding chairs and tuned their instruments. People walked up and down the aisles greeting friends, stopping to talk. Paolo wondered impatiently when things were going to get started. With the sisters there, Francesco could not give Dora any compliments. He merely caught her eye and winked. She blushed, pretended slight annoyance, and looked away; her sisters smiled for her.

The stage filled with musicians dressed in tuxedos. The chairs on the ballroom floor were full. On the second floor of the ballroom people peered over the rail at the stage. The house lights dimmed and a stocky figure with a leonine head walked out. When the applause subsided, he turned to the orchestra and led them in the overture to *Il Trovatore*. From the floor people called out "Viva Verdi," "Viva Sacco e Vanzetti." Others hushed them, but the orchestra continued until the final notes, and then pandemonium broke loose. The conductor acknowledged the applause and then marched into the wings. A tall man stepped to the podium.

"Today in a jail in Massachusetts sit two men convicted of a crime that they did not commit." A huge roar of applause, whistle and yells. "Why are they being persecuted? Because they are Italians, immigrants, and because they are anarchists." More yells and whistles. He went on to talk about the crimes of the upper classes, how capitalism was grinding up these two innocent men. "Are we going to let them be crucified by this rotten system?" A long echoing "No" resounded. "Each day the lawyers prepare briefs, make motions and legal documents are filed. And each day the poor innocent Nicola Sacco and Bartolomeo Vanzetti count the days--the hours—remaining until they may be destroyed by that vicious machine and its stooges, the judges and prosecutors."

One by one, speakers rose and spoke. One of them was a rabbi whom Francesco had seen on Rivington Street. Even though his Russian accent was heavy, Francesco thought he was convincing.

The conductor came out and the orchestra played some Italian arias. Paolo stood up and cried *Bravi, bravi.*

The tall man introduced Chiari, who came to the podium, took out a handkerchief and wiped his brow. The air was filled with smoke. He began by talking about Italian workers. How they came to this country, many of them in steerage. Some even died in the crossing and never were able to enjoy the freedom and the modest prosperity that hard work brought in America. They died in the holds of the ships in the same misery and despair that they left behind. As he went on the crowd became still. Chiari's eloquence impressed everyone.

"Each day," he said, "I go to the stone yards"—Francesco squeezed Dora's hand—"and collect pennies from the envelopes of workers, peasants, Italians. They take away from their children some of the food they work to give them. I go to the factories and instead of buying lunch, people give me their money. I have people going from house to house, store to store, building to building, and cart to cart, all raising money for Sacco and Vanzetti's defense." He used his hands for emphasis, gesturing like an actor. "I have raised five thousand dollars and sent it to Boston to defend our brothers. Tonight reach into your pockets, fill your hands with your change. Give a dollar if you can...." Then the ushers came by passing wicker baskets. "Just like church," Silvio said disdainfully.

At the end of the program the crowd filed out, a flush of enthusiasm and pride on their faces. Francesco literally had emptied his pockets since he had already bought the tickets for everybody and felt awkward about having no money to buy coffee. They walked the many blocks downtown. As they neared Dora's house he asked if she would accompany him in the evenings to collect money. "Only if one of my sisters could accompany me," she replied.

Each night Francesco took his jar with the slit cut into the top and went to the streets. In one hand he held the jar, in the other a sign that said in English on one side "For the Sacco and Vanzetti Defense Fund" and on the other *Per la difesa di Sacco e Vanzetti.* They picked a street and went all the way to the end stopping in each store, clubhouse, and recreation room. People reached for their pocket change. Occasionally someone gave a dollar bill, but that was rare. Some asked, "How do we know you won't take the money for yourself? Take it and go back to Italy?" Francesco looked up, hurt. "I do not betray Sacco and Vanzetti. That's how."

Dora and her sister could only stay for a few hours. At the end of the evening, they went by Chiari's room. He was home and welcomed them in. The two sisters felt ill at ease at entering the room of a strange man.

"But Chiari's not a stranger, Dora," Paolo insisted. "He's a leader, an anarchist, a lover of humanity." Chiari beamed as he heard all this. "*Venite, ragazzi, venite,*" come, he said, welcoming them. Then Francesco unscrewed the jar top and dumped the money into a trunk he kept under the bed. "Don't lose faith. We shall never abandon our brothers," Chiari told Francesco. The money clanged into the box.

"Five thousand dollars," a fortune anywhere, here or Italy. In Italy, I would be as rich as a king. I would save the family business. I would," Francesco paused, "own the town."

Some nights with Dora at his side, holding her hand, squeezing it, he would brush his cheek against hers, seemingly accidentally, inhaling the clean smell of her skin, He brushed her cheek and ear with his lips as she pretended that nothing was happening. Her sister looked the other way. Each night he wanted to put his arm around her shoulders, her slim waist, but he didn't dare. Each night he left her and her sister at their door.

Dora noticed Francesco's steadiness, his controlled passion. He was responsible. He believed in the Sacco and Vanzetti cause and gave it everything. Each day the newspapers talked about the case but the appeals were failing. More money was needed. Francesco spent all his time raising money when he was not working.

After collecting one long night, when he was tired and depressed by the failing appeals he went as usual to Chiari's. He was not at home, so Francesco went home and placed the jar under his bed. The next night after going in and out of bars, restaurants, and taverns, he went to Chiari's, but no answer. He realized he hadn't seen Chiari at noon at the stone yard or any of the other places where he was usually found. For a week, night after night, there was no Chiari. The last night Francesco went there a basement door opened and the landlord, with a sleepy face, looked up the dark stairwell.

"What do you want?"

"I'm looking for Attilio Chiari. I'm from the defense fund." The landlord wrinkled his brow.

"Chiari? You look for Chiari? Don't you know? Chiari, he leave. Go 'way."

"Go away?" Francesco queried. "He's the head of the Sacco and Vanzetti Defense Fund."

The landlord shrugged his shoulders. "He go to Italy."

A year later, Francesco saw their picture in the newspaper. "Sacco and Vanzetti Die in Electric Chair." He closed his eyes. *Vergogna*! He repeated it to himself, "Shame!" He thought of Chiari in his white striped pants, folded newspaper clippings in his pockets, now most probably sitting regally somewhere in the Piedmont. "There is no justice."

———————————

One Friday afternoon, the old Jewish owner called the workers together just before he gave out the pay envelopes. The workers were shocked to hear that they were going to be laid off. Business was bad and all but one stone cutter, one letterist and one manual laborer—Murphy—would be laid off. The brothers had been afraid of this but none of them had really believed that they would ever be out of a job. Weren't they the best workers and the most experienced? Wasn't America the great land of opportunity? Paolo had noticed that the large stones were not arriving as regularly as before. These large stones would be brought in and then cut up in smaller sizes. In the hands of the brothers these stones became gravestones and large building stones. Usually the owner could be heard gleefully talking about stone contracts he had. But the owner uttered no more of these remarks as the brothers and others sweated to produce the stones whose incised messages would last forever. Glumly, the owner gave out the envelopes. He shrugged his shoulders when they asked questions. He seemed genuinely sorrowful. What could he do? If there was no work, then he didn't need that many workers.

Each man returned to his bench and started packing his tools. The hammers and chisels dropped clanging into the bags. What was the Calabrese going to do? He had a wife and several children, or the Abbruzzese, with his aged parents, a wife and children? The brothers would no longer be able to send money home as they had since coming to America. One by one the workers nodded good-byes and filed out of the yard to return to their homes. Francesco thought that now Murphy had good reason to get drunk since he was one of the few who had a job.

The weekend usually meant shopping and cleaning their rooms on Saturday, maybe going to the church dance on Saturday night. Sunday was spent lazing, reading the newspaper, and going around the corner to play cards with some of the other Baresi at the club. If the opera was on, the brothers usually went and stood on the side, the cheapest ticket and often the best, right beside the orchestra.

That weekend they sat wondering what to do next. Silvio was morose and thought about the money spent at the Turkish bordello. He counted up in his mind how much money he had left there and winced. That money, he thought, could have been a cushion precisely for days like these. It really did not add up to much, but what bothered them was the idea that they had betrayed their mission. Silvio regretted the times he went to the opera, sometimes on Friday nights after work when he practically fell asleep standing up—a habit, Mastro Paolo used to say only practiced by horses.

But Francesco was most irritated that he would not be able to go to the church dance on Saturday nights. It was an unspoken agreement that he and Dora would meet there under the watchful eyes of her sisters. After the Sacco and Vanzetti disappointment Francesco felt himself growing closer and closer to her.

The brothers hadn't managed to save their father's business for the family in Giovinazzo, yet Francesco often thought about what it would be like to come home to Dora, to see her large with child, to have his own family. His children, he thought, would have her dark hair and beautiful, dark eyes. He didn't think anyone would get his green eyes, those same green eyes that caused people to say, "but you don't look Italian." Those dreams were a long way off, now more than ever.

The weekend was a gloomy one. At the stores, they bought the cheapest cuts of meat and the cheapest fish; things they usually said only low-class people ate. Now the brothers felt the need for thrift.

Monday morning the brothers decided that they would go down to the union hall and see about work. Ideally, this way they would lose only one day's work. On Tuesday, they could possibly start work at another yard.

The union was something that Francesco had been wary of. The brothers would be listed as apprentices even though they had more experience than most full-fledged workers. They were told that their experience in Italy didn't count toward being official master granite cutters. Before they became full members they had to be apprentices and then journeymen. Paolo did not trust the delegates or the union bigwigs. When he and his brothers were working in the yards the union people hobnobbed with the owners rather than the workers. They went visiting from yard to yard, and then played cards afternoons in the back of the union hall. The brothers and many more like them would pay their dues month after month, but for what? He distrusted the union people.

At the hall they recognized a few people they had known from previous jobs. The air was thick with cigarette smoke. Francesco looked for someone nicknamed *Spellato*, Baldy. He was not sure of his real name. *Spellato* seemed like an important person, wearing his fedora hat inside the building. His shirt collar was open, his tie loose and he smoked short, dark Toscano cigars. Baldy would get them their first union job.

Several people gathered around Baldy as he spoke in Italian to them. The brothers moved near. What impressed Francesco about Baldy was not that he spoke Italian but rather that he also spoke creditable English. Silvio had overheard him with the owners.

"What do you want me to do?" Baldy yelled. "It's not the union's fault. You think we want to see you without work?"

"But what are we paying dues for?" A short, dark man with large hands stood in front of him.

"Look, we can't control the market," said Baldy. No one really understood what he was talking about. "Stone yards in Wilkes-Barre, Stonington, Maine and Montpelier, Vermont—that's where they are doing a lot of the work. That's where they cut the stones right out of the mountains. They used to send them to New York but now they're not coming here. That's why. You got families; I know you got families. We all got families and mouths to feed. But right now work is drying up in New York. You wanna work? Go to Wilkes-Barre; I can get you a job tomorrow." The men murmured unhappily. Baldy threw up his hands and shrugged.

"What we pay these bastards for?" said Paolo. Francesco took his brothers aside. "What are we going to do?" he said. "We can't be without work. Baldy says it may last through the winter. What do we do until then?" No one had an answer. Slowly they moved toward Baldy who had just finished giving this same talk to another group of workers. Silvio hailed him: "Baldy, you said something about going away to work. We came here to New York because we had some *paesani* from Giovinazzo. Where are we going to go? We don't have nobody."

"Whatsamatta? You babies or something? You wanna stay drinking from your mother's teat forever? You gotta go, you gotta go. You came here, now you go there." Baldy tipped his fedora back on his head. He made a gesture as if drinking from a baby's bottle. Nobody found him particularly funny, least of all Francesco. "If you wanna go, tell me, if not I gotta go take care of them other *paesani*."

The brothers looked at each other and nodded.

"Okay," Silvio said. "What you got?" Baldy took out a sheaf of papers from his pocket.

"Let see," he hummed, "let's see---Wilkes-Barre, Pennsylvania," and he looked up. No response from the brothers. "Stonington, Maine," he said, chuckling. "Stonington, Maine, you will freeze your little balls off. They will be like the tin balls on the Christmas tree. Well?" Still, no response. They didn't want to go, really. Baldy shrugged. "Oh, here's one. Montpelier, Vermont. If you don't take this one, that's it. I can't send you to heaven, boys. That's it." They looked at each other.

"Okay," Francesco said. He had no idea where or what Vermont was.

"All right," Baldy said. "Go to Starwell Stone Company in Montpelier. Ask for Steve Culler and give him this paper. Tell him I sent you. Try to get there soon so he doesn't hire anybody else. Goodbye and *buona fortuna*." He shook hands with the brothers.

"Where is Vermont?" Paolo asked putting the accent on the second syllable as if it were an Italian name. Nobody knew. "Mister," he stopped a stranger on the street. "Where is Vermont?" The man looked at him and kept walking. "Mister, tell me, where is Vermont? Montpelier, Vermont?"

At Penn Station, the clerks knew how to find Vermont and sold the brothers three tickets to Montpelier. This time they took a taxicab to move their things. They loaded it up with a big trunk and several other bags and their tools. They were not sorry to leave the dingy apartment.

When the train got moving, they settled into the seats. In one bag they had their food for the trip. The train would stop in Boston early in the morning, then they'd change trains. By six the next day they would arrive in Montpelier, Vermont.

Once the train was out of the station, Paolo opened one bag and distributed its contents: sandwiches, fruit, and several small cakes. That was supper. Wine in a carefully corked bottle was passed around with small glasses. The people around them looked without commenting as the brothers polished off the sandwiches, fruit, and everything. Francesco didn't like to eat this way because it reminded him of being on the job. He liked to sit around the table, chatting, making jokes and reminiscing about home. Here on the train they felt conspicuous and thought people looked on them as oddities, three guineas eating with gusto and drinking wine.

The steady motion of the train, its muffled hum, the contentment of the food and the wine put them to sleep. Waking in the night they looked out the window and saw isolated houses, their lights lonely in the night. They wondered who lived there. Occasionally, they could make out forests. The train hummed along. By ten, the lights were lowered.

By eleven, there was just a little light at the end of the car. Paolo had long since fallen into a deep sleep, softly snoring.

Early the next morning Silvio woke and saw the beginning of the day unfold, the train racing along through the grey morning. Outside, they could see farms and cows. It was fall and the air crisp. He thought of the train trip from Bari going inland, passing vineyards and olive groves.

At the station in Boston, they emerged tired and rumpled, dragging their suitcases and boxes. It would be a two hour wait before the train to Montpelier. In the waiting room others sat in dull silence, some smoking, some napping, all counting the minutes and hours.

The brothers were tired of sitting and sleeping in their seats. They wondered if anyone else was going to Montpelier or was a stone cutter. The fall weather had given way to cold, and the radiator whistled tunes. It sounded to the brothers as though the people in Boston spoke English differently from New Yorkers. One of the loudspeakers broadcast a list of names, one of which Paolo thought was Montpelier. He ran in panic to a conductor and showed him the ticket, saying "Montpelier, Montpelier" in his heavy Italian accent. "Platform eight in five minutes," he was told. The brothers boarded the train and settled in. As the sun rose, the light revealed gray fields and groves of white birches gleamed in the light. At the stops, people shuffled on and off. The cold air became sharper.

At Montpelier, the brothers watched people stepping into carriages and cars. They waited, looking around for someone to direct them to the stone yard. They looked for somebody, a conductor, anyone to tell them where the Starwell Stone Company was. A porter finished packing luggage into hacks and carriages and told them that the stone yard was a little bit out of town and that it was probably closed at this time. They conferred among themselves and then Paolo asked in broken English if there was a hotel or boarding house they could go to. The man suggested Mrs. Borden's. It was in the middle of town. The wagons that would take them to work stopped by there, and the place was clean and served decent food. They picked up their grips and headed downtown. It was a small town with a few streets and dour people, no more Turks walking the streets selling lemonade. The food at this Mrs. Borden's, it didn't sound like there would be spaghetti. They all sighed.

Mrs. Borden's house was plain but clean. They would be placed all three in one room, just like in New York. They had missed the evening meal, and Mrs. Borden offered fruit and some bread, which they took. From one of the other boarders they were told how to get to the stone yards; the company wagon came at six, and would take them there, a trip of thirty minutes.

They took a walk in the early evening, strolling around the square, looking at the stores. No *provoloni* hanging on hooks next to hams and salamis. No fish stores with *stocco*, cod, nailed to the door, just groceries and hardware stores. They knew they would stay just long enough for the situation to get better in New York then they would return there.

When he thought of home, Francesco now thought of New York and of Dora, whom he missed terribly. He missed her softness, what little of it he had been able to savor and her beautiful eyes. In the evening light, people walked past clothed in heavy jackets, collars up and hats tipped down to ward off the wind. This was another country, it was another land.

Mrs. Borden's breakfast was what Paolo had heard that Americans ate: wheat cakes, sausage, pots of coffee with smoke swirling out of the spout. They felt full like after Sunday dinner.

The wagon brought them to its last stop. From there they had to walk until they saw the work sheds. They carried their tools and each had a small bag filled with lunch from Mrs. Borden. Paolo had peeked in, there was no loaf of Italian bread, no smell of green peppers. It would be a long winter.

They were each given a work stall. The voices around them spoke Italian, some Southern dialects and other dialects as well. People didn't greet them at first, just nodded. The brothers were strangers, outsiders. They knew that it would take time to be accepted; it would happen a little at a time. The Southern-Italian accents meant that at least they could communicate with people other than themselves. Francesco looked for the manual laborer, fearful he might find another Murphy. Silvio wanted to get to know all the Italians there. Maybe he would go to their homes and get the smell of rich tomato sauce in his nose again.

At lunch there was small talk. This one was from Calabria, this other one from Basilicata, that one from Tuscany. The Tuscan had a high opinion of himself, always talking about *La Toscana*.

The brothers watched the other workers furtively, measuring their competence. These artisans were proud of their talents and were watching the new arrivals also. By the third day it was obvious that the brothers had passed inspection. At lunch time they shared stories. Most of them had come directly to Vermont from Italy. Those workers were met at the pier and taken to the railroad station. Had the brothers seen New York? Their only glimpse of New York was tall, grey buildings disappearing as they sped away. Now they got up, came to work, went home, got up, went to work, and came home. On their day and a half off, these workers had to see to their laundry, do special tasks and look after the children.

On Sunday the brothers usually napped on and off all day. Their lives were empty. Sometimes at night they would sit at the dining table after it was cleared and play cards. Francesco sometimes read. Paolo and Silvio spoke about opera. They remembered whole arias which they recited not quite singing, *"Recondita armonia," "Un bel dì,"* and others.

One of the residents, a certain Mangano worked as a handyman at the town department store. He came from outside Rome and was illiterate, uncouth, and generally unpleasant. At the boarding house table, he grabbed at everything like it was his last meal. Mrs. Borden watched him, wondering where his manners were. He gobbled his food up and reached for more. Mrs. Borden finally told him he would have to wait to ask for dishes to be passed to him. Paolo murmured to him in Italian that Mangano was a pig. Mangano heard him and grunted.

Mangano did a lot of work around the store; in fact, there wasn't anything he didn't do. At night after dinner he stood outside the boarding house watching people who walked by. Often he was asked to carry bundles out to a waiting hack or to a car. No one ever greeted him; he was the least likely person that anyone would ever want to greet. He did this until it was time to retire and then he went to his room and slept. Mangano fell into deep sleep and snored for the whole night. The brothers slept in the room above his and all night they heard him snoring. Paolo was a light sleeper and all night he tossed and turned while Mangano slept and snored.

One night he listened to Mangano snore minute after minute, hour after hour. He got up and crept down the stairs, along the corridor to Mangano's door. He turned the knob slowly and felt it giving and then opening. Paolo slipped in, stepped close to his bed and pressed Mangano's nostrils closed. Mangano started choking and coughing. Paolo stepped back against the wall where he could not be seen. When he heard Mangano's breathing become slow and rhythmic, he slipped out of the room, returned upstairs and went to bed. He no sooner slipped under the covers that he heard Mangano snoring again, and after a few minutes he was back at his peak of loudness.

Each night that Paolo could not sleep he went downstairs to his room to tweak the man's nose. Mangano coughed and always went back to snoring. Someone told Paolo that if you got a glass of water and put someone's fingers in the glass while he slept they peed in their bed. One night Paolo had a glass filled with tepid water ready and went to Mangano's room. Mangano was all curled up like a fetus and there was no way Paolo could get at his fingers so he tickled the sleeping man. Mangano scratched himself but always made a fist afterwards. Each night, the snoring soared up the walls into the brothers' room.

All Paolo's attempts had failed at stopping him. Paolo noticed the wooden floor of their room and the next day he brought a drill home. When Mangano was outside watching people walk by Paolo drilled a hole in the floor right above his bed. He didn't quite manage to get through the floor's thickness so when he finished he covered the hole with a throw rug they had in the room. The next day he got an extension, and connected it to the drill and quietly and surely turned the drill. Mangano never noticed the accumulation of plaster on his bed. When the hole was made Paolo waited until he heard Mangano snoring, then he lay over the hole with his penis in the hole and peed on him, aiming as best he could for his face. He could hear Mangano sputter and get up out of bed. He put the light on, and found himself and the bed all wet. Paolo watched through the hole, heard Mangano cursing in his Roman dialect and then slipped the rug over the hole. If he couldn't sleep, then Mangano wouldn't sleep either. After a few days Mrs. Borden noticed the discolored sheets. At first she was nervous about talking to him. Finally she took Mangano aside. With Mary Margaret, the Irish housekeeper, standing beside her, she told him that if he couldn't control himself he would have to move out. Mangano didn't know what to say. He had never had this problem but he would wake up and find himself all wet. By the second week Mrs. Borden told him he would have to be out by Friday. Finally, Paolo got to sleep at night.

It was late November, the trees lost their leaves and the ground was hard with frost. Soon, the other workers said, the snows would come. The stone cutters worked at their benches that were only partially covered by the shed. There was always a fire in a big barrel where the workers went to warm their hands. They worked all bundled up. Between puffs of his cigarette, Silvio coughed. He always coughed because he smoked a lot. When he chipped at the stone, a cigarette dangled from his lips as if it were stuck there. As he hammered, he coughed. When this persisted some of the other workers began to talk. They said he had silicosis or worse, tuberculosis. Silvio paid no attention and went about his business. The next week he felt weaker. and weaker. One day as he leaned against his stone Francesco walked over and asked what was wrong. Silvio didn't know. An hour later he fell to the ground at his work place. Back at Mrs. Borden's, Francesco put him to bed and felt his face burning with fever. In his delirium he would talk to his father and mother; or call out to his sister. They were finally able to get Dr. Slocum, who had an office nearby, to come. He said that Silvio had a bad case of pneumonia.

Francesco and Paolo took turns at watching over him. Outside it got colder and colder as the windows frosted. At intervals Francesco took a wet cloth and sponged Silvio's face, but the fever became worse. The next day Dr. Slocum returned and shook his head.

"I thought once the fever broke he'd get better, but it didn't happen that way." Silvio was delirious, shouting incoherent words and phrases. The brothers wiped his face and body with alcohol but he radiated heat. Through the night they sat quietly, hoping and saying prayers. Another day passed and through the night Silvio hardly moved his parched body. At daybreak the breathing stopped, the body lay still. Francesco ran to Dr. Slocum's. He came, listened to Silvio, ruefully shook his head and pulled the sheet over Silvio's head. The brothers wept silently at first, then loudly.

After the funeral, the most difficult thing they had to do was write home and give their parents the news. They didn't know how to say such bad news. Finally, they composed a letter and sent it off.

━━━━━━━

Six months after they returned to New York from Vermont, Francesco asked to meet Dora's two brothers to discuss his wish to marry her. Her older brother Manfredo was in charge of this meeting, due to his rank in the family, in the absence of her father. Paolo sat behind Francesco as if he were a second to a prize fighter, not uttering a word but strong in silence.

"It is clear that I love Dora, and I believe that she feels the same about me. I am twenty five years old. I have a trade from which I live—*scalpellino a granito*—granite cutter. I have worked everyday that I have been in America. I help support my family in Italy, but together with my brother I can help support them and still have a family of my own."

"Would your family approve of and accept Dora?" Manfredo asked.

"When they hear about her, yes. Dora is warm and affectionate and physically strong. I believe that she cares for me and will stand with me."

Manfredo went into another room to confer with the rest of the family. When he returned, he stood in the door with a solemn face. Francesco and Paolo got up to face him.

"We accept you, Francesco, as a husband for our sister, Dora."

Manfredo's seriousness seemed funny to Francesco. He wanted to laugh but knew he should not, fearing he would offend him. Inside he felt liberated, he knew that soon he could kiss Dora without fear or embarrassment; he could bury his face in her dark hair. He would love her and make love to her ceaselessly. She would be his, and they would kiss and kiss.

Manfredo shook hands and then all hugged each other.

Francesco felt he was in a new world, his thoughts no longer hesitant. No more wondering and worrying if he would lose her or if he and his brother would go back to Italy. Paolo and Francesco lived in a dingy room in Mott Street. He couldn't take her there, but he felt bad at leaving Paolo alone. Paolo told him that Dora's younger sister Nicoletta often made eyes at Paolo. He would not be displeased if she read his thoughts and accepted him as a suitor.

After work Francesco walked around the neighborhood looking at rooms and small apartments. They all looked the same, more or fewer rooms, all dark and the bathroom in the hallway. He often thought of his house in Giovinazzo with its courtyard, sturdy stone walls and windows that let in the sun all day. He imagined Dora holding up a child, offering it to his mother and father. "Behold the next generation. I give you another son, Mastro Paolo. He is yours. I am yours. We are all one." Francesco felt his fatherhood deep in his bones, in his every gesture.

Dora now was also freed. She would be a wife and have new liberties. Her thoughts would not be quieted in her mind, snuffed out to conform to what befit a woman of her age and class. Now she could think it all and feel it all; someday Francesco would be hers. His kisses and caresses, now so controlled, had been dampened by fear or apprehension. She didn't know what lovers did, but she knew that Francesco would know, and whatever that was it would involve their whole selves.

Francesco spoke of living in Brooklyn. He spoke of streets lined with trees and less traffic. With the subway nearby he could get to work easily. It would be, he thought, a better place to raise a family.

Francesco and Paolo spent the weekend looking for a place to live. Everywhere he went he found houses, some made of brick or stone, some of wood. Behind the houses he saw fig trees casting their shadows. In the front yards next to flower beds, green leaves of sweet basil stood up strongly. These had to be Italian houses, he knew.

Paolo kept seeing Dora's younger sister, Nicoletta. Most of the time the two brothers and two sisters met and went to the opera or for a walk along Broadway. Nicoletta looked a lot like her sister but was smaller and energetic. She had the same dark brown hair but her looks were less lustrous than Dora's. Together they walked, talked, drank coffee and planned their lives.

This time it was Francesco who sat as a second to Paolo. The same words were said to Manfredo as if Francesco's words had also been scripted for his brother. He worked, would work, be strong, reliable, a tower of strength for their sister. They would have a large family and bring honor to them all. Manfredo excused himself and went into the next room. It seemed like he stayed a long time. Francesco and Paolo both smoked cigarettes endlessly. Manfredo reappeared with a somber face. "Paolo, we respect you as we respect your brother and would embrace you as a brother but there is one problem." It was like an icicle jabbed into Paolo's heart.

"What is that?"

"There is this fellow in Italy who once showed an interest in Nicoletta."

"When was that?" Paolo asked.

"That doesn't matter. What is important is that we agreed to acknowledge his interest."

"But that had to be when they were children." Paolo said impatiently and angrily.

"Agreements once made cannot be rejected, otherwise we would lose honor and that would hurt Nicoletta."

"Nicoletta loves me, I know it. She told me that she cares for me and I care for her. I want her to be my wife."

In another part of the house Nicoletta and her sister Dora sat listening. Nicoletta cried silently into her handkerchief. Manfredo would not budge.

"Agreements cannot be thrown away like rags," he said.

"I recognize your wishes but we must also recognize Nicoletta's," Paolo said.

"They are hers" Manfredo said sternly. "What we have decided to do is to write home and ask my cousin Biaggio to talk with the boy to find out his intentions," Manfredo said. "Who knows what has happened to him? We shall ask Biaggio."

Walking home Paolo was burning in anger and impatience. Why hadn't Nicoletta told him? She probably doesn't even remember him.

For days Paolo didn't speak. Now only Francesco went to see Dora because it seemed there was no point in Paolo going.

"What if that fellow in Italy wants to marry her? What then? Then I'm out, that's what."

Francesco continued looking at houses in Brooklyn. Paolo accompanied him but with his situation uncertain, they could not think of buying an old house that they could fix up. Now they would try to find a house that they could rent. They went to Staten Island, took the ferry from the Battery and then a trolley car. There it was the country—trees, hills, an occasional house. How would they get to work? Along the route they saw an old rickety house. A sign said Giuseppe Garibaldi had once lived there. They couldn't believe it. Back in New York the brothers still couldn't believe that Giuseppe Garibaldi, the great patriot of Italy, had lived in that house. He was a hero and he should, at least, have had a much bigger house they thought.

They waited to hear from Nicoletta's cousin in Italy. Each day Francesco went to her house full of expectations. As he came in the door her brother shook his head. "Nothing." Nicoletta was never to be seen when Francesco came to call. She too waited and wondered what the mails would bring.

One day Francesco came and Nicoletta ran in and told him they got the news. This fellow emigrated to Australia and married somebody down there. She was free. Francesco immediately ran home and sprinted up the steps, all five floors to tell Paolo. When he answered the door Paolo looked at Francesco's face. He did not have to say anything; Paolo knew.

Nicoletta's brothers had insisted on a full six months wait but Francesco told them that the time they waited for the answer from Italy had to count. It was decided that they would be married in a double ceremony.

Francesco and Paolo started looking into wedding preparations. They would also have to write home and inform their parents. There was the church, a reception and a honeymoon. All of this would cost but these were the inevitable expenses of life. They would call Il Leccese who had a car to bring them to the church and reception in style. Then of course they would get Angelo, the Master of Ceremonies. His cousin

Mauro, would get a band. No, Paolo wanted opera singers. They would work it out, and maybe have both.

The day came that they were married, Francesco first since he was older. They rented two tuxedos with boiled, starched shirts. The couples were each other's best man and maid of honor.

At the reception, people danced, the band played, and the singers sang. Francesco and Paolo held their spouses proudly and possessively, there were no longer any barriers.

After the reception, Il Leccese drove them to a hotel on Broadway. Paolo and Nicoletta sat in the rumble seat and Francesco and Dora in the passenger seat. When they got out Il Leccese refused any money and said that was his present. He turned away as they went in, out of delicacy. He didn't want to embarrass the brides by watching them go in the hotel to do what they all knew they were going to do. The next day they would take the train to Atlantic City for a few days, and then return to the city to work and start building their families.

—————

Nicoletta sat by the window. Outside it rained; it would be that way for the rest of the day. The drops ran down the window pane, and she accompanied the downpour with her own tears.

Downstairs in Francesco's apartment, she could hear his children's voices as they played. She had not borne Paolo any children. Each month she hoped that she too would feel the stirrings in her womb, feel, as she had heard so many times, the painful pleasure of the breasts swelling, feel a sickness of the stomach that meant that a child would be born. Their house had a sterile stillness and order. No one disturbed that order and made messes with paper and toys. She gave her love to Francesco's children without reservation but she could feel the role of a childless woman closing around her. She wanted to have the feeling of a life growing inside that was uniquely hers but time was passing with every day, month, year. She sewed clothing for her nieces but not for children of her own. Her husband came home to a warm meal, and a clean house. Their only distraction was a canary that sang all day in a chilling, high warble.

Nicoletta went to the doctor because at night she wakened, feeling alternately hot and cold surges. She gasped for air. She went to Father Flynn, who coldly assured her that God had a plan for everyone. With or without children she would be God's servant and serve Him as He thought fit.

Paolo never said a word but he too wished for his own offspring. He wasn't sure if this was part of God's plan or not; that did not interest him. At least, they had each other. She imagined what it would have been like if she had never married and one day she would face her death in solitude.

Feeling this desolation of body, she went to Dr. Weinberg, a specialist who had no particular interest in God's plan. He told her what she hoped she would never hear, that she was sterile. He said she would never have any children.

Nicoletta realized what she had to do. She had heard from one of the *paesani* that in Bensonhurst there was an old woman who practiced her own kind of medicine. Donna Concetta was reputed to have saved the lives of old and young. People told that they had a month to live, saw the light of day for years with her help. Some people called her a witch and would have nothing to do with her. They blamed her for the death of their family members, but those who believed in Donna Concetta of Bensonhurst never hesitated to recommend her.

Paolo tried to convince Nicoletta that the woman was a witch and it was a waste of time to see her. "The doctor said you would never have a baby."

Nicoletta said, "I want to go see Donna Concetta. I never believed him."

In the basement of an old house, Donna Concetta received people. As Paolo and Nicoletta went down the steps, another couple was coming out.

"*Venite, venite,*" Donna Concetta said, waving them in. Nicoletta began crying into a handkerchief.

"*Figlia bella, non piangere, non piangere,* don't cry," she said soothingly.

"*Non posso avere figli,* I can't have children," Nicoletta choked out.

"Is that all? Do you know how many women I gave babies to? You wouldn't believe it. After a few times with me, they go home and they make baby. Two gave them my name! I have a Concetta Dora and a Maria Concetta," she boasted.

"All I want is to have children, Donna Concetta, please help me," Nicoletta pleaded.

Donna Concetta motioned Nicoletta to come near her. She was sitting in an old easy chair, whose cover was worn by the years. "Now, Nicoletta, come here, come close to me."

Nicoletta came close and Donna Concetta rubbed Nicoletta's stomach, while she hummed and sang a tune. Paolo was embarrassed by all that was going on. He didn't think that there was magic in her fingers and that rubbing Nicoletta's belly was nonsense but he said nothing. He looked around the basement apartment with its faded wallpaper, votive candles blinking in the darkness and pictures of saints on the wall. He was disgusted. Donna Concetta still rubbed Nicoletta's belly intoning her song. At the end, Paolo paid Donna Concetta five dollars, which she folded and put into her brassiere.

At home, Nicoletta continued to say her rosary. Sometimes Dora would come to her sister's apartment, and they would both pray for Nicoletta to become pregnant.

After two more treatments with Donna Concetta, one day Nicoletta felt terribly ill and ran to the bathroom to throw up. She couldn't keep anything down for several days. Once again, she asked Paolo to bring her to Donna Concetta's house.

"Oh, *figlia mia bella*, now we are moving," Donna Concetta said and she waved her hands in the air. "Come here, *figlia mia bella*, let me rub you some more."

Nicoletta said that she wondered if she was pregnant. Paolo made a face. "The doctor, a real doctor, told you you couldn't have babies."

"I don't believe him. I believe Donna Concetta."

Paolo threw up his hands in anger.

Three months later she began to feel something kicking in her belly. Paolo did not believe it until she guided his hand on her swollen belly and he felt a kick. He too was overjoyed. "So," he said, "the doctor was wrong and a witch from Calabria was right. We're going to have a baby."

PART VI

A letter from Francesco and Paolo came to Giovanni at his job in Italy. It spoke about the brothers' work and their wives and children. Giovanni read it several times and remembered what it was like to be at the wharf in Naples ready to go to America and then to be detained because of this business of tuberculosis. He sat back and remembered it all.

The four of them had left for Naples full of anticipation.

"There certainly is a problem with your brother," the examining doctor said to Silvio. "He is tubercular."

"Are you sure? No one has ever mentioned anything like this," Silvio said.

"He is in the incipient stages of tuberculosis, and as such," the doctor said with great emphasis, "I cannot approve him for emigration. He will be turned away at the port of entry when he is reexamined."

Silvio was stunned by the word "tuberculosis," and by the fact that Giovanni would have to return home. His brothers stood there wondering what they should do.

After conferring together, Silvio, who was the eldest brother, said, "Giovanni, he won't let you go. Perhaps in a few weeks or months you can try again. Go back home and explain everything to Mamma and Pappa, and go with them to see a doctor in Bari. Once we get established in America, we can send for you. That is the only way out of this," and he looked at the doctor, who had buried himself in his papers again.

Once Giovanni was on the train going home, he lost himself in his thoughts. The noise of the wheels was hypnotic. He would not arrive in Bari until the next morning and since he couldn't sleep he rehearsed what he would say to his parents.

What would people think? After all the fuss about leaving, and people coming by to wish them luck, he now had to return. All through the night the words of the doctor rang in Giovanni's ears, "Tuberculosis, tuberculosis." This would make him a leper in the town; nobody would have anything to do with him for fear of contracting tuberculosis from him.

When light began to appear, the train was going through the lush fields of Cerignola. He saw the very things he would have missed in America, the groves of almond trees and their white buds, giant fig trees that bore figs the size of a fist; olive trees loaded with fruit of green olives, ready to be pressed. This is what they meant by "*I beni di Dio*," God's gifts. At eight in the morning the train reached Giovinazzo and with a long whistle made its presence known to all.

At the train station was Giacomo the carter and his wagon with the dog tied to the rear axle. "Giovanni? You just left and now you're back?"

He thought it best not to say why he was returning but he couldn't think of anything to say. "Giacomo, I am tired. When they bring my trunk out, please bring it home."

"I hope some Neapolitan whore didn't take all your money," he guffawed.

"Just bring the trunk home and my father will take care of you."

His next ordeal was to walk through the town. He could have ridden with Giacomo but he knew that sooner or later he had to face the curiousity his return would arouse. As he walked along the curved and ancient streets, head after head emerged from the houses to see who was walking by. Donna Giuseppina, then Donna Beatrice, each with their head covered with a black kerchief, leaned out of their closed houses. Giovanni did not look up to greet them.

The town's longest street, Via Garibaldi, led to his house. He looked up, his mother was on the balcony hanging out wash to dry. His sister, Filomena, was watching people go by from her window. With each step Giovanni rehearsed his defense. He even practiced repeating things that were said by the doctor in Naples. He was at the door. He banged strongly with the knocker, which had the face of a lion. The noise echoed through the house.

"Mamma, it's Giovanni, he's back from America already," Filomena said.

Her mother knew better. She kissed her son and led him into the house, closing the heavy door behind him.

"Mamma, I am so ashamed," he said.

"What is there to be ashamed of, my son?"

"We all set off to go to America. I looked forward to working so as to keep you and Pappa in some comfort. I wanted to become a millionaire like so many people I have heard about, but when we got to the port of Naples a doctor examined me and told me that he could not approve me for leaving because he said," he paused here, it was difficult to say the words, "I had tuberculosis."

He waited with his head averted. His mother brought a handkerchief to her lips and made the sign of the cross.

"But you have never been sick a day in your life." She leaned up and put her hand on his forehead. "See, you have no fever."

"The doctor in Naples said that he was a specialist and knew I had tuberculosis. He was a miserable Northerner who laughed at me and Silvio when we tried to reason with him. He was surrounded by other Northerners and they laughed at us when we protested. I was afraid that Francesco was going to get violent." His mother closed her eyes and seemed to be praying.

"Mamma, what am I going to tell Pappa?"

Just then, Mastro Paolo came in and kissed Filomena. Giovanni was dreading this moment. His father was startled to see Giovanni.

"Pappa, they didn't let me go to America. They said that I had tuberculosis."

"Tuberculosis?"

"Yes, the doctor in Naples said that he could not approve me to go because, according to him, I had tuberculosis, and once I arrived, the Americans would send me right back home. He said he was doing us a favor."

"Who was this doctor?" he asked.

"Pappa, he was some Northerner. I tried to get him to reconsider. We even said that we could go into Naples to get another examination, but he laughed and said better go to the mountains for clean air."

Mastro Paolo thought a minute.

"I don't know that the mountains are any better than the sea with its pure salt air," his mother said and began to cry.

"What are you crying about?" Mastro Paolo said angrily. "You were the one who was always saying that God will provide. What about now?"

The next day when his mother and sister were busy doing something, Giovanni took his cap and walked quietly out of the house. He went down to the square, and entered the town café. All conversation stopped when he entered and everyone looked at him. Giovanni thought they were entertaining thoughts of a possible illness or even a crime that prevented him from leaving Naples.

"*Giulio, un caffè, per favore,*" Giovanni said, not flinching. Giulio prepared him his coffee. "*Servito.*"

"*Grazie.*

Giovanni felt the weight of the silence in the room. After taking a sip or two he turned to the others that watched his every move for evidence that something was not right. He swallowed the rest of the coffee and headed out the door.

As he walked the streets he could see people stepping back into their homes in order to avoid him. An old woman gave him the horns of the *malocchio,* the evil eye, when he passed her house. There were a lot of reasons as to why he might not have left with his brothers but everybody knew the cause was usually illness or mental deficiency.

At home, his father sat at the table with a pencil in hand, writing down figures, columns of them. He did this for a while, until Giovanni said:

"Pappa, what are you working on? You are going to wear the pencil down."

Mastro Paolo did not say anything and did not look up either. He kept working away at the figures. Finally he looked up at Giovanni and said: "It will work."

"What will work?"

"You will work," he said with a sly smile.

Mastro Paolo realized that dry, pure air could restore health to his son's lungs and he remembered an old client for whom he had made two gravestones. They were for the man's parents and they were masterfully done. The customer, a Don Andrea, was very happy with the work.

The client answered Mastro Paolo's letter quickly assuring him that he could in fact use Giovanni in any number of jobs in his hotel and restaurant in the mountains outside Rome.

Giovanni's mother once again went through the throes of watching a child of hers leave. Marta went to the cathedral and stood before La Madonna di Corsignana.

La Madonna had come to Giovinazzo town long ago in the rucksack of a crusader only to be abandoned because a death penalty had been declared for soldiers found with loot. The icon was found near Giovinazzo but Molfetta also and both towns claimed it. The dispute threatened to break out into violence.

La Madon' was placed on a bed of straw—imagine it, Marta thought—Our Lady in a cart pulled by two oxen. The agreement was that whichever city the oxen turned toward at the crossroads, that city would claim the icon.

In this miraculous way, her beloved Madonna found her way to Giovinazzo. Today, Marta had come to ask for a miracle of health for her son, Giovanni. She knelt to pray.

━━━━━━━━━━━━━━━━

Giovanni took the train again and kept his eyes open for con men and other things that his parents warned him about. He didn't worry about such things when he left with his brothers because he knew that Silvio was a very shrewd person who could not be taken for a fool.

Arriving at the Rome railroad station, he looked around for his trunk and did not see any one with it. The noise of the station was louder than anything he had ever heard. The whistle of the trains deafened him, and he saw the porters pushing their noisy wagons. Giovanni kept looking for his trunk and finally, he asked about it. The porter pointed to the baggage claim.

Suddenly, a man stepped forward. *"Paesano,"* he said reaching out with his arms. "How good it is to see someone from the old town here in Rome! What brings you here?"

Giovanni could not remember this person at all, but his effusiveness was convincing and Giovanni went along.

"I am here to work in a hotel and restaurant outside of Rome."

"Is that so? Well, let's see what I can do to help a *paesano.*"

"Thank you," Giovanni said politely. "I need to find my trunk and then find a way to go to Torresanta."

"Torresanta? I have other *paesani* there that are going to help you when you get there. Leave it all to me. First of all, we have to get your trunk. Do you have the ticket they gave you when you checked it?"

Giovanni searched in his pockets and finally found a crumpled brown ticket with the numbers on it.

"Here let me have it."

Giovanni handed it over to him.

"Now you know that you will have to pay a small amount to the clerk to handle it for you?"

"How much should I give him?" Giovanni asked.

"Three lire," he said.

Giovanni reached into another pocket and took out three lire and gave them to him.

"Now you wait here."

Giovanni went to a bench and waited. The noise and hustle-bustle continued and he felt a little lost. He wondered how he would get to Torresanta. Would it be by horse and carriage or would it be by cart? The *paesano* surely would know. He waited until he became uneasy. Giovanni went to the baggage claim to see for himself. There he found a clerk dressed in a grey smock, pushing boxes and luggage in a cart.

"I am looking for my trunk. I brought it on the train but...."

"What is the number? Where did you come from?"

"Giovinazzo, Bari, to Rome."

"Do you have the ticket, the tab that they gave you in Giovinazzo?"

"I gave it to a fellow I met in the station. He said that he was from my town."

The clerk looked at him. "What did this *paesano* of yours look like?"

"He was about my height, heavier than I and dressed well."

"And he had a large cravat, didn't he?" the clerk interrupted. "He is one of the biggest con men we have in Rome. You gave him the ticket and he said that he would be bringing the bag to you, right?"

"That's correct."

"My friend, you won't see him and you will not see your belongings again in this lifetime."

Giovanni was crestfallen. His first trip alone and he had been taken for a fool. What would he do now? He had no clothes, nothing. "I am going to the police, that's what I am going to do," Giovanni said sternly.

"Go to the police? They will take down your statement and then file it somewhere they themselves could never find. It's a lost cause."

Giovanni walked away from the baggage depot, feeling desolate, not so much for being a trusting fool but because he did not have a thing to call his own. What would he do when he got to the hotel and restaurant? They would know that he had been tricked.

Giovanni saw a policeman and decided that he would report the theft. He told the details to the policeman who asked, "If I found him and showed him to you, would you be able to identify him?"

"Of course. He was my height, a lot heavier than me. Dressed well, with a large cravat."

"If you go outside, do you know how many people like that you would find? Thousands, thousands. Don't forget you are in Rome."

Giovanni realized what the clerk had said was true, he would be laughed at for his stupidity.

"I see," he said. "I see. Thank you."

While he had the attention of the policeman, he asked if he knew the way to Torresanta.

"Torresanta, Torresanta," he mused, "there is a coach that leaves in an hour. You get a ticket for it at the station, then you go to the corner of Ognissanti and San Benedetto. It will stop there and pick up passengers. And don't," he insisted, "don't strike up conversations with people you don't know."

The trip to Torresanta was even more tedious than the overnight train. Here, he heard the crunch of rocks being crushed under the wheels of the coach while the passengers around him slept. Giovanni was wide awake from embarrassment due to having his trunk stolen. What would he say to his new employer? He made up a tale about how his trunk got lost during the trip, or better, it didn't make it on the train when it departed from Giovinazzo.

He fell asleep for what seemed like a long time but it was in reality just a few minutes. The coachman yelled out, "Torresanta, Torresanta." Giovanni shook himself awake and started to get out of the coach.

"Did you have any luggage?" the coachman inquired.

Giovanni thought about trying out his new excuse on the coachman but was too tired to do it, he simply shook his head.

At the late hour there was no one to be found at the hotel or the restaurant, which was closed. Giovanni could see a sign that said, Albergo e Ristorante Lentino, Andrea Lentino, Prop. He walked around the building several times wondering how he was going to get in for the night. He was afraid that he would awaken the owner who might be annoyed.

Unexpectedly, an old man appeared holding a shotgun. At the sight of the shotgun, Giovanni's heart began to pump faster. "I am a new employee and not a burglar," he said. The watchman kept the shotgun aimed at him.

"I mean no harm and I'm not a thief."

The watchman lowered the shotgun. "Where do you come from?" he asked.

"Giovinazzo, in Puglia. I am here for a job that was promised me."

"Who promised you a job?"

"Don Andrea is a client of my father and he agreed to give me a job working here. I would like to be in the mountains." Giovanni regretted saying that because once again he might become the pariah he had become in Giovinazzo.

"I don't know where I am going to put you. As you can see, it is very late and everything is closed. The best I can do is put you up in the storeroom."

"I don't need much right now, just a place to sleep. I'm dead tired, *stanco morto*."

They walked through the darkness to an outbuilding. From what Giovanni could see there were sacks of potatoes and onions and boxes piled up along the wall. The watchman pointed to the sacks of potatoes and said: "That's going to be your bed tonight."

Giovanni winced.

"Beggars can't be choosers," the guard said.

The next morning Giovanni woke feeling tired and sore. How he wished he could bathe and then he remembered that he had no clothing to change to; that was another sore point.

The watchman came and opened the door letting in the light.

"My God, I couldn't sleep with no bed."

"Oh, I guess we have a *signorino* here, a *figlio di Pappa,* a daddy's boy. You didn't like the bed?" He pushed aside some boxes. "You had better get up. Don Andrea wants to see you."

"Is it possible to wash, maybe even take a bath?"

"A bath? That's for Saturday night! Right now you go see Don Andrea and and then you go to work. We don't waste time around here. Don Andrea won't allow it."

"Surely, I can wash my face."

"Follow me, there's water out back here. See what you can do."

After splashing his face with water and drying his face on his shirt, he plastered down his hair with what was left of water and followed the watchman.

———

"Come in, come in," Don Andrea greeted him. "Why didn't you tell me last night when you arrived? What is your father going to think of me?"

Giovanni thought of the night sleeping on the sacks of potatoes but thought better not to say anything. "I didn't want to disrupt the household having arrived so late."

Don Andrea was a big man, large in body and voice. He was still wearing his nightshirt and a robe, made of red silk. His factotum stood by in the background.

"Have you had anything to eat?" he asked.

"No sir," he said. His stomach growled with hunger, since he had not eaten since yesterday afternoon. "Giulio, don't stand there. Bring Giovanni into the kitchen with the other help, and give him something to eat."

Looking around him, Giovanni saw the kitchen help, six or seven people, all *contadini,* country people, who went about their business. Some seemed to look upon him resentfully as an interloper, some were unconcerned because they had seen many people come and go.

Feeling the strain, Giovanni got up after he ate, and turned to someone who could have been the manager of the kitchen and said,

"Are you the majordomo?"

They all broke out into laughter. "A majordomo? Who? Him?"

The man stiffened up and said that he was in charge of disposal. More laughter. "He's the sweeper and garbage man," someone howled.

Giovanni felt sorry that he began with that question, because the man was obviously humiliated by the reaction of the others in the kitchen.

"I'm sorry I made that mistake," he said apologetically.

"The others are happy to see anybody embarrassed. That's their pleasure."

Giovanni repeated his apologies. "My name is Giovanni, and I am here to work in the hotel and restaurant."

"A pleasure to know you," he answered taking off his cap.

Another of the kitchen help called out to Giovanni, "What kind of work will you be doing?"

"I don't know. Whatever Don Andrea needs, I suppose."

"Don't worry. There's plenty of work to be done here inside or outside," answered another.

Don Andrea's property consisted of many acres of land, on which grapes, tomatoes, almonds, olives, figs and other vegetables were grown.

He was one of the biggest landlords in Torresanta. The family of Don Andrea had increased their wealth through a series of marriages of convenience with distant relatives. In this way lands were brought together, as well as houses, hunting lodges, and a summer house farther up on the mountain.

There came a time came when some of the family lands had to be sold to make ends meet. Don Andrea was driven to create a hotel and restaurant which would provide the family with cash income. Don Andrea, without help from anyone, had mastered the basic administration of a hotel and restaurant.

His day began with going to market to purchase the food. His majordomo always accompanied him, sitting on the buckboard with the coach driver. Don Andrea, in his small splendor, sat back in the carriage and when they came upon people, especially people of greater category, he sat straight and tipped his hat. He had a special look he adopted, half smile and half serious. If the person were very important, he would stand and give a slight bow.

Don Andrea's marriage to Adelaida Correa, had not brought the economic solvency he expected. He thought at the beginning that she came to the marriage with a sizeable dowry, but her father did not have all the resources that he pretended to have. Although Signor Correa was adept at maintaining a good house and an appearance of wealth, he had no economic fluidity. There were small amounts of property but these had to be shared with two other sisters, so Don Andrea had to resign himself to the idea that he had not become wealthy through marriage.

He sustained his ego and his pretensions by having many servants and by associating with the wealthier people in Torresanta. He was also careful to maintain the friendship of those in political power in Torresanta and in the province at large. On occasion, a representative of the king came through town and Don Andrea could not do enough for him. Thus Don Andrea reigned as a kind of lord over his domain.

Once in the kitchen, Giovanni was given an apron and brought to a work station where many sacks of onions lay.

"Okay, *signorino*," one of the cooks said, "start peeling these onions, and when you are through, I want you to chop them up for cooking."

Giovanni thought that this was an easy job until he had peeled a dozen onions. The others were snickering as Giovanni doubled up in convulsions of weeping and coughing. Giovanni kept on working, though his tears flowed. He didn't want them to have the satisfaction of seeing him walk off the job.

"Eh, what's the matter? You got a problem?" the others asked, watching Giovanni wipe his eyes.

As best he could, Giovanni tried to answer: "I'll get over it. I'll finish the job." he said in a choked voice.

"You're damned right you will, because if you don't, you will be out of here right away."

Giovanni continued to peel the onions, one after the other, until all eight sacks were done. He stepped outside.

"Giovanni," the chef called. "What are you doing, you lazy bum? I need you in here, not outside. What are you doing, keeping the flowers company? Get in here now."

Giovanni finished wiping his eyes and went to the chef.

"Now that you are finished crying like a baby, I want you to start peeling those potatoes, and don't take off more than just the skin, do you understand? The last bum we had here removed as much potato as skin, goddamn it. Get on with it now."

After washing his hands and face, Giovanni looked at the small mountain of potatoes he had to peel, grabbed one and started peeling it. The cook came by and examined the skins.

"Look at all you left on the skin here? What do you think, that we're made of money?" He threw up his hands in exasperation. "What sin did I commit to get this lazy dumbbell?"

"I'm peeling the potatoes, aren't I," Giovanni answered.

Don Andrea was told that Giovanni arrived without any clothes, nothing except the shirt on his back.

"I don't understand how a man as wise and correct as your father could send you away for an extended period of time without giving you clothes," Don Andrea wondered out loud.

"Don Andrea, I told you that my baggage was lost in transit. I had all the clothes I would need for a long time," he answered defensively.

The watchman took Giovanni to a back room on the estate where there was pile of old clothing and he rummaged through looking for some clothes that Giovanni could wear. Shirts, their collars lined with sweat and a couple of shapeless coats were gathered for Giovanni to call his own.

After Giovanni performed his kitchen tasks, he was told to go to the dining room where he would get lessons in serving.

Carlo was the maître d'hôte, and he had been with Don Andrea for many years. Carlo got to wear a uniform similar to a soldier's, a long coat with shiny gold buttons and braid on the shoulders. Giovanni came in, still in his cooking smock and reeking from onions.

"And whom do we have here?" Carlo asked with a sneer on his face.

"I am Giovanni, the new man in the kitchen…."

"And the restaurant and the hotel, *mio caro*."

Giovanni knew that he would have several jobs but he began to wonder how much work was expected of him.

"Right now, the first thing you have to do is learn how to serve and to take away dishes," Carlo said. "You bring a plate to the left side and take it away from the right." Giovanni nodded. "You place the water in front of the fork and the wine in front of the knife. You put the fork on the left side of the dish and the knife, the blade facing the dish on the right. Understand?" Giovanni nodded.

As Carlo explained all this he picked up each article with the delicacy of a surgeon. "The napkin on the left side under the fork, folded in an elegant fashion." Then he stepped back and looked upon his creation with the satisfaction of an artist. "There. You see? It is my job to keep the standards up. When people come in and sit down, you greet them: '*Buon giorno, buona sera,*' you nod lightly. Then you bring mineral water: one bottle for two people, two for four people. You ask, '*bianco o rosso?*' Usually they have an idea if they are going to have meat or fish. Then you come to me and tell what kind of wine I should bring them. *Capito?* Understood?" Giovanni kept nodding. "When they finish, and you must make sure that they are finished because there is nothing worse than taking away a plate when they haven't finished. Keep your eyes on their mineral water. If the meal is at the beginning and it looks like they have drunk most of their mineral water, then you ask the oldest person at the table, '*Ancora, acqua minerale?* Let them tell you. You must not hover over the table while they are eating, you are there but you are not there, *Capito?* Of course, you will be assisting other tables."

He would do his best, Giovanni assured Carlo. Giovanni himself had a uniform, not like Carlo's which was military; Giovanni's was plain, a white jacket, black pants, and a black bow tie.

After his jobs in the kitchen in the morning, he went and got his busboy's outfit and then laid out all the forks, spoon, glasses, and napkins on all the tables. He also had the job of getting flowers to put in a vase on each table to add to the elegant atmosphere.

Dressed in his uniform Giovanni waited at the door for people to come in. An older couple from Modena came in. He was a music conductor with white flowing hair down to his shoulders. His wife was matronly, short, and stocky with hair piled high on her head. Giovanni greeted them, but then Carlo swept in and bowing greeted the Maestro and wife, including kissing her hand, which he did in one swooping motion. His arm motioned to the left and they followed. Carlo turned to Giovanni, *"Attenzione!"* Giovanni rushed to the table, bringing a bottle of mineral water.

"This is *gaseosa*, I want plain," the signora snapped.

"Sorry," Giovanni said and rushed off into the kitchen to get regular mineral water.

"Bianco o rosso, White or red wine?" Giovanni asked.

"Cretino," she carped. "We have no idea of what we are going to have, so how can we choose?"

Giovanni felt deflated. He had memorized his routine so that it would come out cleanly.

"Sorry," he said and left the table.

Carlo told him to fetch white wine. Giovanni rummaged through the wine rack and pulled out one bottle that looked white in the light. He quickly brought it to Carlo, who had the bottle opener at the ready. He looked at the bottle, and through clenched teeth, said, "Giovanni, I said white wine, this is rosé."

"Wait, I'll go and get you a nice, white wine," and Giovanni rushed away. He came back with a bottle dusty with powder and spider webs.

"I am so sorry, Maestro, but he doesn't know anything," Carlo said. "Nothing!" Carlo opened the bottle and poured a little in the Maestro's glass.

He savored the wine, licking his lips, "Nice, if however slightly on the sweet side but still drinkable," the Maestro said.

All the while Giovanni was working each table, running back and forth to see that there was enough mineral water and wine. As the patrons left the dining room, Carlo stood at the door, thanking them and telling them what the main specialty would be the next day. Some even passed him a tip which Carlo acknowledged with a smile.

That night in his room Giovanni could feel his feet sore and his legs tired. He had started out the day by doing kitchen chores, then he worked the dining room and then he helped the scullion wash all the dishes. It was a long day. He wondered just how much good mountain air he was breathing for his problem.

The next day it all began again, this time there was a change in his activities. Instead of going to the kitchen he was sent to the hotel, where he found an attractive woman, Miss Curti, who directed all the hotel activities. She had a small office where she gave out orders to the help. She looked up and said: "Yes, what is it?"

"I was sent here to work with you today," Giovanni said cautiously.

"Where were you working before?"

"I was working in the kitchen."

"Why did they send you here, I would like to know?" she said with her hands on her hips.

"I don't know why, but here I am. What do you need me to do?"

She gave a look of exasperation. "They want to make me crazy, that's what they want to do."

"Put me to work. I'm getting tired of waiting," Giovanni said impatiently.

"Oh, so you are tired of waiting, are you. Well, I am glad to hear that. Then, if you are so tired of waiting, I'll solve your problem," and she came out of the office smartly hitting her heels on the parquet floors. They walked the whole corridor, and she pulled out a ring of keys from her pocket and opened a dark room. It was filled with laundered bed sheets.

"What do you see here?"

"Looks like bed sheets to me," Giovanni answered.

She stood tall and looked him in the eye. "What you will do is to fold all these sheets and pillow cases. Fold them nicely and when you are finished, then come to me and I shall have a few more odd jobs to do so you don't get bored." She swung around and walked out of the room.

The room smelled stale, like it had never been opened to the pure mountain air. He noted that they did not believe in ironing the sheets like his mother did. Giovanni pulled out one, folded it and put it in a pile, a boring job but he kept at it.

Two hours later, the house mistress passed by and gave a cursory look in the room and asked, "Well, *mio caro*, how is the work going?"

"Not bad. It beats cleaning pots and pans. But soon I have to go to the dining room."

Miss Curti looked at the sheets that Giovanni had folded. "You know, you could do better. Look," and she grabbed the topmost sheet in the pile, "here is how I learned to do it." She folded quickly until what was large became a small package. "You see?" she said with satisfaction. As she moved she brushed against Giovanni. He could feel her body against his; he even could see the profile of her breasts in her uniform. Miss Curti had a very officious manner but Giovanni did not forget how she walked by and brushed against him. It left him uneasy and excited. "I guess I should be going otherwise Carlo will have a fit," he said.

"Oh him! He thinks that he is the most important person around here, and you should see how he plays up to Don Andrea."

"Is he a member of the family?" Giovanni asked.

"He might as well be." She stood closer to Giovanni, "Don Andrea lets him get away with murder. I have even heard it said that Carlo has his eye on Don Andrea's daughter."

Giovanni did know that Carlo worked Giovanni to death and browbeat him regularly over small things.

"You don't know the half of what goes on here," Miss Curti said and brushed past Giovanni. She looked back at him and said, "When you get a minute again come over and I'll find you work."

"Yes, okay," he stuttered.

Over in the restaurant, Carlo saw Giovanni and yelled, "Where the hell have you been?"

"I was sent to help out in the hotel and Miss Curti put me to work."

"Miss Curti has no business telling you what to do. I'm the person in charge here not Miss Curti."

"At the desk they told me to go to the hotel this morning instead of working in the kitchen, so I went."

"From now on I am the one who tells you where to go. From now on you check in with me and I'll tell you if you should be in the kitchen or the hotel," Carlo said. Looking over his shoulder, he said "and don't believe a word that Miss Curti says. She is a malicious gossip," and walked away.

That day there were some new guests and Carlo stood by the door in his uniform greeting people as they came in. "The table," he snapped at Giovanni who hurried with mineral water and nearly tripped over his own feet to get there right away.

"Ah, from Naples, are you? I have been there. How wonderful to live in Italy's nicest and liveliest city," Carlo said. He always tried this bit of flattery on everybody, even if they came from the bottom of the sea and they believed him most of the time. After going through the food for the day, Carlo took the liberty of asking why they were in Torresanta. Quiet ensued. Giovanni butted in, "*Rosso o bianco?*"

"I'll tell you when to bring the wine," Carlo snapped.

Carlo smiled and asked if they were on business or holiday. With a strong Neapolitan accent the man said that he should mind his own business. Carlo stepped back. Taking his order, Carlo snapped at Giovanni, "*Rosso.*" As Giovanni poured the wine, he noticed that the man had a black band on his sleeve. Giovanni understood that he was a member of the Fascist party. He made himself scarce except to replenish the mineral water.

On his two hour break, Giovanni would take walks in the forest nearby. He liked the quiet and especially he liked to get away from the restaurant. It was a time of freedom for him.

At the beginning of his free time, he walked past a window and saw Miss Curti talking excitedly. Giovanni could not see to whom she was talking but she waved her hands energetically and her eyes spit fire and hate. Giovanni would love to have known who the person was that was receiving her venom. At one point she yelled something and walked out of the room.

When Giovanni came back toward the hotel curiosity led him past Don Andrea's house. The door was partly open and Giovanni could hear Carlo's voice. He was ranting about being destroyed by Miss Curti and cursing the day he ever saw her.

'Now it is my turn to talk." Miss Curti said. "And I have a lot to say." She continued, "You say that you are being destroyed, what about me? You told the last man who was interested in me that I was a *puttana*?" She didn't wait for an answer and continued. "He liked me in a marrying way and you stuck your nose in and ruined it. Don't you remember, you filthy son of a bitch? From that day on, I declared war on you. He never came back to see me. You killed it and me at the same time. I almost saw the way to get out of here and have a life of my own."

"Lies, lies," Carlo said turning to Don Andrea.

"Lies, you have the audacity to call them lies?" Miss Curti asked. She turned to Don Andrea, "I could have had a life, but this scum poisoned it all, and you know why."

Finally, Don Andrea spoke, "I will not have this nonsense going on here on my property. If you can't get along, both of you will be let go. I am trying to run a respectable hotel and restaurant. You carry on like children and I won't take it any more. Is that understood?"

"But, Don Andrea," Carlo said, "I can't have her talking against me all the time."

"They are not lies, but the truth," Miss Curti answered. She turned to Don Andrea, "One day you will get rid of this snake." And she left the house.

Giovanni hid himself. He had witnessed this battle between the two most important managers there. No one seemed to win and Don Andrea did not seem very convincing that he would get rid of them both.

The next day Giovanni went to the hotel to see if he could find out more. He walked past Miss Curti's office and said, "*Buon giorno, Signorina Curti*."

She looked up at Giovanni. "I thought I could trust you, you miserable worm."

"Me? What did I do?" he answered.

"What did you do? What did you do? Do I need to tell you what you did? You went and told Carlo what I said about him, that's what."

"Miss Curti, I don't know what you are talking about."

"I am afraid I cannot believe you. Carlo, he went to Don Andrea and accused me of saying terrible things about him. How did he know what I said to you?"

"Who knows? Maybe the walls have ears. I swear to you that I did not say anything to anyone about our conversation."

"He is a bad person, you can't trust him. He told Don Andrea I had insulted him and was attacking his character. His character! What a joke, his character!" As she said that she held her hands on her hips swinging from side to side. "Well, how did he find out?" she asked.

"How do I know? I didn't tell him," Giovanni answered defensively. "Look, Miss Curti," Giovanni said, "don't you think that he suspects you tell people about him?"

"You could be right. Frankly, I can't afford to lose this job. I have people depending on me."

Back in the restaurant Carlo watched Giovanni with great suspicion. Giovanni now had a slight advantage because he had heard the conversation at Don Andrea's and knew that there was a puzzle to be deciphered.

"Where have you been?" Carlo asked. "Just make sure that you don't go to Miss Curti's office, because if I hear that you did, you're finished around here. You can go back to the swamps of the South or wherever in the hell you come from."

Giovanni contained himself, there were no swamps where he came from, but the insult was clear, he was a Southerner and that meant that in the eyes of Carlo, he was a primitive.

"Yes, sir," Giovanni murmured.

That day Giovanni overheard that an important political figure, a high-ranking member of the Fascist party, a Minister, was coming to the hotel and would be taking his meals there. Carlo knew the extent of

Don Andrea's ambitions. Don Andrea wanted to be everybody's friend, that is, if they were important people, so Carlo went to the kitchen and harangued the chef. Whatever the Minister asked for he was to get; no questions asked, and the chef had better be prepared for anything he might want, even regional dishes. He exhorted the kitchen help that the napkins had better be spotless and the dishware as well.

When the Minister came to the dining room that evening Carlo went up to him, gave a slight bow and introduced himself. The Minister smiled when Carlo told him that it was an honor to have such an important person come to this dining room and his every wish would be granted. Carlo turned to the wife and kissed her hand. Even though the Minister was not of any noble rank, Carlo treated him as if he were a Count or Duke.

He led them to the best table in the dining room and seated them. Carlo looked at Giovanni, "*Mi raccomando*, Giovanni." Giovanni, eager to please Carlo, hurried to bring mineral water to the table.

"You know, Excellency, these days we simply do not have people we can count on for the kind of service that you expect. This clod here can't do anything right. I have had to teach him even the smallest things," he said and looked disparagingly at Giovanni. Giovanni swallowed his pride and helped the people unfold their napkins. For this occasion Carlo wore the best uniform he could find, all buttons shining and shirt starched stiffly.

"Excellency, today our chef, who trained in France, has made a soup in your honor. It is a true country minestrone, made from our own vegetables and with a meat broth from our own stock. I recommend it highly, followed by some egg pasta with our own butter that is so rich it will melt in your mouth. Also, brought in from Civitavecchia we have fish so fresh you can smell the salt water. The chef can make it any way you like." The Minister nodded. After Carlo finished, he turned to Giovanni, "*Rosso* to start. Remember where I put the special bottles for His Excellency," and turned toward the Minister. "We shall do everything we can to make you happy at this table."

Giovanni rushed into the wine cellar where Carlo had shown him the special bottles of wine. Not just everyday wine, but the best they had, vintage wine from their own grapes. He picked up one, held it to the window to make sure it was red, and brought it upstairs. Carlo turned to Giovanni, "Let me see this wine," and he gave an exasperated gesture, "What did I do that God has punished me to have this cretin here in my dining room? Excellency, I'll have to go the cave myself and bring you only the best." He turned to Giovanni, "Idiot, when are you going to learn where I keep the best wines?" and disappeared for ten minutes, whereupon he returned with a bottle covered with dust and cob webs.

"Excellency, this wine is so good it will wake the dead." With a cloth he cleaned the bottle, opened it and served the Minister a taste. The Minister sipped it slowly, swished it around in his mouth and approved it with a nod. With a smile and flourish, Carlo poured it out for the Minister and his wife. One after the other, Carlo brought the plates to the Minister's table. Carlo's every move was accompanied by his smiles.

Giovanni observed them from his place near the wall. The Minister wore a dark suit with a dark shirt and dark tie. He was of medium build, bald and wore a large pin in his lapel with the symbol of the Fascist Party on it. His wife was a matronly woman, made up in a manner that Giovanni's mother would never have approved. Carlo insisted that the Minister and his wife try a special cake that the chef had prepared for them. This, of course, was a lie, but Carlo worked that way.

Giovanni knew nothing about politics. Every now and then in Giovinazzo there was an election in which very few people participated. Most people did not want to get involved with politics because they believed it was a sham. All they ever voted for was a mayor who did nothing. He in turn appointed his friends as "advisors to the mayor."

The Minister commanded so much respect that before he and his wife had finished eating Don Andrea himself, all dressed up, came and paid his respects to them. He kissed the wife's hand. Don Andrea turned to Carlo and said,

"Why are there no flowers on His Excellency's table?"

Carlo's face flushed, and he turned to Giovanni,

"Didn't I tell you to put flowers on the table, idiot? These clods from the South, what do they know about any manners or class?"

Giovanni said nothing and left the table.

"I apologize for this oversight, Excellency, it will not happen again," Carlo said.

The Minister looked up and said nothing. As they prepared to leave Carlo helped the *signora* with her chair and bowed all the way to the door. The Minister nodded and sent his best wishes to Don Andrea.

Later when the bill for the dinner was made, Don Andrea ripped it up, put it on a little dish and told Giovanni to bring it to the Minister's room. Giovanni knocked on the door. The Minister, no longer in his dark suit and outfit, answered, "Yes?"

"Don Andrea asked me to bring this to you, Excellency."

The Minister lifted the silver cover off the dish and picked up the bill now in two pieces. He read that Don Andrea had written "void" on the bill and tore it up. A slow smile came to the Minister's face. He reached in his pocket to give a few coins to Giovanni and said, "Tell Don Andrea that my wife and I thought the dinner was excellent."

A letter arrived for Giovanni. "Caro Giovanni," the letter read. "Since we have not heard from you for a while your mother and I have decided to write to you. We hope that you are well and are taking advantage of the pure air of the mountains. Your health is a matter of our constant concern. So please write and tell us how you are. How is Don Andrea? Did he remember me? He was thankful to me at the time, and I presumed to take advantage of our friendship and send you there. What kind of work are you doing?

"We are all well here, thank God. Your mother is constantly worried about money and how we will do on the olive harvest and later the almond. That is what we are living on, to be sure. I do hear regularly from your brothers who, it seems, are making a good life for themselves in America. I worry that they will work too hard and get sick like poor Silvio, may he rest in peace. We do not even have his remains here so we could go and pray for his soul. He is buried in a place called Vermont. Your brothers send us money in the form of a money order, a *vaglia*. I take this and go to the Maldoni bank and they give me the money in *lire*. God knows how much your mother and I depend on that money to survive. If we have a drought, we are finished. Your sister Filomena, is doing well in school. Her teacher says that she is becoming very skillful at reading, and she writes with a good hand. The other day she wrote a story and gave it to your mother and me. It was about a lamb that got lost and the gypsies stole it. We laughed throughout. I dread the day that she may say that she wants to go to America. I don't know what I would do.

"Please look after your health and write to us. Your mother and I wait to see your handwriting on an envelope. Also, please give my respects to Don Andrea. With all our love, I am, your loving father."

Giovanni read it many times. He folded the letter and put it in his pocket to be reread. He felt that it contained his parents' souls.

The Minister came and went and after him others of his party visited. The weather began to change and instead of hot weather they enjoyed a delightful coolness. In his walks through the forest Giovanni saw the leaves fall and the forest take on a different face. He could feel his face flush as he walked up the side of the mountain. He felt the air come into his lungs with its sharpness and he breathed deeply. He kept doing this until he reached the mountain top and sat down at the foot of a large elm tree. He let his mind wander, anywhere, everywhere. He closed his eyes and felt the caressing breeze go over his face and body. He thought about Carlo and his obsequious ways, of Miss Curti and her flirtation. She was a fine specimen of woman, a face of chiseled features and hair the color of chestnuts but she seemed a cold person. Yet why did she brush against him when she went by? He wondered if there was anything to the gossip about Don Andrea's daughter being no beauty, but for Carlo's sheer opportunism, she would do. Eventually Carlo would become the owner of the restaurant and hotel if he succeeded in marrying her.

He wondered if he was getting better with his so-called tuberculosis. He had no fever, no sweats and he breathed easily. He still thought that the harbor doctor in Naples was wrong. His father had brought him to see a doctor in Bari who thought that it might be some kind of infection or a cold that clouded the lungs, his examination was inconclusive. He had said time and a healthy life would tell.

What must his brothers be doing in America now, he wondered. There was talk of them getting married. That meant they would never come back to Giovinazzo. With the burden of their own families, then it would be difficult to support their parents too.

Mastro Paolo had always told them the story of the son who married and then all but abandoned the father. One day the father and the son went for a long walk. The father told him that he was very tired and could his son carry him. The son did that for a while then he stopped and put the father down near a stone and began to walk away. The father called out and said "Just as you have abandoned me, your son will do the same to you."

Giovanni did not know what his next step would be if he lost his job at the hotel and restaurant. Until he could resolve the problem about his health, there wasn't much he could do. He sent money home to his parents; a small amount but at least it was something. He had seen pictures of New York and would like to live in such a great city The thoughts came and went, until he realized that he had better get back to the restaurant.

Giovanni placed the silverware and stemware on the tables. To avoid the complaints of Carlo he made double sure that there were no errors. He didn't want to hear Carlo talk about him being a clod, a Southerner and an idiot, so he did his job with perfection.

There was a young man from Rome who worked in the kitchen as a dishwasher. His name was Fabio and he and Giovanni were about the same age. Fabio did not say much and when he wasn't washing the dishes, he stood at the sink and smoked cigarettes. They had gotten into a routine of nodding to one another. When Carlo was browbeating Giovanni, Fabio's looks said to Giovanni, "Why don't you kick him in the teeth?"

In time Giovanni and Fabio became friends. He would walk with Giovanni in the woods and they talked and gossiped about everybody. Fabio came from a poor family in Trastevere. He had to work and gave his money to his parents—all of it. Fabio had an attitude of self-assurance. "They can go to hell," he would say about Don Andrea and everybody.

One day Giovanni told Fabio about how Miss Curti had walked past him and brushed her breasts against his chest. "I don't understand her. On the one hand she seems so distant and cold to everyone, but then she goes ahead and flirts this way."

Fabio shrugged. "Who knows what she's all about? All I know is that I don't get involved."

"Yes, but I have to work with her. So I slip away from Carlo's scut work and say that they need me at the hotel. I end up folding bed sheets with Miss Curti, and sometimes she talks; I mean, she really talks."

"What does she say," Fabio asked.

"Basically, she harps on what a son-of-a-bitch Carlo is," Giovanni answered briskly.

"What does she say about Don Andrea?"

"Nothing, really. Except that she thinks that Carlo has him in his pocket, and that is why Carlo gets to stay, even if Don Andrea says that he will sack the two of them if they don't stop fighting."

"I see," Fabio said shaking his head. "Miss Curti knows a lot more than she is saying, I think," and he stopped.

Giovanni didn't know what Fabio was hinting at. "It sounds to me that you know more than you are saying," Giovanni shot back.

Fabio was startled by Giovanni's directness. "Don't we all?" he said and pushed Giovanni in the shoulder.

"*Mio caro figlio*: It has been some time now that we have not received any letter from you. Your mother and I worry all the time and hope that your silence is not due to any health problem. How is your health? Do you have any fevers? Do you sweat at the wrong times? Do you, God forbid, spit blood? These are the signs of tuberculosis, and you should know them. Have you gotten the name of a good doctor nearby? Naturally, you do not want to tell Don Andrea about this. Use your good judgment.

"Your sister Filomena has reached the age of finishing her schooling. Now she will go to the house of Francesca Scotto and learn how to cook. God knows that her mother is an excellent cook but they say that it is always a good idea to learn how to cook from a different person. Signora Scotto will also teach her how to sew and embroider. At the end she will be a fine young woman and then I am sure because she is a very pretty girl, there will be young men gathering around to court her. I saw my sons go to America and now your mother and I, who had waited to enjoy the fruits of our labors, live like old crones. How I wish that we all were together.

"Well, Giovanni, please send us a note or two to calm down our fears. In the meanwhile I send you all our love, your father, Paolo.

"P.S. I have received a letter from your brothers in New York. They have settled in a place called 'Brooklyn,' where they say that they live among other Italians. They say that economically there are problems in America, the Depression. Since they can cut stone, they have work. I pray that it lasts."

Giovanni discreetly asked around about a doctor. Someone told him that there was a doctor in the town of Torresanta. An old fellow but supposed to be good. Taking advantage of a two hour break between the dinner and the evening tea, Giovanni walked to town, at a good pace, proving to himself that he wasn't ill. When he got there, a young woman with an apron and lace cap on her head answered the door. She spoke Roman dialect which he now understood through his contact with Fabio.

"Yes? Can I help you?"

"I would like to see the doctor," he answered.

"What is the problem?"

Giovanni was annoyed. He didn't want to discuss his health problems with her. "I'll talk about that with the doctor," he answered. "Can I come in?"

"Come in and wait until the doctor calls you."

When Giovanni's turn came, he was ushered into the doctor's office. The doctor looked like a priest they had in Giovinazzo, Don Felice. Giovanni felt reassured because he had confessed often to Don Felice.

"Doctor, I have a problem which I would like to discuss with you in the strictest confidence."

"Everything that happens in this office is done in the strictest confidence, young man," the doctor answered.

"Doctor, some time ago my brothers and I went to Naples to go to America. When we were there a doctor said that I had tuberculosis and he wouldn't let me emigrate. I had to come home like a beaten dog. My father suggested that I go to the mountains and that pure mountain air would cure whatever it was that was bothering me."

"Tuberculosis is a very difficult illness to diagnose correctly."

"Could you please see what my condition is, so that either I can stop worrying or I can do what I need to be cured."

"There is no cure for tuberculosis," the doctor said matter-of-factly, "Just treatment to contain its spread." That was cold comfort to Giovanni.

"Doctor, I think that the doctor in Naples was wrong. I don't have the symptoms."

"Most of the so-called symptoms that people cite are wrong anyway," he said, again with a scientific certitude that rubbed Giovanni the wrong way. "Here, take off your shirt and I'll give you a look. Then we'll know what your condition is."

Giovanni took off his shirt and undershirt and stood there, thin as a rail.

"Do you get out into the mountain air?"

"Yes, doctor, I try to go for walks in the woods near the hotel of Don Andrea."

"Ah, you work for Don Andrea. What kind of work do you do for him?"

"I am a waiter and busboy, and I also work in the hotel doing odd jobs."

"Is his daughter married?"

"I don't think so."

"He has done almost everything to marry off his daughter, but nothing seems to come of it," he said with a chuckle.

The doctor started tapping Giovanni's chest with his fingers. Then he asked him to cough. The doctor moved the stethoscope around his chest in front and in back and to Giovanni's heart and listened there. When he was through, he put the horn down and looked at Giovanni.

"Son, I don't think you have tuberculosis, but there are sounds there that might convince the unprepared that it is. Where were you examined?"

"It was in Naples, and then I went to a doctor in Bari."

"Ah, Naples! he harrumphed.

Giovanni was waiting for him to go to work on the doctor in Bari, the kind of treatment a Southerner would get from Carlo, but he didn't.

"I would say that while you do not have tuberculosis, you do have a wheezing condition that could be thought to be tuberculosis. It also means that you must watch this condition carefully; not let it go so that one day you will maybe find yourself spitting blood."

The thought made Giovanni's mind spin. "What should I do?"

The doctor slapped his knee. "Well, for one thing, don't marry Don Andrea's daughter."

Walking through the woods Giovanni took deep breaths. His visit to the doctor left him dissatisfied. He wanted a clean bill of health and only got a partial one. He had been smart not to tell anyone here about it.

When he saw the mountain of onions waiting for him in the kitchen he slipped out quietly and went to the hotel. There were more than the usual number of guests there and the cleaning staff was bustling about from room to room. He walked past Miss Curti's office and cast a glance in. She was there as usual with her papers, shuffling them, exasperated with it all.

"What a miserable life I have," she said. She put her hand up to her forehead. "People come here and then steal the sheets." She threw a pencil against the wall. "I am short seven sheets!" She looked at Giovanni standing there. "Don't just stand there for heaven's sakes," she said. "Start folding the sheets in the utility room."

Giovanni nodded. "As you wish, Miss Curti," and went down the corridor.

"How are you doing?" she said when she came in later. "Look at this *miseria*. You are not neat. Is this the way they do it in your home?"

"Miss Curti, I take that kind of stuff from Carlo because I have no choice, but I don't expect it from you."

"Oh, you mean I don't count?"

"I didn't say that. I simply said that I don't expect it from you."

"Isn't that the same thing? Giovanni, listen. I have to be angry otherwise the people around here think I am soft. If I were not tough, I hate to think what Don Andrea and Carlo would do."

"Please don't talk to me about Carlo. I know all too well what he's like."

"Giovanni, you are probably the only person around here that has some decency."

"When I was sent to do the sheets you treated me no better than Carlo did."

"Poor thing! I didn't know you were so sensitive. Didn't I tell you that I have to maintain this toughness? I am sorry," and she put her hand on Giovanni's cheek. She purred, "Poor thing, so sensitive."

Giovanni enjoyed her soft hand on his cheek and her special smell, a mixture of talc and perfume. "I thought that we could be friends. Who do I have for friends here other than you and Fabio," Giovanni said.

"Listen, don't trust that Fabio either. He comes from the dregs of Rome, a real *cafone*."

"I didn't like him at first, but then we started talking I saw that he was the only person I could talk to. Who was I going to talk to, Carlo?"

She started to remove her hand. Giovanni held it. He turned his body so he could lean against her. She leaned into him too and then the two of them were kissing. Giovanni sent his hands running up and down her back and slowly pushed his pelvis against her. He reached into her blouse and took out her breast. Giovanni looked at the raspberry nipple and leaned to kiss it. Miss Curti pushed him away.

"Now, don't go getting any ideas after this bit of stupidity do you hear?"

Giovanni could say nothing; he was as hot as a pistol and she was pushing him away. This was the stuff that he dreamed about, meeting a woman and having sex this way, not like Fabio talked about, going to a whorehouse in Rome.

Miss Curti fastened her blouse and turned to him. "If I hear that you said a word about this to anyone I shall never forgive you. Do you know what that means? You insult me and you'll be sorry." With that she left quickly and shut the door behind her.

"Where have you been, you son-of-a-bitch?" Carlo was screaming. "Where have you been?" He was livid, his eyes popping out of his head. "Perhaps *il signore* would like to tell me where he was all this time."

Giovanni panicked for a minute, wondering if some spy had tattled on him "We have a whole new group of people staying at the hotel this week, and they didn't have time to do all the rooms, so I went to help fold the linen."

"Didn't I tell you that only I decided where you went?"

"Yes, but I figured that this was important too."

"I'll tell you what's important around here."

"All right, if that is the way you want it," Giovanni answered sullenly.

"And what did the bitch tell you this time?"

Giovanni feigned surprise and ignorance.

"You know who I mean, don't act dumb with me. What did she tell you?"

"If you mean Miss Curti, she and I did not talk. She came by and saw me folding sheets, and she went away."

"Oh, you don't expect me to believe that? Since when did Miss Curti not take advantage of a moment to attack and insult me behind my back?"

Giovanni played dumb, and shrugged his shoulders. "If you don't believe me, then go talk to her; ask her what we talked about," and he started to walk away.

"I am still talking to you, cretin, don't walk away from me."

"Look Carlo, what do you want from me? I just work here. Do you want me to go talk to Don Andrea? He's a friend of my father, did you know that?"

Carlo quieted down. "I can't imagine Don Andrea being friends with some goddamn Southerner."

"If you have any questions, just ask Don Andrea who Mastro Paolo of Giovinazzo is. He'll tell you."

"I have had enough of your crap for today. Go set up the tables and make it fast. Also, get a fresh outfit. Last night your outfit had stains on it."

Giovanni walked quickly away and started folding napkins at a table.

"Can you imagine the gall," he overheard Carlo say, "A father that knows Don Andrea!"

When the evening serving was over, Fabio motioned Giovanni to go outside He made a motion of cigarette smoking. Giovanni was glad to go.

"Well, Fabio, what do you think of that bastard, lambasting me like that?"

"What are you complaining about? You know what he's like. Once he gets on that miserable uniform with its fake military buttons, he goes wild. Stay out of his way. Did you go see Miss Curti?" he asked.

"Yes. She walked by and then kept walking."

Fabio snickered and pushed him affectionately.

"Look out," Fabio said. "Look, Giovanni, next week there is a holiday when Don Andrea closes the restaurant and even the hotel. I'll be going to Rome to see my family. Why don't you come home with me. I know a great cathouse in Trastevere. Wonderful girls! Girls from all over. I once had a black woman from Africa. Was she something!"

"Fabio, I'm supposed to be sending money home to my parents. That's one of the reasons I came here and you want me to go spending money on whores."

"It's not that expensive. Three *lire* for these girls."

"Three lire, is that all?" Giovanni asked. "If I can get a tip of three lire, I can use that to screw that African."

"Hey, don't fool with her," Fabio said. "She's mine."

"A whore is nobody's. She is married to the lira, and that's it."

"We have a little space where you can sleep, but don't get any ideas that you are going to a hotel. I am working for the same reason as you—to give money to my family.

"Don't worry about things like that. I am not the kind of person who needs luxury," Giovanni answered.

Giovanni had been to Naples once for a very short period of time, but he had never been to Rome. To him, Rome existed only in books at school. To get there, Fabio and Giovanni spent a good part of the day riding in a wagon owned by a butcher who made deliveries to the restaurant.

When they arrived at Fabio's house, Giovanni realized immediately just how lucky he had been. His own home was clean, well-lit and had comfort. Fabio's house was dark and dank and was on a back street that smelled of urine.

When they entered the house, Fabio said, "Here it is, just like I told you."

"That's all right, just like I told you," Giovanni stressed. "I can get along anywhere, besides, I think it is an insult to your family to be ashamed of your house. They are doing the best they can."

"Thank you for reminding me," Fabio said sourly.

His parents were peasants who had moved to the city. His father was a small, stocky man, with large hands, the kind of hands that are used to hard work. He greeted Giovanni with a nod of the head. When Giovanni reached out his hand to shake he got a limp hand not used to such amenities. Fabio's mother was bigger than her husband and more energetic and dignified. She dressed in black and wore a black head scarf as she moved around the house.

"We are poor, as you can see, but thank God, we get along thanks to my husband and my son who sends us money when he can. For the rest, we just get along. Please feel at home," she said. Giovanni nodded his head in thanks. "*Signora*, I am pleased to be here with you and to share your house for a few days."

They had a meager breakfast of some left-over, hard bread and coffee. Then Fabio and Giovanni went out to the street. Giovanni marveled at the noisy fruit and vegetable vendors and the many carts with meat and fish. He was used to going to the market to get food, but here in Rome everything seemed to take place in the streets. He noticed the ringing sound of trolley cars which whooshed past. Fabio was well-known in the neighborhood; every other person greeted him and people stepped out of the stores to say hello to him.

"Eh, Fabio, how are things in the country?"

Fabio became another personality, more relaxed, more outgoing. "There is nothing like the countryside, my friend, but there is nothing like Rome either," he answered with assurance.

They crossed the bridge to get to the center of Rome where Giovanni saw ancient statues and monuments that he had read about. They walked for miles but neither Fabio nor Giovanni tired from it. Fabio knew the city from narrow streets to grand piazzas, dropping in one place and then another to greet someone. In front of the Pantheon, they bought food from vendors. Giovanni was not used to eating standing up but that was the way you did it in Rome he was assured by Fabio. In the middle of the day they lay down in the cool of a tree by a Roman monument. A yawning lethargy came over them because of having wine. They slept for an hour or so. When they woke Giovanni noticed that the noise level and the activity had not abated.

Near the Quirinale, they began to see many men in uniform. They were dressed all in black with sleek boots, and greeted each other in the street with an upraised arm. They looked impressive to Giovanni in their hats with braid and tassels, eagles on their military caps and medals on their shirts.

With Fabio serving as guide, they sauntered around Rome. This was not the quiet Fabio of the restaurant. Much to Giovanni's surprise, Fabio talked about some of the Roman emperors and could name a few yet he knew that Fabio had very little formal schooling.

In the evening, Fabio suggested that they go to a special place, but was insistent that this was going to be the most special place of all. Giovanni's mind started whirring; he had an inkling of where they were going.

They arrived at an old building like the others, but once the door was open Giovanni saw fine furniture and gilded objects in a velvet-draped room. The pungent smell of perfume permeated the place. An older, matronly woman walked in and greeted the boys.

"*Ma, chi si vede?* Well, look who's here. Fabio, is it you?"

"Of course, Emma, it's me. I came to Rome for a few days and I couldn't simply ignore you, my love."

"Oh, *mio caro*, and who is this handsome man here with you?"

"Giovanni, a friend from work. I told him that if and when we go to Rome we are going straight to Emma's place."

"You know that little thing from Africa? She's still here," she said. "Every now and then she asks me, where is Fabio? I miss him."

"Well, Emma, here we are. Let's go see the girls."

Giovanni was all eyes, looking around the bordello. There were a half dozen girls sitting rather bored. One was doing needlepoint, another just looking up at the ceiling. Emma came in and gave a clap of the hands. They sat up straight and fixed their hair.

"Girls, who do I have here?"

"It's Fabio, my favorite," said a dark woman.

"That's right, and you are my favorite. I am always talking about you, isn't that so, Giovanni?" Fabio said.

Another girl, all painted up, smallish in build, and pretty, said, "And who is your friend, Fabio?"

"This is Giovanni." Turning to Giovanni, Fabio said. "She is called L'Algerina. There is not another like her," and he quickly added, "that is, after my lovely, ebony woman," and stroked L'Africana.

Emma cut short the small talk, "Why don't the four of you go upstairs and get to know each other?" As they moved ahead, she grabbed the men by the elbows and whispered, "Three lire each, payable in advance."

Each one searched his pockets and came up with the money. Upstairs there was a long corridor with doors on each side of it. Giovanni's door was number two, Fabio's three.

L'Algerina had slipped out of her dress and into a silky shift.

"Are you ready," she said.

"As ready as I'll ever be," Giovanni answered.

She removed her shift, and Giovanni stared at her. He got into the bed and started touching her. She kept a discreet smile on her face as Giovanni explored her body. Giovanni did his work and when he was through, L'Algerina went into the bathroom and emerged all dressed again.

"Do you ever have any time off?" Giovanni asked, thinking how pretty she was.

"Sometimes during the day we go out and help *La Signora* with the shopping."

"I wish I could be in Rome more often so that I could see you."

"Where do you live?" she asked.

"Torresanta."

"Torresanta is not around the corner, it's a way off."

Downstairs Giovanni joined Fabio and they said goodbye to Madame.

The next morning they had to get up very early to get back to Torresanta. At the appointed time, Giovanni could see the butcher's creaking wagon filled with meats covered by a canvas. They jumped on the buckboard and off they went.

At the hotel, Giovanni was sleepy yet full of life. He felt so much better. He could smell the soft skin of L'Algerina and her perfume. He would smell that for days to come. He was setting up tables when Carlo came to him.

"Well, Don Giovanni, where did you disappear to?"

"We had the time off just like you," Giovanni answered with some surliness.

"I don't know where you get the idea that you get every feast day off."

"Don Andrea is the boss around here. Whatever he tells me, I do. Even Miss Curti tells me to come to do work there when they have a lot of guests."

"She does, does she? She doesn't run this part of things."

Giovanni continued to go about his work never looking up at Carlo.

"*Signore,*" Carlo said sarcastically, "as soon as you are through setting up these tables, go inside and Mesiù has some work for you to do."

Inside the kitchen Mesiù was the boss. All the kitchen help, including Fabio did what Mesiù, the chef, told them to do. Tall, robust and red faced, Mesiù stalked around the kitchen carping at everybody. Fabio washed everything that was brought to his sink and never said a word. As Giovanni walked into the kitchen looking for Mesiù, he spotted a mountain of onions. Mesiù handed him a knife and said, "Peel and chop them up."

So Carlo had gotten Mesiù to help punish Giovanni by putting him to work on onions again. Every now and then Carlo came in and looked at Giovanni. He and Mesiù got a great kick out of Giovanni crying while he cut the onions. It took Giovanni three hours to peel and chop the onions.

"Yes, my friend," Carlo said, "this will teach you to go off to Miss Curti's office. You work here, do you hear that?"

As far as Giovanni was concerned they were both guilty of persecuting him and he would find a way to get even.

Later, finding an excuse, Giovanni went to the hotel. He found Miss Curti in her office. She read the anger in Giovanni's face and said, "What is the matter?"

"I'll tell you what the matter is. Carlo was getting even with me for coming and working here and he got Mesiù to have me peel and chop up a mountain of onions, that's what."

"They are both pigs. One is worse than the other."

"They had a great time laughing at me while I choked and gagged over the onions. A great joke for them, but not for me."

"What are you doing here then? If Carlo finds out that you have come here, he will do it again."

"If he does, I'll make him sorry." Giovanni said.

"Giovanni, there is no good to be expected from him. He has nothing in his life except the job that Don Adrea has given him"

All Giovanni could think of in this state was getting even with them both. He would have to wait for just the right time and in the end it might cost him the job and the mountain air if he were to be caught, but his anger sat in him like acid.

When he calmed down, he looked at Miss Curti and got close enough to her to smell her perfume. "Miss Curti, I can't forget that wonderful taste of love you gave last week."

"Forget that," she said in a matter-of-fact way. "Don't think it will ever happen again."

"Miss Curti, didn't you enjoy it?" and he moved closer to her. She pushed him away and went back to her ledgers. "I have work to do now, so if you are finished, you can go back to the kitchen."

One day Carlo came bustling in calling all the kitchen and dining room staff together. When it was quiet, Carlo looked at each person and said, "This weekend everybody will work. There will be no leaves or trips. You will all be here." Silence ensued. "You are probably wondering why I am saying that. The answer is that the Minister of the Roman Fascist Party is coming here with a group of his friends and our job is to see to it that they have a good time. No effort will be spared in making the weekend pleasurable and unforgettable for them. Don Andrea told the Minister that he will look after everything. I don't want any slip-ups, understand?"

No one said anything.

"Mesiù, I want you to arrange two wonderful dinners, is that clear? Make up a list for me to approve. Understood?"

Mesiù said nothing.

"Hey you, clod, understand that I shall not go looking for you. If you are not here all the time, then you can pack the few things you cadged when you came with only the shirt on your back and go back to wherever-in-the-hell you came from. Understand?"

Giovanni said nothing. He simply looked Carlo in the eye.

"You, Fabio, don't think that you are going home to carry on like you do in Rome. You think I don't know what you do when you go there? You better make sure that you don't come back with a disease."

Fabio did not say anything.

"Now, little clod, if Miss Curti asks you to fold linens, you had better tell her that you are otherwise occupied in the dining room, is that clear?"

"Why don't you tell her yourself so she won't ask me?"

Carlo's face and neck got red.

"I will not stand any insubordination from you, do you understand? One more answer like that and you will be out. And for the rest of you, make sure that your uniforms are clean, especially you, Mesiù, because these people like the high life, and they like good food. I wouldn't be surprised if they come into the kitchen and they won't want to see you with stains all over your apron."

Mesiù was not happy to be ordered about.

"I am the king in the kitchen," he said slowly. "No one gives orders in my kitchen. Do you understand?"

"Am I to stand here and take this insolence, not only from the clod but also from you? Don't you know what my authority in this hotel is?"

"I don't care what your authority is in this hotel, I am the ONLY authority in the kitchen, and if you get on my nerves like you are getting on my nerves now...."

"This is something that Don Andrea will hear about."

"I don't care if he hears about it or not, I am the boss in this kitchen."

After the meeting, Carlo disappeared, and Giovanni and Fabio met outside behind the building for a smoke.

"How did you like that?" Giovanni muttered.

"He certainly is a true *figlio di puttana*," Fabio answered as he lit a cigarette.

"Who the hell does he think he is? In that silly soldier uniform, it's as if we were in the army and he were the general. What kind of power does he hold over Don Andrea that he can act that way?" Fabio did not answer. "You've been around here for a while, don't you know?" Giovanni asked. When Fabio didn't reply, he said, "Well, I suppose that we should start thinking about this meeting that the Minister will be having here. I can just imagine the nonsense that will be going on."

Giovanni was given the job of cleaning the silverware and the stemware. Don Andrea sent word down that everything had to be perfect. He also said that some day the Minister and his cronies would be in charge of things in Rome. Giovanni cleaned each knife, fork and spoon so that there were no stains on the silverware that might make Don Andrea look bad. Don Andrea liked to hobnob with the big shots from Rome. All he had to know was that somebody important was in his restaurant or hotel and he fell all over himself making a new, powerful friend.

When Giovanni was finished cleaning, he got all the best, embroidered napkins and started folding them. He was missing a few napkins, so he decided to go to Miss Curti. First, he wanted to tell Carlo about it so he didn't catch hell for it later, but Carlo had gone out. Who would be his witness? He turned to Mesiù and told him, "Mesiù, I have to go get some more napkins, okay?"

"That's fine with me. But you had better tell Carlo."

"He is not around, but you know that I asked?"

"Fine," he said and returned to his sauce.

"Miss Curti, I need to have more napkins. We are getting set up for a big dinner, and Carlo told us that there could be no slip-ups."

"If Carlo wants more napkins, I invite him to come and ask me for them."

"He didn't send me to get them, Miss Curti. I know that there are not enough for the tables and I need some."

"I understand that Carlo had you all against the wall to make sure that there were no slip-ups."

"He's panicked, I think" Giovanni said.

"Carlo's a fraud."

"So what, I still need napkins," Giovanni reminded her. Giovanni didn't know what to make of Miss Curti. She let him kiss her more and now, she acted like nothing happened.

"You better be quick about it because if Carlo knows you were here you know that he is out to get you."

"What did I do to him?"

"He knows that you have no respect for him. He is the kind of person that will beat you into respecting him."

"He's already made an enemy of Mesiù; so I expect to see them fight it out soon."

"Remember my words, *Signore*. If he puts his mind to it, he will do whatever he can to get rid of you."

"Miss Curti, this is not the only restaurant and hotel in the world, you know. If he sacks me, then I can look elsewhere for work. Right now, all I want is to be in the mountain air."

"You want to be out on the street right away?"

"If he sacks me, he sacks me. I'll look elsewhere, but before that I would like to keep my job, make my money, as little as that is, and keep busy."

"That's a good philosophy, Giovanni, a good philosophy indeed. Did you study?"

"Not really, just eight grades and then I went to work for my father cutting stone. I really don't have a great education; just enough to get along."

"Why did you come here to work if your father had a business?"

"Things soured. My brothers went to America, and I wanted to stay here in Italy so I could look after my parents, an aunt and a little sister."

"How can you look after your parents here in Torresanta?"

"Miss Curti, it's a long story."

"Well, you better get those napkins and get back to the dining room otherwise *figlio di puttana* will be howling."

"Thank you," he said and left.

The day finally arrived and one by one the Minister and his friends came in. They all wore black suits, black shirts and black ties and greeted each other with an arm raised in salute and then an embrace. Giovanni could tell from their accents that the men came from different regions of Italy.

For the evening Mesiù made *tortelloni verdi alla panna* for the first course. On the kitchen table they looked like little green pillows stuffed with various cheeses. For the second dish Don Andrea had ordered roasted boar.

Carlo wore a brand new jacket, shiny with gold buttons and tassels on the shoulders. As each person came in he gave them the fascist salute, his right arm straightened and went up. The salute was always returned. He led each person to a table and then would snap: "The water, the water, please." He was especially attentive if the man was accompanied by a woman. This time the women were not matronly, but young and flashy. Some of them looked like the made-up whores Giovanni had seen in Rome, smoking cigarettes in doorways.

Giovanni went from table to table to see that everything was in order. The *tortelloni* in a rich cream sauce smelled wonderful but Giovanni knew those were only for the guests. He and Fabio and the rest of the help got pasta with whatever sauce was left over and a small piece of meat.

These were sleek, sharp men, their hair shiny and in place. They all had the Fascist pin in their lapels. There was a great deal of loud talking and gesturing. When occasionally a glass of water was knocked over, Carlo would call, "PSST! you. Come clean this up," which Giovanni did.

At the end the Minister called for the cook and congratulated him on what a wonderful meal he had prepared and slipped him a tip. Carlo was there smiling as ever but received nothing.

The next day Don Andrea called the group together and spoke to them: "I want to thank you for doing such a good job. The Minister came to me this morning and said that the meal was unforgettable. Thanks to you, we have made a good impression, and the Minister will not forget us. Thank you very much. Mesiù, thank you for the good dishes. That boar was stupendous. And thank you, Carlo, for your good supervision. I am very proud of all of you."

That evening the scene was repeated. A wonderful first dish, pasta
with bits of the boar cooked in a tomato sauce with tomatoes from
Don Andrea's own garden. This was followed by fish that was brought
in that morning from Civitavecchia. Carlo trolled the dining room,
smiling as ever, seeing to it that things went well. One person said he
wanted a drier wine, and Carlo went to the wine cellar and fetched a
bottle. When he opened it, pouring some for the person to test, he
smiled and nodded continually. Giovanni watched and despised him
for his servility.

The last day, they had a meal at midday of cold lamb accompanied
by a thick soup. Then one by one they left, all of them embracing,
saluting. Some gave a tip to Carlo and some called for Mesiù to give
him a tip. Nobody tipped Giovanni or anyone else in the kitchen.

Don Andrea had tears in his eyes as he wished each guest a farewell.
He had proved his worth by satisfying the Fascists. Giovanni didn't
think much of them, but he had to admit that all dressed in black they
cut an impressive figure.

Things calmed down after the visit of the Fascists to the usual
travelers that came and went. They were salesmen who carried cases
full of their wares, decent people, not ostentatious, who liked to stay
and eat at the Lentino.

Everybody at the restaurant was on a cloud because the visit with the
Minister had gone so well; Carlo more than anyone else. He had taken
on a new aura of importance. There was certainly a strain between him
and Mesiù. Each one would try to bring the workers to their side and
this began to create a lot of tension in the kitchen.

Carlo began to make a habit of going through the kitchen, picking
up a *bruschetta*, say, or a cutlet. Then depending on what it was, he
would taste it or put it back down. Mesiù watched glowering and then
went to talk to Don Andrea.

"Don Andrea," Mesiù started with a heavy French accent in his
Italian, "I am not happy with Carlo, and I want you to do something
about it. He has decided that he is the boss of the kitchen."

"Mesiù, you mustn't take him so seriously. Let him come in and act
like the boss. It doesn't mean anything," he assured Mesiù.

"I do take it seriously. He comes in the kitchen and picks food up, tastes it and then he throws it down like it is dirt. I don't like it one bit."

"Let us say that Carlo takes on a role that really isn't his. I am the only supervisor of things in this place, not Carlo, not Miss Curti, nor anyone else."

"Then why don't you tell him yourself, that I don't want him in the kitchen?"

"I can take care of that if you wish, Mesiù. I want you to be happy here. Didn't I tell you that the Minister and his friends were joyful at the food you served them? So you see, dear Mesiù, you are much cared for here. I will see to Carlo, don't worry about that."

"*Parola d'onore?* Word of honor?" Mesiù asked earnestly.

"*Parola d'onore,*" and Don Andrea shook hands with the Frenchman.

The next day Carlo came in the kitchen and started walking around picking up slices of melon. Mesiù looked at him out of the corner of his eye.

"Yes, do you want something?" he asked.

"No, not really, I am looking around," he answered.

"I have had a talk with Don Andrea and I don't like you coming in the kitchen and snooping around."

"Yes, I know, Don Andrea spoke to me about that. But you know, dear *Francese,* that I am the most important person in this restaurant," he preened.

"The most important person in this kitchen is me," and he emphasized his point with a bang of his fist on the cutting board.

"Dear *Francese*, I will come in here all I want, do you hear that? All I want."

Mesiù was getting red around the neck and face "I was told by Don Andrea that I am the one and only important person in this kitchen. So, if you would do me the favor, you should please get out."

"I will get out when I want to, not when you want me to," Carlo replied.

"In that case I will have you thrown out."

"Oh, really, and who, pray tell, is going to throw me out?"

Mesiù looked at Giovanni and Fabio and said, "They will."

Giovanni and Fabio looked shocked. "Look," Fabio said to Carlo, "we don't want any trouble. Why don't you leave if Mesiù tells you to?"

"Why you little turd, you little *pezzo di merda*, you little whoremonger, are you telling me what to do?"

"Mesiù is the boss of the kitchen."

By now, Carlo was purple. All activity stopped in the kitchen and focused on the four of them.

"I will stay here as long as I want," Carlo said with authority, stamping his foot.

Don Andrea came in. "What's going on here? You can be heard in the hotel."

"Don Andrea," Mesiù began, "you told me that I am in charge of the kitchen, isn't that right?"

"Yes, I did."

"Well, then, would you please tell this man," pointing to Carlo, "to leave?"

Carlo was waiting with intense impatience.

"Carlo, come here with me," and Don Andrea led him into a small office and shut the door. After a few minutes the door reopened. Don Andrea and Carlo came out, unsmiling and tense.

Don Andrea turned and said, "The kitchen belongs to Mesiù, is that understood?"

Carlo was furious. "Don Andrea, I have served you loyally for many years, and now you put a dagger in my back?"

"There are no daggers here. Mesiù is the boss of the kitchen. You come in here only when he says it's all right. Is that understood?"

Carlo swiftly left the room not looking at anyone. Giovanni looked at Fabio and they nodded in satisfaction.

Now that Carlo's grasp on Giovanni had loosened, he felt freer to go and see Miss Curti at will, which he did one day.

"My dear Miss Curti, how are you?" he said with a flowery voice.

"What do you want?" she answered curtly.

"Miss Curti, I came here to say hello and to tell you how pretty you look."

She looked up with a wry smile. "Look who's trying to be the Romeo. Does Carlo know that you are here?"

"No, and I don't care if he does."

"Yes, I heard that Carlo was put in his place," she said with obvious satisfaction. "Finally, Don Andrea had the guts to show who's boss."

"Miss Curti, I don't understand how things are around here. Why should you have such satisfaction in seeing Carlo put in his place? What do you have against him?"

"Listen, why don't you go back to the kitchen, if you are so full of questions?"

"It's that I'm curious, because everything seems to belong to some kind of plot that I know nothing about."

"Curiosity once killed a cat, don't you know that?"

"Miss Curti, I am here to talk to you, to say hello, and to see if we can do something together."

"Like what?"

"How about taking a walk in the woods some time?"

"I rarely have time to take walks in the woods or anyplace else."

"It's great to get out of this place and go where there are no people. The air is pure and we can see trees and flowers that have been there for many, many years." He moved toward her.

"*Basta*. Don't get chummy with me or you will be out of here."

"What did I do to deserve this kind of cold treatment, Miss Curti," and he moved even closer, putting his arm around her waist.

"Who do you think you are?"

Giovanni tried kissing her behind her ear.

"There is work to be done and I don't have time for this silliness," she said. She didn't move away and he drew her closer. When she no longer resisted him, he turned her around and kissed her on the lips. He couldn't stop now. "I can't stay away from you," he said, kissing her ears and mouth. He could feel her softening to him and he walked to the door and locked it.

He embraced her and could see that she was passionate, too.

Miss Curti turned her head away from him. "I hope you are not like other men. Can I trust you to keep quiet about this?"

"Of course," he said. "Do I have to call you Miss Curti? What is your first name?"

"My first name is Ada, but you are never to call me that here in the hotel."

"I understand. No one will know," he said.

———————

Giovanni was bursting to tell somebody but he knew that if he did it would get back to Don Andrea or Carlo or God knows who else, and it would be the end for him and probably for Ada. When he ran into Fabio, he feigned disinterest in things.

Fabio said, "Where have you been? I haven't seen you for two days. What are you up to?"

"Nothing. Just trying to figure out how things are going to be since Don Andrea kicked Carlo in the ass." Giovanni said.

"Don Andrea has threatened him with being kicked out, but that never happens. He must have something on Don Andrea."

Fabio waved his hand. "Where are you going now that we are on our midday break?" Fabio asked.

"Probably to help Miss Curti, if she needs me."

"While you are there, why don't you ask her a few questions?"

"Fine, and if I find out anything, you'll be the first person to know about it, okay?" Giovanni said sarcastically.

———————

"Good day, Miss Curti," Giovanni said in mock courtesy.

She looked up at him and said nothing.

"Well, my friend, I expected you to be coming around. Close the door, please. I knew you would be coming again after our meeting the other day. Do you know how I knew that?"

"No, please tell me, Ada."

"You see, once you make the mistake of getting into confidence with someone, then they come around like a dog sniffing."

"Why are you saying all of this, Ada?"

"Because I know men. I know what they are like. They talk to you, they make love to you and then in the end they are not there, except to make love, isn't that so? I have to think of the future."

"Ada, it takes time to get to know each other; then we can talk about it."

There was a long silence. Ada sat with her arms crossed. "My experience with men is that they promise you much but give little."

"Ada, let's get to know each other. These questions will be answered later."

"I do not want to be taken for a fool."

Giovanni did not know what to reply. The question of marriage had never entered his head but Ada seemed to be thinking of it. Something kept telling him to be careful, but he felt a pull toward this woman.

"Ada, we need to get away from this place. I try to go to the woods every time I get the chance, why don't we go?"

"Oh no, I wouldn't want Don Andrea or Carlo to know that I went anywhere with you."

"Why can't we just slip away?"

"Because I am afraid of Don Andrea. Less so of Carlo." she repeated.

Her answer piqued Giovanni's curiosity again about her relationship with both Don Andrea and Carlo.

"Why are you so afraid of them? I don't understand."

"You don't know them like I know them."

"I usually take my afternoon break at about two thirty. We can meet and go to the woods."

Finally she gave in. "All right, but we must be careful, very careful, do you understand?"

"About two thirty you start walking down the path that goes to the woods. The path will start to turn near a huge oak tree. No one can see you once you go beyond the turn in the path. Wait for me there."

Ada nodded and Giovanni went back to the dining room. During the dinner he couldn't keep his mind on his work. Carlo berated him for clumsiness. His mind was on Ada and how he hoped they would be successful in getting away together. Giovanni finished his work and set his tables for the next meal so that if he dallied he wouldn't have to worry. When everyone was gone, including Carlo, Giovanni slipped out and walked along the path.

He reached the twist in the path, looked back and saw no one. He could see the figure of Ada in the shade and felt light and happy to see her. When he got there she smiled at him in a way that he had not seen before. He noticed the neat, colored blouse she was wearing. He only had seen her with her work smock on and never truly got a look at what she was like without it. Today she looked less like the ogre she was supposed to be and more like a girl, younger looking than when he saw her at the hotel yelling and carping at people. Her brown hair and brown eyes shone in the sun.

"Ciao, Ada," Giovanni said.

"Ciao, Giovanni."

Together they entered the woods through a grove of pines. In the dappled light and shade it could almost have been twilight. As they walked their bodies brushed together and they held hands, walking like the lovers they had become.

"My home is near a forest. I am from a small town called Giovinazzo, near Bari, in the South."

"I could tell you were from the South. Your accent."

"Yes, my accent. That's the first thing that Carlo noticed about me."

"Let's not ruin our time talking about someone we both detest," as she spoke, her soft appearance turned hard.

They stopped at a place hemmed in by trees in an intricate lattice of leaves and branches. There Giovanni put his arms around Ada and began to caress her. She submitted to his kisses and they slowly fell to the ground. It must have been two hours that they were hidden in this paradise. When they realized it was time to go back to work, they were unwilling to return.

Back at the hotel, Ada walked into her office feeling light from their love making in the woods. Giovanni went to the restaurant. Carlo was there and he was quieter than before. Whatever bad feelings he harbored for Don Andrea, he kept them to himself.

Mesiù now assumed a very prominent place in the restaurant. Instead of going to Carlo for instructions the workers now went to Mesiù. Although Mesiù got Don Andrea's support, he wanted no enemies in the operation so occasionally he went to Carlo to ask advice. Carlo was reluctant to give in to Mesiù's game and he maintained a dignified but cold front.

"Back from a foray into the woods, clod?" he said. "At least you had the good sense to make sure that the tables were all prepared for the evening meal," and walked away.

He could no longer anger Giovanni, but he never dropped the word "clod" from his conversations. Giovanni claimed that he was not bothered by Carlo's bad humor in referring to him as a bumpkin, but it did hurt him inside. With Carlo reined in, his principal tormentor now became Mesiù. The Frenchman never lost an occasion to call attention to Giovanni's carelessness.

"And you," he said, pointing to Giovanni, "make sure that when you put plates on the table that you serve from the left and remove from the right. I saw you the other day doing it the other way."

When Mesiù corrected Giovanni, Carlo had a quiet smile on his face. Fabio stood by the sink and watched as usual.

"Giovanni, when are we going to go for a walk in the woods like we used to do?"

"Whenever you want," Giovanni answered dryly.

"I used to look forward to our walks," Fabio said.

"There will be other walks."

"How about tomorrow?" he asked.

"Fine with me," Giovanni answered.

Giovanni knew that sooner or later Fabio would catch on that something was going on with Ada but Giovanni wanted to keep his love life with Ada to himself. Once Fabio knew there was the possibility that every one would know and then Ada's job could be in jeopardy.

During the off-moments Giovanni thought back to Ada and how she maintained that tough front on the job. A lot of people didn't like her because they thought that as an employee she worked too much in Don Andrea's interests. They wanted her to be more like them—taking advantage of the little things, moments when there was no one looking and they relaxed in the rooms that they were supposed to be cleaning, or ate some food that was available. It was Fabio who put a cake or salami aside and gave it to a scullion or to a housekeeper. Some employees managed to steal things and bring them home even though both Don Andrea and Carlo kept their eyes open for thievery.

The next day Fabio reminded Giovanni that they could go for a walk on their break. Giovanni nodded agreement, and at two thirty they put their uniforms aside and headed for the woods. From the window in her office Ada saw them disappear into the forest.

"I looked for you yesterday and I couldn't find you," Fabio said.

"Yes, I needed a little time off by myself," Giovanni said.

"Yes. I also looked for you in Miss Curti's office but the door was shut."

"Oh? I guess she was busy too," he shrugged.

Giovanni could tell from the tone of his voice that Fabio knew what had gone on. Silence ensued. Finally Giovanni couldn't take the silence any more.

"Okay, now you know. She and I came for a walk here in the woods."

"That's what I guessed."

"All right, what's next?"

"You have to figure what this is going to mean for Don Andrea and for Carlo, once they find out that you and she are sweet on each other."

"Could you tell?"

"Of course I could tell."

"I guess I'm not as clever as I thought."

"One of the things you have to keep in mind is that nothing remains a secret around here."

Giovanni thought about it for a few minutes. If his friendship with Ada became common knowledge, then he was putting her and himself at risk but they had already gone too far to stop.

"Well, Mr. Detective, now that you know, are you going to blow the whistle on me?" Giovanni wondered.

"Don't be stupid. I am not going to inform on you," Fabio said.

"My main problem is with Don Andrea and Carlo," Giovanni said. Fabio's silence perplexed Giovanni. "I can't figure you out. You know more than you say, but you won't tell me what is going on here."

"You must find out for yourself. Nobody is going to tell you," Fabio said.

"What kind of friend are you?"

"That's life, my friend. There are certain things that it's best you find out for yourself."

They got up from the grass and made their way back to the hotel. Giovanni wondered what secrets Carlo had. What about Ada? What secrets did she have? Giovanni's secret was now known, at least to Fabio, but he wondered if anyone else knew. He figured that if Carlo found out, then everybody would know about it. He would have to be very, very careful.

———————

"My Dear Son: I hope that all is well with you. How are you feeling? I hope that the mountain air is helping you. From here there is little to tell. Filomena is through with her schooling, and we have to decide what comes next. She is very intelligent, maybe too intelligent for her age. Always asking questions. When is Giovanni going to come home from Rome? Can I go to Rome to see him?' The questions are never-ending. You have to be very careful that a girl doesn't become too smart for her own good.

"Your mother and aunt get very worried about your brothers in America. We know that they work, because they send us money which is a gift from God. Things are not any better for me here. No commissions in a long time. My tools are getting rusty on my work bench. The money they send is much appreciated, and the money that you send also helps us. Your mother and aunt help a great deal by making clothes for us all and practicing little economies around the house. Our property in the country gives us some fruits and vegetables, not enough to keep alive on, but enough to go from day to day without having to buy everything."

"Do you think that you will be able sometime to come home to visit us? People ask about you but I don't tell them why I sent you to the mountain. Best not to tell people too many things, don't you think? Stay well and please write to us more often. Your mother and aunt are happy when they get your letters. With much love, I am your affectionate father, Paolo."

Life in the hotel and restaurant was starting to get boring for Giovanni. He craved some sense of surprise. He made it a point to stop by and greet Ada each day. He no longer cared what others might think of his interest in her, although it must be obvious to all that their relationship was more than just platonic. They continued their walks whenever they could and out there in the heart of nature they practiced the most natural of things. Ada loved their intimacy and Giovanni wondered how she got along before he entered her life.

"Do you ever go home, Ada?" he asked innocently.

"Why do you ask?" she said.

"I wondered, that's all."

"Some times I do," she answered.

"Whom do you have in that town where you came from?" he inquired.

"Giovanni, why do you ask so many questions?" Every time she avoided answering a question she stimulated Giovanni's curiosity all the more.

"Ada, I am asking to get to know you," he explained.

"I have my mother and my father, okay, now you know. Are you satisfied?"

Another day when they had planned on going to the woods for their tryst, Ada gave him a quiet signal when he came by her office. Don Andrea had come around asking a lot of questions about where she went in the afternoons so Ada decided that they had to stop their walks in the woods. Giovanni blurted out how much he was going to miss her, and it was true. "What are we going to do now?" he asked. She had no answer. "I think that it's time to abandon the walks," Giovanni told her, "but I think that I can slip up to your room, late at night and we can be together."

"It's risky, Giovanni. We'll have to figure a time when Don Andrea is out of town."

Giovanni sensed that there was more to tell, but he didn't know what.

"Fabio, what's the relationship between Don Andrea and Miss Curti?"

"Is that what you call her when you are in the woods?" Fabio asked.

"Don't be a silly ass. I think that there is something more than just the owner-employee thing between them. You, yourself, once said that even though Don Andrea threatened to fire her and Carlo, he never did it. So, are you going to tell me anything?" Giovanni asked.

"Giovanni, I don't like to repeat gossip. What if I said that she is Don Andrea's lover and Carlo is a former lover of hers? Would you believe me?"

"No, I don't believe you."

"Then why do you ask me? It's time to go back to work" Fabio said and walked away. Turning back, he added, "The next time we have some time off, I mean, not just two hours in the afternoon, I want to bring you to a small town not too far from here."

———

Giovanni and Fabio set out early one morning to go to Assunta Alta, a very small town not far from Torresanta. A bus took them from the hotel to the town square in front of a church. They went through the small winding streets until they arrived at a house no different from the others. Fabio carried a small package under his arm. An elderly woman answered the door.

"Hello, good day, I'm Fabio. I work with your daughter Ada. We were nearby and Ada asked us to drop off this package for you."

An older man came in wondering who they were.

"These are friends of Ada, and they brought a package from her."

The old man nodded a greeting to Giovanni and Fabio.

"How is my daughter?" the old man asked.

"She is well, working as usual," Fabio said.

"She is a good person who has always worked hard to help us," her father said. "I can no longer work, you see but we must keep going along."

Giovanni could understand the father's predicament. "Certainly, your other children could help you too, couldn't they?" Giovanni asked.

"We have no other children; just the little one that Ada gave us."

Giovanni froze. She never said anything about "a little one."

"Ah, yes," Fabio said knowingly, "the little one. How old is he now?"

"He is five years old and a joy to us. He's a wonderful boy, full of life," the old man said. "Mamma, go call Andrea."

A child came in. He had brown hair and was tall for his age.

"Andrea, greet these gentlemen. They brought us a package from your mother."

The boy merely nodded shyly. He went and sat with his grandmother, leaning on her shoulder affectionately.

Fabio said, "Here is a little something for the boy that Ada sent."

The grandmother unwrapped the package and he immediately took the toy in his hands.

They spoke a moment until Fabio got up, saying that the bus would be coming by soon.

Giovanni said nothing as they boarded the bus and bumped along the country road. Fabio looked out at the countryside, silent also.

━━━━━━━━━━

Giovanni was left cold in spirit. Who was the father of Ada's child? He had suspicions that tortured him. The Lentino ceased to hold any interest for him. He was tired of the fights, the quarrels and petty affairs. If Giovanni had no enthusiasm for the job before, now he had even less. He had to decide what he was going to do about Ada. He realized that he had come to love her. His glimpse behind the façade that she had built for herself made him aware of this. Later that day he went by her office and she looked up expectantly.

"Where have you been?" she asked. When he didn't answer she rushed on.

"Giovanni, I sense that Don Andrea is watching me, because now he comes by much more often that he ever did before. I am afraid he knows. I cannot lose this job. If I did, it would be a personal disaster for me."

"I understand. We shall have to be so careful or not see each other." Giovanni immediately felt sorry at that prospect. "Tonight around ten o'clock I am going to come to your room, so keep the door unlocked and I can just slip in quietly. And then we can be together again."

The Fascists had another meeting at the hotel. The Minister was there with his wife and the rest of the group. Don Andrea had put aside some of the best rooms for them, especially a large room where they could meet for their business.

Mesiù had made up a menu for them. He hadn't forgotten the fact that he was tipped handsomely for his work the last time. Carlo groused that he wasn't consulted in the making of the menu. Mesiù reminded him that the only person who made up the menus, with or without Carlo's approval, was Mesiù.

When the Minister arrived, Don Andrea was there to receive him with a bouquet of flowers for his wife. "Viva il Duce," Don Andrea said. "Viva il Duce," the Minister said and gave him the long arm salute.

The rest of the staff was made to understand that they should be at the beck and call of each of the Fascists. Carlo made himself available for anything they needed and wanted. Fabio in his usual way watched silently how Don Andrea and Carlo played up to the Fascists.

Each meal was a masterpiece by Mesiù. Each course was delicately cooked, the pasta hand-made by an old woman in the next town, tortellini some white and some green. As Giovanni served the dishes he noted that the guests loved their food. They asked for more wine, which Carlo ran to the cellar to get.

That evening Giovanni waited until about ten o'clock, then, he tiptoed upstairs where the hotel staff slept. He walked in the shadows until he got to the end of the corridor where Ada had her room. Then he turned the door handle and opened it silently. Across the small room he could see Ada against the window in the dark. He could barely make out her features but he could see the swoop of her hair and the turn of her body. It was so dark and quiet that he could hear Ada's breathing. They embraced and moved over to the bed.

Later as they rested, their breathing became regular and they touched each others' faces. Giovanni caressed Ada's long hair and turned to kiss her every now and then. There was a long silence until Ada said, "You and Fabio went to my town, didn't you?"

Giovanni's first reaction was to lie. After a silence, he said, "Ada, I wanted to know as much as I could about you, as much as Fabio knows. I told him that I had great affection for you."

"How could that little whore-monger know about me?"

"He said there are no secrets in this hotel and restaurant. He told me Mesiù is on the run for having killed someone in a kitchen he worked in years ago in France and Carlo has designs on Don Andrea's daughter, hoping that some day he will inherit this whole operation."

"And me? What did he say about me?"

"He said nothing. All he said was that we were going to visit somewhere."

"And what did you see?"

"Ada, why are you torturing me and yourself this way? You know where we went, and you know what we saw."

Ada started to cry and hid her sobbing in her pillow. Giovanni tried to console and comfort her but she shook his hand away.

"You weren't satisfied were you? Who are you to want to find out about my life? What right did you have?" she asked.

"I am very fond of you, and I wanted to know more about you," Giovanni said defensively.

"Do you love me?" she said.

Giovanni was stopped in his tracks.

"It is not that I don't love you, but that is a great step forward. I am afraid to take it, that's the truth."

"Here we are, making love like husband and wife. In those wonderful moments in the woods, I loved you. When you first arrived I could see that you were not like the rest of them. You looked and acted like you had some class, no simple *cafone* like the others. Why do you think I let you touch me that first time in my office? It was because I saw something in you that seemed sincere."

Giovanni listened in silence. "I have one question only. You can answer it or you can forget it."

"Let's hear it," she said.

"Why do you hate Carlo so much?"

"You haven't given up the snooping."

"It's not snooping. Your hatred for him is so intense, I'm curious." Giovanni said.

"You pride yourself on your curiosity, as if you were some kind of special person. I detest Carlo because he deceived me. Such betrayal and such guile that I can't forgive nor forget. I keep waiting for the time I will be able to answer him in kind."

"Please tell me what happened between you," Giovanni implored.

"It started out innocently, he met me, he sought me, he regaled me with stories and I believed them all. One day he told me we were going to visit a friend that was a very wealthy man, and that I would like him. I never questioned Carlo. We came here and he introduced me to Don Andrea." With intense anger, Ada said, "You can imagine the rest. Later, Don Andrea said to me. 'Don't worry, my dear, you will have a home here for as long as you like. You are a wonderful woman. Don't worry about anything, do you hear? Now, you will have a home and a job here,'" he said.

After a few moments, Ada continued, "I did not know what to do, who to go to. Don Andrea took care of me, but I became pregnant. I could not go home to my family in that condition. Carlo, on the other hand, avoided me like a leper. I never felt so betrayed by someone. And you wanted to know why I hate him so much. Now you know, having found out everything else. How do you like that?"

"You were honest in telling me everything."

"What will happen to us now?"

"I don't know, Ada, I don't know."

They both fell asleep. During the night Giovanni woke, took his clothing and left the room as quietly as he had come in.

Giovanni pondered the future of his relationship with Ada. Ada was a real thing going. By now, she entertained ideas of marriage. His choices were difficult. Either he made his situation with Ada formal or he left and found another place to clear his lungs. He wanted to get to America and join his brothers, but that was far in the future.

As he reviewed his options, he thought of Carlo and Mesiù, knowing full well that he owed them both something. Carlo, for his betrayal of Ada and for treating him as if he were dirt just because he came from the South, and Mesiù for taking pleasure in giving him the worst jobs in the kitchen. He thought of all the mean things he could do, but nothing seemed to take the sharp edge off his desire for vengeance. Giovanni remembered his father saying *"la vendetta è un piatto che si mangia freddo,"* vengeance is a dish that is eaten cold. So be it, he would have to wait.

He tried several times to go to Ada's office but she saw him and turned away.

Carlo, in his imperious fashion, called together all the dining room and kitchen staff. It was at least two hours before the dining room opened but he was dressed in his uniform.

"I have called you together to make sure that you know what will be going on here soon. The Minister will be having one of his meetings. But I have been told that this one is very, very important. The people who will be here are highly placed." He paused for effect. "In fact, Mussolini himself, will be here," he announced. He looked around. "For Don Andrea this is the most important day of his life. There must not be, and I repeat even if I have to repeat it a thousand times, and I mean you, little clod, there will be no mistakes. Miss Curti will be looking after all the arrangements for the hotel, but we have to see to it that their experience in the restaurant is perfect. Mesiù, I want you to sit down and prepare a menu for Mussolini. Nothing too regional, I want it to be the best in the world, dishes that are served in the best hotels of Paris and London. For this occasion Don Andrea is getting out the gold service." Looking directly at Fabio and Giovanni he said, "I will personally count every single piece of tableware and at the end of the meal, I shall count again, in the event that anyone thinks that he might," he paused looking for the right word "how shall I say it...."

"Steal it," Fabio answered cheekily.

"Shut up, you little whoremonger. When I want your ideas I'll ask for them. Exactly, steal them. I'll be watching each and every one of you. Now, as far as your appearance is concerned, you will go to Miss Curti's office and get a fresh change of jacket for each meal. I don't want to see any stains from midday on your jacket when you are serving the evening meal." Carlo's instructions went on this way until the staff became restless.

As for Giovanni, he had greater issues on his mind. After having spent many hours at night turning over the options that he faced, he knew that if he married Ada she would take the child into the marriage. Then he would have to emigrate to America where the three of them could start a new life. He decided to pursue this possibility with Ada to see if she would go along.

When Carlo's lecture was finally over Giovanni went to see Ada. For a week since their meeting, Ada had assumed that everything was finished between them. Giovanni, for his part, knew that with her history he could not bring her home without causing great problems with his parents. Going to America was the only solution to their problem.

He obtained the name from Fabio of a doctor in Rome to see if he could pass the physical examination in Naples. Getting the doctor's name was risky because now Fabio could add this to his information file that he kept mentally on everyone. Giovanni tried to make it seem like nothing but in his heart he knew that Fabio had the ability to see through his lies and fakery.

Before he went to Rome he managed to get Ada to listen to him. It was his turn to reveal his secret. "I know how you feel, Ada, and I am determined to do the right thing by you."

She did not look up from her papers.

"I am going to propose a solution for our situation, and I hope you will weigh it carefully. Marrying here in Italy poses too many problems for us both. Do you know why I came here to Torresanta? It was because a doctor in Naples declared me to have tuberculosis. He would not approve me for emigration to the United States along with my brothers."

She listened intently but did not look up.

Giovanni said, "You know the depth of my feelings for you and I want to make sure that I'm doing the right thing. We would go to

America and marry there. You would bring your son. I am going to Rome to see what the doctor there thinks of my lungs."

—————————————

On his return from Rome, Giovanni found an excuse to go to Ada's office. She had just finished having a difficult exchange with one of the maids because they did not have the beds made up on time. Don Andrea was counting on everything being in place for Mussolini's arrival.

"I am waiting for a moment when I can get your attention," Giovanni said.

"You have my attention," she said, sorting her files.

He snatched the papers out of her hands.

"I'm listening," she said sulking.

"I went to the doctor in Rome and he says that I do not have tuberculosis, but in lesser hands, it could seem like tuberculosis."

"So, what are you going to do?" She asked without looking up.

"I am going to go to Naples and see who the doctor is there. Try to butter him up, and even offer him a bribe if I have to. If he approves me, then we both go to America," Giovanni said.

—————————————

Giovanni requested permission to go to Naples, but did not tell anyone why he was going there. This was for him the most important visit he would make. He claimed that he had to go to the funeral of an uncle who died in Naples.

In the Rome train station there were many Fascist soldiers. They wore black uniforms with tall, shiny boots. He found that everything was linked to the Fascist power in the city. In public buildings there were large flags with the sign of the fasces. It seemed as if there were more people in uniform than not. All of this added a feeling of threat to the atmosphere.

The arrival in Naples was even more chaotic than it had been in Rome. Here the porters screamed as they ran through the crowd with rumbling carts. From the station he went to the the offices of immigration and health affairs. He presented an official request to emigrate to the person in charge. These papers were stamped with pictures of King Victor Emmanuel and Mussolini. There he got the paper he needed and was told to go to a room and wait.

Every now and then a person would return from the medical exam. Giovanni tried to gauge how successful he was by his face. Finally Giovanni's name was called and he followed the clerk down a corridor and into a room.

The doctor looked over Giovanni's papers.

"What have we here?" he said. "An application to emigrate to the United States. Do you have people there that are going to take care of you?"

"Yes sir," Giovanni said.

"I get letters from people that tell me that life in America is not like they thought it would be," the doctor said.

"My brothers are there and they are working. I need to go there too so that I can help my parents who need help these days."

"These days?" the doctor asked. "What do you mean by 'these days'?"

"My father has had to close down a stone yard that he had for many years, and his father had before him. They don't have work any more, and we must go out and work to keep them and ourselves alive."

"I am more concerned with what you say about 'these days,'" he said, sternly. "These are great days thanks to our King and Mussolini who have given us a new way of looking at the world. Now Italy is a country that others have to reckon with. We are a great nation, thanks to Mussolini."

"In that case, how was it that we lost the stone business to the English and the Scandinavians?" Giovanni dared to ask.

"That can happen. There are ups and downs. But now we stand as a strong country and I can tell you, you are not going to find that kind of stability in America."

Giovanni wasn't there to discuss politics. He simply wanted the doctor to grant him permission to go abroad and then he could solve matters with Ada.

"Well, let's see what you have here?"

Giovanni stood while the doctor examined him from head to toe. He stopped particularly around his chest and back. Giovanni's blood chilled for a moment, afraid that he might have heard the kind of wheezing that the first doctor heard and turned him down. The doctor asked him to breathe deeply and exhale. After he went through this, the doctor looked over the papers and said,

"It looks all right to me, as far as your health is concerned so I am going to sign these papers," which he did, and handed them to Giovanni.

No one could imagine the joy Giovanni felt at having those papers in his hands signed by the doctor, and he didn't even have to bribe him. He rushed back to Torresanta to give Ada the news. When he told her, he could read in her eyes that she was pleased with the possibility of having a new life.

"I see that the little clod is back from the funeral," Carlo said. "How did they bury the poor bastard? With the same clothes he had on his back his whole life I suppose?"

"He was buried with honor," Giovanni said.

Carlo laughed. "Get back to your work. We still have the big dinner for the Minister to do today."

Since he would be going to America with Ada, Giovanni saw that the dinner for the Minister with the possible attendance of Mussolini might just be the opportunity for his revenge. As he walked around the dining room he racked his brain thinking about what he could do to mess up the dinner without falling under suspicion. In the kitchen, he saw cauldrons boiling and skillets heating. He remembered that Epsom salts were often used as a purgative. The more he thought about it, the more attractive the plan seemed to him. Off the kitchen was a supply room with sacks of flour and sugar and other spices. He looked around for Epsom salts but only managed to find garlic and onions. Then in a tin up on a shelf he found the Epsom salts. When he saw no one around he grabbed the tin of Epsom salts and hid it behind a door. Giovanni kept his eyes on Mesiù stirring and mixing sauces. When Mesiù went out of the kitchen and left it empty, Giovanni grabbed the tin of Epsom salts and emptied it into the large soup cauldron. Moments later Mesiù walked by and stirred the soup. The Epsom salts were now part of the soup.

As it came close to dining time, Carlo and Mesiù checked things to make sure that there would be no mistakes. Don Andrea stood outside the dining room dressed in his tails and starched shirt. Lesser Fascist figures were posted to see if Mussolini was coming. They were dressed in black with their lapel button shiny and their hair plastered down. When one of them ran into the hotel to say that Mussolini had arrived the place became alive with excitement. Even Giovanni, who had heard so much about this Mussolini, became excited. Don Andrea rubbed his hands together nervously.

A black car came to a stop in front of the hotel. The Minister ran out to it, and opened the door. A man dressed in a black suit and coat stepped out. He removed his hat from his balding head and faced the crowd. The Minister's group raised their arms in a salute and Mussolini returned the salute. Then Don Andrea came forth and the Minister introduced him to Mussolini. Don Andrea bowed to Mussolini who made a gesture of false impatience with the bowing and they shook hands.

From where Giovanni stood he could see Don Andrea pointing things out to Mussolini who looked admiringly at the hotel and the hills around it. Don Andrea was in his best form with Carlo following him around like a puppy.

After the introductions, Mussolini was brought to his room. Fabio was used as a porter to bring Mussolini's bags in. The others stood straight as ramrods, always waiting for some sign of recognition from the great man.

Later, Mussolini met with the Minister in a separate room. Here a few were invited to join and others were told to wait outside to make sure that the room was safe. These were tall men, blue eyed, with alert faces. Every time Mussolini appeared they snapped to attention and saluted. Mussolini returned the salute perfunctorily and kept talking to the Minister.

The Minister gave the signal to his men that they would go to dinner shortly. Don Andrea started snapping his fingers all around. Carlo went to the kitchen. Giovanni wondered if he had put enough Epsom salt in the soup to achieve the desired effect. As the notables came in Carlo ushered them to tables. Giovanni brought bottles of mineral water and wine to each table. He had developed the habit of bowing slightly when he addressed people, just as he had seen Carlo do.

Before starting to eat, the Minister got up, tapped a glass with his fork to get attention and said, "Today marks a new phase in the development of the *Fascio*, not just in Italy but in the world." Mild applause. Mussolini smiled modestly. "Italy has been chosen and blessed to have a great leader, Signor Mussolini," and he extended his hand to him, and everyone else applauded. Standing at the back, Don Andrea was all smiles.

"What is it that we're asking for? What do we see or rather not see in our current government? The King is largely unable to join the country in an expansionist mentality for one thing. Our industrial output is low and cannot compare with that of France, Germany or England. That must be changed. The impoverished South needs an injection of vitality to get agricultural output up. There is nothing happening in the South. All of these issues will be addressed by Signor Mussolini."

When the Minister finished, Mussolini stood up and embraced him,

"Thank you my dear friend and colleague," he began. "All that you said is true, and it is slightly embarrassing for me to think that I can change it all, after all, these conditions have existed for years, even for centuries."

He stood now, his hands on the table. What the Minister said about the South had an impact on Giovanni because he knew how poor it was.

"Why shouldn't we have factories like England that produce steel and iron? Why shouldn't we have factories that produce goods for us all to enjoy? Why shouldn't there be a place where our citizens can go to start new lives?" Applause. "Italy can be the new leader of the world. The English, French, and Germans will look up to us. It will all depend on how well you can put into place those things basic to the running of a modern corporate state. It is you who will do this, not me. I can only watch and guide you like a good father, but it is you who must be at the forefront of this massive effort." And then he sat down, with everyone applauding. The Minister turned to Don Andrea and said "Let the dinner in Signor Mussolini's honor begin!"

At this sign, Carlo went into the kitchen to tell Mesiù to start serving the meal. One by one all the servers were sent into the kitchen and came out with the soup bowls full of the puree of carrot that Mesiu said would wake the dead. Then they began to serve the wines that Carlo had chosen for this meal. Everyone was happy and proud, and Signor Mussolini partook of it all smiling occasionally to express his satisfaction with the quality of the food. After the soup Mesiù had prepared a pasta dish with a rich tomato sauce recipe. By the end of the meal, the guests sat there satisfied and happy. Don Andrea brought around bottles of cognac and other cordials to take with their coffee. He could not be happier with the evening. As the evening wound down, the guests began to leave.

In the night the maids were called to several rooms because they needed more toilet tissue. By midnight all the lights from the special group of rooms reserved for the Fascists were burning. All of the Fascists, including Signor Mussolini, spent the night sitting on the toilet as their systems were churning. The maids had a terrible night being called from their rooms to clean up messes. From his part of the dormitory reserved for the help, Giovanni heard the scurrying about and talk by the cleaning staff and he hid his smile in his pillow.

The next morning Mussolini's car was waiting for him. He decided not to take breakfast there because as he said his system was not well. Carlo had the staff bring fresh flowers for the tables to be occupied by the Fascist group, but one by one they came to the desk and departed.

The Minister called Don Andrea and they went to his office. You could overhear the loud voice of the Minister and Don Andrea's defense of the food.

"But Mesiù is a genuine French chef who has cooked in some of the greatest hotels in Europe. I can't imagine that it was something in the food that made you ill, Excellency," Don Andrea pleaded. The Minister continued yelling that it was probably a plot by their enemies to poison them and above all to poison Signor Mussolini.

"But that cannot be," Don Andrea said. "I have highest quality food for you. I saw to it myself that the meats were the best and everything else is absolutely fresh. I assure you that I shall find out what happened, and if there was foul play, I shall strangle the culprit with my own hands," he said, accompanying his words with a wringing motion of his hands. Giovanni could hear the Minister counting out bills to pay for the hotel and dinner, but Don Andrea handed it all back to him imploring that he would rather be killed before he accepted money if his clients, especially the Minister and Mussolini, were not completely satisfied. The Minister rushed out of the room, pocketing the money that Don Andrea had refused. Don Andrea ran behind him, pleading with him to understand.

Later that day Carlo called everyone together, including Miss Curti and her staff. They were all brought together in the dining room awaiting the arrival of Don Andrea. Earlier, Giovanni heard Mesiù and Don Andrea arguing in Don Andrea's office. Word had gotten around that something happened which sent most of the Fascist council rushing to the toilets, even the great Mussolini. Don Andrea came in, and Carlo stood at attention at his side.

"You probably have heard that we had a major disaster last night." Don Andrea started walking around as he spoke with his hands clasped together behind his back. "This is a dishonor that I shall never live down. We were so lucky that the Minister preferred to come here whenever he had a major meeting. It was good for all of us, not just me. People were taken care of by them, either in payment or through tips to individuals. I prided myself on having them come here. Last night when we had the dinner and the Minister introduced Mussolini I felt that my day of fame had come. Little did I know that somewhere there was a bug, a worm who was not satisfied that this would be a proud moment for me." He stopped and loudly said, "I want to know who screwed things up. I want to know who did something to the dinner that sent the Minister, Mussolini and his men to the toilets all night. What lowlife did something that caused this?"

Carlo came forward, "I, too, want to know. If Don Andrea was proud to have these individuals come to our hotel and restaurant, I was equally proud, and I did whatever it took to make them very happy with their stay."

Giovanni looked around at people trying to read their thoughts. But all were silent. He looked at Ada who had a very long face. Everybody was sullen.

"I would give a small fortune if I knew who may have done something to bring this about," Don Andrea said. "And when I find out, I pity the evildoer." He stalked out of the dining room with Carlo following in his footsteps.

———

Giovanni had to begin making his arrangements. Now that he had passed the physical examination, he began to plan for his departure.

He went to Ada's office. She had no idea what had happened to the Fascists that sent them all to the toilets, but Don Andrea suspected everyone. The one person who might have known was Fabio. Later that day Giovanni brushed past Fabio who whispered to him, "You are the only one." This was like an icy blade going into Giovanni's heart. He was sure there was no one around when he dropped the Epsom salts in the soup.

Giovanni spoke to Ada. "We have some big decisions to make."

"I'll meet you at three o'clock in the forest where we usually go," she said in a whisper.

At three o'clock Giovanni had finished preparing the dining room for the next meal and put his jacket aside. He slipped out the back door and headed for the woods. After some twenty minutes of walking he came to the forest that they had come to call their own.

"I'm so glad you are here," and he reached for her shoulders and kissed her. "It seems like years since we have been close."

"We both have had lots of things on our minds. What have you decided to do?"

"I think that I should go to America and then call you and little Andrea to come to meet me there."

She thought and then said, "You'll never call me there if you go there alone. Don't tell me I don't know what I am talking about. Out of sight, out of mind and I won't be the first one to be left behind like that."

"You have no reason to doubt me. I am determined to do well by you."

"If you are so convinced that you want to do well, why don't we marry first and then go to America together?"

Giovanni had no answer to her question. He had thought that he could best face his family by not facing the situation directly. A nice letter from America would have been his solution. He knew that this was not very heroic but he was not in a very heroic mood at this time.

"I am not going to be waiting here for a letter inviting me to go to America." She got up from the grass straightened her skirt and went back to the hotel.

———————————

Things had not lightened up at the hotel. Don Andrea and Carlo were threatening anybody they thought had something to do with the indigestion incident with the Fascists and Don Andrea lamented the loss of business from the Minister. He had tried to make it up to the Minister by inviting him and his wife to the hotel as his personal guests for a long weekend. His letter went unanswered.

Giovanni kept his mouth shut about the matter. He was thinking about his next step with Ada. He realized that he loved her and did not want to lose her, even if this meant that he had to assume the responsibility of little Andrea. Now he had to meet his parents and deal with the matter.

Claiming another death in the family, Giovanni went home for a weekend to face his parents. He knew his parents would never accept such a marriage. Nevertheless, he had to be the good son and sit down with them to explain the situation which now was beginning to haunt him.

Once at home, after dinner, he asked to meet with his parents. His father sat there impassive, sensing something important. His mother was used to leaving these things up to her husband.

Giovanni began by saying, "I have been at the job in Rome now for some time and certain things have happened that touch upon my life. I need to discuss these things with you before I take any steps." He paused. "During this time I have met and have gotten to know a very nice young woman and she has returned my affection. We are seriously thinking of formalizing our friendship through marriage."

His father said nothing and merely nodded to what he was saying.

"However you must know that this woman, her name is Ada, has a child from an earlier experience. I would be ready to assume him as a son. She's a very good person, intelligent, loyal, and loving. I believe that she and I can make a good marriage. As far as the child is concerned—he is five years old—he does not know another father and I would be his father."

The silence in the room was overwhelming.

Mastro Paolo spoke. "Am I to understand that you want to marry someone who has already had a liaison with someone else and on top of that has a son from it?"

"Yes, father, that is the way it is."

"Dear son, do you think that I have raised you to become the husband of a person of disrepute?"

"I have come to know her very well and I believe that in spite of this earlier mistake she is a good person, who loves me and is willing to entrust the raising of her son to me."

"Where is the child's father in all of this?" the father asked.

"I know who the father is. He is a very bad person who took advantage of an innocent young woman who knew nothing of the world and its ways. He has been supporting the child financially and the child lives with his grandparents outside of Rome."

"Why doesn't he marry her?"

"Because he is already married and has a grown daughter."

His father gasped. "Please tell me, dear son, why you should be the," and he hesitated, "the savior of this woman? Why can't she find someone else to save her and her child?"

"Because we love each other. We have a great need to be with each other."

"Love? Is that what they call it? I have another name for it and were it not for the dignity of your mother I would use it now. Love? Is that it? So she had managed to capture an innocent young man who will be her savior and that of her child. Have you learned nothing in this house? An appreciation of innocence in a woman? A sound family? Could we bring her into our home? Could her children be our children? It seems to me that you have forgotten everything we taught you. Where is your common sense? Where are your brains, that is, if you have any? If this young woman, whose qualities you appreciate so much, fell to the desires of another man-- and at that a married man--what is to stop her from doing the same by putting a pair of horns squarely on your head?"

"Father," Giovanni started to say.

"Keep still. I am talking. I want to tell you that you are making a mistake that you will carry for your whole life. You will never be rid of the humiliation that you bring upon yourself and us, your family. This, this..." he hesitated, "this *puttana* will now be your wife. Won't you look grand walking around with a whore on your arm? Won't you look the ninny talking about 'my wife' and 'my son'. You will be laughed at until the end of time. Didn't any of these things occur to you while you were falling in love?"

Giovanni wanted to debate his father, but the words wouldn't come.

"If you persist in this relationship, you will gain, yes, a new family, but you will lose your real family. You will be unwelcome in this house and in the houses of your brothers. You will cease being a son to me and to your mother. If you think that you, your woman and child will be part of this family, you are wrong, dead wrong. If on the other hand, you desire to terminate this relationship honorably, whatever that means to a *puttana*, you will continue to be our beloved son."

Giovanni thought best not to answer the things his father said. It hurt him profoundly to hear Ada being called a whore. Giovanni had feared that the scene would be just like this. His family lived by a certain code. Ada's situation belonged to the scenario of bad novels, wayward women, innocent women led down the path by lecherous and opportunistic men. But this did not relieve Ada of guilt. According to the code, she had agreed to whatever had happened, otherwise she would still be a virtuous woman. As for little Andrea, Giovanni knew that he would never be accepted into the family.

Giovanni returned to Rome. Ada would be waiting for his final decision, and he knew in his heart what it would be. He felt that he had spent a lifetime on the train from Rome to Giovinazzo and back.

He traveled at night so as to get back to work the next day but he also needed the dark and quiet to go over his thoughts.

Back at the hotel, he was confronted by Carlo. "Well, my dear clod, you don't seem to be running out of dying relatives. How many are left to die so you can have a little time off? We needed you these past few days, and where were you? 'I had to attend a funeral in my town'," he said, mimicking Giovanni's voice. "Well, you better get this into your thick skull. One more absence and you no longer work here."

"You didn't hire me. Don Andrea did. If anybody gets rid of me it will be him, not you," Giovanni answered.

"Oh, that's the way it is, is it? Well, let me tell you a thing or two. I never welcomed you here from the beginning. Imagine, arriving here without even a shirt or underwear! 'You didn't hire me, so you can't fire me'," Carlo imitated Giovanni again.

Giovanni's patience was wearing thin at this point, but he knew that he had to keep quiet for now.

"Get back to your work, and I am going to be keeping a special eye on you. No more funerals in the family, do you hear?"

Giovanni had spent a restless night ruminating on what his father said and what his next step was to be. He said to himself, if you and Ada marry, then you will be the father to the boy, and you will never enter the house of your parents, except perhaps when they die, and even then, you will not be welcome.

When he got off from work, he went to Ada's office and sat her down.

"I have had a talk with my parents, and it did not go well," he said. She lowered her head. "I have decided to formalize our situation. We are going to marry. We will take Andrea with us to America, and then we both start a new life."

Her face brightened. "I am so happy. Now we can leave this horrible place and start over," she said.

Giovanni felt so relieved that he let out a long sigh. He had chosen what his life would be.

Giovanni and Ada had to begin thinking about their departure from the hotel. In the back of Giovanni's mind there was a lingering taste for vengeance against Carlo. He wanted to pay him back. He wanted revenge.

When a particular couple from Brescia came to the hotel each year, Don Andrea always played up to them. The man was a mining engineer and had made a lot of money. Giovanni knew that when they came to the restaurant Carlo always brought them to the same table. He sat the gentleman facing north and his wife facing south. Being alone in the dining room, Giovanni took the chair that would be for the engineer's wife and began to loosen all the screws.

That night with a great flourish Carlo brought the engineer and his wife to their table, first carefully taking out the chair for the wife. When she sat down with her corpulent bulk the chair collapsed and she went thundering to the ground. Carlo turned pale as he stood there with the back of the chair in his hands and the wife on the floor flapping like a fish. The husband screamed at Carlo calling him an imbecile and idiot, claiming that he deliberately moved his wife's chair. Carlo, with tears in his eyes, denied everything. The wife was crying. It took several people to lift her up, among them Giovanni, who held her hand and waved a napkin in her face trying to give her air. Carlo was pleading with the engineer to believe that it was an accident.

Don Andrea arrived huffing and puffing. "What happened here?" he asked.

"I'll tell you what happened. This idiot of a waiter moved the chair just as my wife was about to sit and look what happened. My wife has been hurt."

"No! I want a complete explanation for this," Don Andrea snapped to Carlo, who was beside himself with fear.

Don Andrea turned to the woman. "*Signora*, what can I do to help you? Shall I call a doctor?"

"No, no," she said as Giovanni fanned her.

"Get another chair, goddamn it!" Don Andrea said. Giovanni went to get another chair and she was eased into it. "You," he said pointing to Giovanni, who experienced a shiver of fear, "go get the doctor and tell him to come immediately." Giovanni rushed away in a whirl of relief.

Finally the doctor came, dressed formally in coat and hat. He took *Signora*'s pulse and asked her some questions. Everyone stood nearby as if her life were endangered. Finally, he suggested that she put some cold compresses on her backside where she had landed, tipped his hat to the lady and to Don Andrea and left as quietly as he had come in.

In the background Giovanni maintained a serious look. He watched Carlo, wringing his hands. Giovanni could remember the searing anger he felt at Carlo's many insults but now felt almost nothing. "Yes," Giovanni thought, "vengeance is a dish one eats cold."

The next day, Carlo arrived, changed into his uniform in his special room and went into the kitchen to see what was happening there. A new idea occurred to Giovanni as he watched.

A few days later, he slipped into the room and with scissors cut off all the gold buttons on Carlo's jacket. He did a masterful job, being very careful not to ruin the jacket. Carlo loved that jacket and had the habit of straightening the lapels to make it look more military.

A few minutes before dinner time, Carlo arrived and went to his room. Giovanni positioned himself nearby. Shortly after, Giovanni heard a tremendous yell. Carlo screamed curses that Giovanni had not heard in all his life. Then Carlo ran out of the room holding the castrated jacket in his hand.

"Who did this? Who did this?"

Giovanni looked up with his smooth, young face a blank. Carlo held out a handful of shiny buttons. Giovanni looked down at the buttons and then up at Carlo.

"Who had the nerve? When I find out, I will rip his heart out with my bare hands," Carlo said.

To get the buttons sewn on Carlo had to go to Miss Curti. "I need to have buttons sewn on this jacket," he said imperiously.

"So? Sew them on yourself," she answered.

"You realize who you're talking to, don't you?"

"Yes, to a fool," she answered.

"I will not take any insults from the likes of you."

"If you want buttons sewn on, take a needle and thread and sew them on.

"I am the maître d' of this restaurant, and you are just a simple....a simple...a simple" he waited, "seamstress, if that is what you are."

"I am the director of the hotel and if you have any questions, go talk to Don Andrea. We cater only to the needs of the guests."

"I don't intend for a slut like you to be ragging me around here," he snarled.

The word "slut" was a terrible slap in her face. "Don't you call me that. Whatever I am, I owe in part to you. You miserable piece of shit," and she slapped him as hard as she could in the face.

Carlo bent over, more in shock than in pain, and a trickle of blood came out of his nose.

"You miserable little whore, you lousy piece of trash, how dare you touch me? Well, you can start packing your things and go back to your town to that little bastard...."

Before he finished the sentence Ada hit him again, full in the face. She ran out and hid. Carlo tried to stop the blood that came out of his nose. Ada shut the door of a broom closet and leaned against it. She didn't know what to do now. She stayed hidden until she could hear no more of Carlo's curses.

In the restaurant Carlo greeted the guests with his oleaginous smile, and led them to the tables, self-conscious about his appearance. In the back of his mind he thought of Ada and was furious. He was determined that she would not get away with it.

The first thing Ada did was to contact Giovanni. They met at the back door of the restaurant.

"Giovanni, something terrible has happened. Carlo came in my office and insulted me. I slapped him in the face twice. I know that I shouldn't have done it but he insulted me. He is angry beyond all belief. What should I do?"

"What happened?" he asked.

"He wanted me to sew some buttons on his jacket, but I wouldn't do it. He called me...." she hesitated, "he called me a whore and called my son a bastard. I couldn't help it. I hit him as hard as I could. I could see blood coming out of his nose. I am so afraid."

"Don't worry we'll work something out. Remember, whatever he says about little Andrea must apply to Don Andrea himself. Right now, the only thing I can think of is for you to go to see Don Andrea. And don't forget to tell him what Carlo said about little Andrea."

"What if he doesn't do anything?"

"He might do something unexpected, like getting rid of Carlo."

"I don't believe that. Carlo has been his right-hand man for many years."

"You don't seem to remember that he blamed Carlo for the toilet fiasco at the Fascists' dinner and then the problem with the chair for the engineer's wife. Don Andrea has already lost two big customers. With him money talks. I think that you should go to see Don Andrea right away and see if you can get your story in first. If Carlo gets there first...."

She thought a moment and then left to see Don Andrea. She knocked on his door. He woke suddenly from a nap and groggily opened the door.

"I have to talk to you about something urgent."

Shaking off the sleepiness of his nap, he said, "What is it? Can't you see I'm busy?"

"We must discuss matters that concern you and me."

His ears pricked up at that.

"It's Carlo," she said.

"Again?" Don Andrea asked.

"Yes, this time things are serious, and whether you like it or not, you are involved in it. Today Carlo came to my office and asked to have some buttons sewn on his jacket."

"So?" Don Andrea asked.

"It is not my job to do sewing for him and I told him so. He started insulting me, calling me some very bad words, and on top of it all, he insulted your son."

Don Andrea came awake now at the mention of his son.

"He first called me a whore," Ada said, "and then called our son a bastard. I won't stand for that."

Don Andrea was not accustomed to being reminded about having a son. As far as he was concerned he had his own legitimate daughter, anything else simply wasn't spoken of.

Don Andrea was truly caught off guard. He had found that the best way of dealing with this problem was to give Ada employment—lifetime employment—just to keep the matter quiet.

"Carlo had no business talking to you that way. I'll speak to him."

"I'm afraid. I hit him. He'll do something to me."

"Carlo is a coward. Leave it to me. Go back to your work and I'll take care of the matter."

"Don Andrea, I am going to confide something very important to you and I don't want you to mention this to anyone."

"What is it?"

"I love someone and I think he loves me too. He works here too, it's Giovanni. We are going to America together and that includes our son Andrea."

Don Andrea was stunned by the news. He never paid attention to the gossip he heard about his employees, who slept with whom and who slipped into whose bed late at night. But at the thought that she would go to America his spirits soared. He would not have Ada around to remind him of his mistakes. "You can count on me to help you in this." He reached out his hand and pressed her arm.

For the next two days Carlo did very little smiling. After an initial reprimand, Don Andrea did not speak at all to Carlo who stood behind him looking crestfallen. Don Andrea stepped in to pay the passage for Ada, Giovanni and little Andrea to go to America. Giovanni went to the nearby church and spoke with the priest who told them that they could not have a regular marriage ceremony because, and he hesitated, "this is not a conventional marriage. She had a child from an illicit affair. In view of these circumstances," he continued, "I can offer you a ceremony in the side chapel, after the banns are proclaimed, of course."

The idea that they would not have a regular marriage ceremony depressed both Giovanni and Ada. She had always expected a ceremony with a white dress which she and her mother would make.

"You and your mother can still make a white dress," Giovanni said.

"Yes, we can. But not go to the altar as others do…."

"It will be a valid marriage in the eyes of the church, even though it lacks some of the proper ceremony," Giovanni added.

They had to wait for the banns to be read three times and after that the wedding could take place. Her father would give her away. Fabio would be the best man, the *compare,* and a childhood friend of Ada's would be the maid of honor.

Giovanni sat down to write his parents and his brothers in America.

"I know that this union," he said in the letter to his parents, "does not please you, but I feel that this is a very good person in spite of a mistake that she made some years ago. I do not believe that marrying her is wrong in any way. I have made up my mind to do this. We are getting married on Sunday, the fifteenth of May before our departure for the United States where I will be joining my brothers. It would give me great pleasure to have you at the wedding ceremony, and if you do decide to come, please let me know immediately. Your loving son, Giovanni."

His parents read and reread the letter several times. His father maintained silence. Giovanni's mother and aunt discussed the matter several times out of earshot of her husband. They could not go under any circumstances. Mastro Paolo had declared Giovanni no longer a member of the family and he was not to enter house again during Mastro Paolo's lifetime.

Later, Giovanni only remembered the dark church and the gleam of the few candles. As he and Ada faced the priest, she held his arm tightly. Her thoughts were hidden from him but they held hands and went out at the end, man and wife.

═══════════

Once in Rome, Giovanni saw more and more Fascists in the streets. Everywhere were individuals done up in black uniform and holstered pistol. The order of the day was war. Italians were living their lives as characters in a play. Giovanni had other plans. He would be leaving Italy for America.

═══════════

In bustling, noisy Naples they felt far from the quiet of the Albergo Lentino, with only the occasional sound of a horse, clip clopping.

Giovanni first had to go to the Health Office to get recertification, then the steamship office to get tickets. He had received a letter from his brothers in America. Since their father had disowned Giovanni, they were put in a difficult position in receiving him, although they would do what they could to assist him in getting started in New York. It seemed to Giovanni that since his affair with Ada there had been nothing but a series of disappointments. He tried not to let his feelings overcome him. His brothers' cool reception of the news that he had married a woman who had a child outside of marriage was another blow.

The clerk read Giovanni's papers several times and said that Giovanni had to go to the government office on Via Roma to get a further certification.

Giovanni complained but it did no good. He told Ada and Andrea to wait for him because there was a slight problem.

To get to the foreign office Giovanni took a trolley car to the center of Naples. At the entrance stood two black-shirted soldiers. Everyone was asked to present their papers to be examined. Then he was admitted into the building and sent to room 108, where he found a waiting room with five people who sat morosely papers in hand. Giovanni became impatient as time moved slowly and the person at the desk seemed not to care about the urgency of his situation.

After an hour and a half his name was called, and he was sent to a room down the corridor. The clerk in the room was also a Black Shirt.

"I see that you are not in the habit of saluting a member of the Fascist Party."

"I didn't know," Giovanni answered feebly.

"In today's society whenever you see a person with a uniform like mine, you salute," and he got up, "like this," he said, raising his arm.

Giovanni nodded and began to state his business. "Sir, I have applied to go to America and had to go through a physical examination, which found me healthy. What is the problem? My family and I are waiting to get on the boat and leave for America."

The Black Shirt got up from the chair and walked around the desk slowly until he sat at its edge, his long black boots gleaming. "We have no quarrel with your health, and recognize that there may have been a mistake in the first place in labeling you as tubercular," he paused. "But when you met the last doctor and were examined by him you must have said something that was critical of the Fascist Party."

"Critical of the Party?" Giovanni asked incredulously. "Critical of the Party?" he repeated. "When did I say anything against the Fascist Party"

"When you met the doctor, according to a note which the doctor appended to his report, you are alleged to have made some remarks that were not respectful of Il Duce and his politics."

"I recall no such thing," Giovanni pleaded.

"*Signore*, we don't make these things up. The doctor, who is a member of the Party and holds the rank of major, a medical officer, felt that you had made remarks that were not consistent with the aims of the Fascist Party."

"As far as I am concerned, the doctor must have made a mistake. For me, if the Party does well for the common people, then I am in favor of it. If it doesn't, then I am not."

"And? Has it done any good for the common people?"

"I can't say because I haven't seen anything."

"His Excellency, Benito Mussolini, made a vow to help all Italians from every region and from all walks of life. Your blindness to his aims makes me wonder if the doctor isn't right about you."

"Well, he's not," Giovanni said belligerently.

"You are suspected of being a dissenter, and Mussolini doesn't want people of your kind going abroad to speak ill of his program."

Giovanni was exasperated. As far as he was concerned, one party was as good or bad as another because it never went beyond the stage of talking and never quite helped the poor *contadini*. All Giovanni wanted to do was get out of Italy and get to America with his new family.

"I am afraid that we cannot approve the departure of a dissident whose political ideas we do not trust. We don't want people in America to get the wrong idea about our party."

Giovanni was livid. "I am not a dissident," he protested. "All I want is to go to America to join my brothers."

"I think that I have had just about enough of you. Be careful or you go to jail. Then you will see what the Fascist Party is like," the officer said as he rounded the desk and took up Giovanni's papers. He took out a large stamp and placed at the head of the paper "Denied for reasons of political deficiency, *irriducibile*."

"Now you can go," he said with a sneer. "Some day you will see the error of your ways. Soon no one will be able to go to America any more because the Party will be involved in a full-fledged war with the enemy."

Giovanni waited outside the building, breathing in the ocean air of Naples. How would he be able to tell Ada about this? When he went back to Ada and Andrea she could tell immediately that something was wrong. He sat down in despair.

"They are not letting us emigrate," he said.

"What do you mean?"

"They said that I am a danger to the state because I said some negative things about the Fascist Party. Not a word about my health and now I am an enemy of the state, and they won't approve me for emigration. All kinds of fools get to emigrate, but me, no, I have to stay." He felt wild with desperation.

"What do we do now? We can't return to Don Andrea's. That is a closed door. What are we going to do?"

"I don't know," he said emphatically.

All they had done was built upon the premise that they would go to America and start a new life there. Giovanni even entertained the thought that if he had stayed in Giovinazzo, he would never have found himself in this dilemma. He banished the thought. They got their belongings, including the large trunk. He would have to return home to his father's house and see what was waiting for him there. Ada did not like the idea because she felt already alienated from them. How would it be for her?

All through the night on the train Giovanni thought up various scenarios. He felt sure that his father would relent.

Arriving at Giovinazzo, he saw Giacomo with his cart always ready to pick up some jobs. Giacomo looked them over, especially Ada and the child with a suspicious eye.

"Who are these?" he asked slowly.

"Giacomo, why don't you mind your own business? Just bring the stuff to my father's house."

Giovanni remembered what it was like to walk through the town when he was sent back because of his supposed tuberculosis. This time he was accompanied by a woman and a child to inspire curiosity.

The porter took the trunk and other belongings and placed it at the door of Mastro Paolo's house. Giovanni put some coins in his hand and he left. Every eye watched them with malice. Ada for her part acted like there was nothing wrong. After all, she had gone through this when she was pregnant with Andrea. She had learned to put up a brave front.

Giovanni knocked at the door. His mother had watched their arrival from behind a curtain at the window.

After what seemed like a long time his aunt, dressed in black, came to the door and opened it a crack. Without even the hint of a smile, she looked out at Giovanni.

"*Zia*," he said and reached up to kiss her on her cheek.

"Giovanni," was all she said, but she didn't open the door to let them in.

"*Zia*, may I come in? *Zia*, this is my wife and our child," Giovanni said.

Tears welled in the corner of her eyes but she did not let them in.

"Your father has said that you are no longer a member of this family." She stopped and tried to compose herself. "He said that we are never to welcome you here," and tried to shut the door. She stopped halfway into the act and reopened it and tried once again to say something but then with tears in her eyes, she shut the door.

After standing there for what seemed like forever Giovanni turned to Ada and Andrea.

"I am going to see Donna Margherita. Her husband is a friend of my father. Maybe he can let us stay with him until we can see what there is to do."

"But won't your father have it against anyone who helps us?"

"Perhaps, but Don Emmanuele has a soft heart."

During the encounter at the door his sister Filomena had watched from the window of her bedroom. She was frightened by the tension of the situation. She loved Giovanni who had always been good to her. She slipped out of her room and went to the kitchen where she took a piece of bread, slathered it with butter and marmalade and opened the window and thrust it at Andrea. Andrea didn't know what to do. Ada reached for the piece of bread and nodded thanks as Filomena shut the window.

Giovanni was touched by her charity and had to choke back a sob. He turned to Ada and Andrea and said, "Let's go. You can wait somewhere while I go see my friends."

"No, I don't want to wait. I am going with you," she said determinedly.

They walked the quiet and crooked streets until he came upon a whitewashed building with a cross over the door. He hesitated before he knocked on the door, but finally overcame his reluctance. After several knocks, the door opened and Don Emmanuele was there pleasantly surprised to see Giovanni.

"Giovanni, *mio caro e figlio bello*," my dear and beautiful boy. What are you doing here? Come in, come in."

"Don Emmanuele, before you let me in, there's a problem here."

"What can such a problem be that you can't come in my house?"

"Why don't you step outside a minute and I'll explain it all to you."

"What's to explain?"

Giovanni tried to find the right words. Finally, he turned and said, "I want you to meet my wife, Ada."

Don Emmanuele was startled, "Your wife? Why didn't you come right out and tell us that you are here with your wife?"

"And child," Giovanni added quickly.

Don Emmanuele frowned. "Look Giovanni, please come in, all of you, and let's talk about this like good Christians."

They entered not sure if they belonged anywhere. Donna Margherita came in and, full of curiosity, looked at Ada.

"Come, sit down, tell me everything," Don Emmanuele said.

"Don Emmanuele, you have known me for a long time, so I hold no secrets from you. You know that I went near Rome to work in a restaurant and hotel after I was refused emigration because some doctor said I had tuberculosis. While there I met Ada and we found a love for ourselves in spite of the fact that she has a son."

"From another marriage? She's a widow?"

"No, not at all. Things happen in life that we can't always control. Let's say that Ada made a mistake, a mistake that any innocent person could make."

As they talked about this, Ada lowered her head. She had gone through this so many times already that she was tired of it all.

"Recently, Ada and I married even though my parents have not blessed the union. In fact, my father has disowned me, and has turned me out of my house—forever. We tried to emigrate but this time I was called a political problem to the Fascist party, so they didn't approve my application to emigrate."

"*Ma che*! You a political liability? I don't believe it and anyone who believes it is a son-of-a-bitch," Don Emmanuele said.

"Be that as it may, I can't emigrate. I can't stay with my father because he has disowned me and does not accept Ada, let alone Andrea. What do I do?"

"Have you have eaten anything? No? Well, Margherita, let's put something on the table for these folks, then we'll talk a little more."

There was ample food left over from the midday meal, and Donna Margherita started to warm it up. Ada heaved a sigh of relief because she was beginning to feel hunger pangs, but didn't want Giovanni to think that she was a whiner. Donna Margherita started to put plates on the table, brought out the bread and the smell of a sauce began to permeate the kitchen. She started to serve the food, preparing a little plate for Andrea. They ate without saying much. Don Emmanuele brought out a bottle of wine he had made.

Then, Don Emmanuele started talking. "I understand the situation. Sometimes parents hold out wishes for their children and if these wishes are not granted, they act very badly. In your case, as I am sure you both know" he looked at Ada, "your parents had expected you to marry someone from Giovinazzo, remember the proverb, '*Donne e buoi, dai paesi tuoi*,' women and oxen, get them from your own town."

"Don Emmanuele, I know that my father will not be happy with you for receiving us."

"Don't worry about that. I know that your father will be unhappy about this matter. He and I have been through many things together, and I don't worry about him. What are you going to do? I have a big question about your life in Giovinazzo. Do you want to end up here?

There is nothing here for the young. One by one they go to America or Argentina. Only we, the elders, are left here to live and die."

Don Emmanuele continued "I have three sons, two went to Argentina and one to Brazil. I hardly ever hear from them. Sometimes I wonder if they are still alive."

"I am sorry to hear that. Life is painful. I would depart today but I have been declared a political enemy and I haven't done anything except say a few things to an examining doctor in Naples. He branded me a dangerous dissident. It's as if I now wear a kind of sign that says 'Antifascist'."

Donna Margherita spoke. "Right now, you, Ada and the boy must stay here. Go to bed and get a good night's sleep, then maybe tomorrow we will have some answers."

Andrea had already fallen asleep in his mother's arms, and Donna Margherita led them to a bedroom in the back of the house. The next day they all woke very late to hear from Don Emmanuele that he had gone to see Mastro Paolo.

"We talked about your situation," Don Emmanuele said.

"What did he say when you told him that I had slept here at your house?"

"He did what I expected him to do. He said I should go looking for friendship elsewhere, and a lot of other things too."

"I am so sorry, Don Emmanuele. I did not mean to ruin your friendship with my father."

"Don't worry. He and I have had some disagreements in the past but it always turns itself around. In his heart, he is a good man, and that is why I hope that he will relent. Giovanni," Don Emmanuele said gravely, "no one in Giovinazzo is going to give you work, knowing that you and your father have a serious quarrel."

"I may have to go to another town."

"Do you remember Don Beppe, he used to have a stone yard on the other end of town?"

"Yes, I remember him."

"He solved his problems by going to Brindisi and opening a restaurant and hotel."

Giovanni had no other choice, so he decided to go to Brindisi and meet Don Beppe.

The ride on the train to Brindisi wasn't long. The railroad station was on the far end of the city, and he needed a hack to take him to the center. Giovanni marveled at the sea that the town opened on to. Brindisi was an old town and the buildings went back to the era of the Christian crusaders and even to the Greeks.

Near the wide steps leading down to the sea he saw a modest sign that said Ristorante Bella Napoli. Inside he asked for Don Beppe.

"Is it important?" the waiter asked.

"Important for me," Giovanni answered.

"I don't know exactly how long you have to wait, because Don Beppe sometimes has to take care of business in town. Why don't you go take a walk and then come back? By that time, Don Beppe should be here."

There were cobble-stone streets near the port and the Adriatic harbor was full of ships and boats. As far as he could tell, the inhabitants spoke Italian as he did, with very little difference from his own Giovinazzese dialect. He understood everybody. People walked up from the seafront holding make-shift fishing rods and twisting fish on a line. He went into a café and had a coffee.

"How's business?" he asked the barman.

"Very busy when the foreign ships are in," he said and went back to drying coffee cups.

"I am here to see a fellow named Don Beppe who has a restaurant and hotel here in Brindisi, named the "Bella Napoli.""

"Ah yes, Don Beppe," he smiled. "Don Beppe. Quite a fellow. He knows everybody, yet he's not originally from here. And what a lady's man!"

"Does he have family?"

"He is in business with his son, Domenico, and another son, Ciccio. Don Beppe's wife is a respected lady."

"Does he do a lot of business?"

"Like everybody else he depends on traffic from the ships. But he has a good restaurant and a lot of people from town go there to get a good meal. He also gets a certain number of businessmen traveling to

Greece or Albania, so they go to his hotel before they leave the next morning."

Giovanni walked back to the restaurant where he found a few people getting the kitchen ready for the noontime meal. He had seen it all many times at the Lentino. There was no one to set up the tables. He walked into the kitchen. The chef was busy filling pots with water, and looking over the vegetables.

"I'm looking for Don Beppe," Giovanni said. There was no answer, so he walked closer to the chef. "I'm looking for Don Beppe," Giovanni said again. The chef looked up and said, "Don Beppe usually comes in at this time, or his son Mimì comes by with stuff that they bought. With Don Beppe you never know." The chef's accent was one that Giovanni had never heard before.

"With Don Beppe you never know. No one ever really knows."

Giovanni went back into the dining room, found a closet where the tablecloths were and put them on all the tables. He found the silverware, which was in a special box lined with green velvet cloth. He set all the places in the dining room.

Some time later some men came in. One of the men walked warily around the dining room seeing everything in its place. He saw the napkins were folded in a special way, a way that was never done in the Bella Napoli. He looked up at Giovanni.

The man said, "Who told you to set up the dining room?"

"Nobody. I figured that it had to be done. So I saved somebody some work. All I want to do is to see Don Beppe."

"What do you want from Don Beppe?"

"I'll discuss that with him," Giovanni answered.

The waiter disappeared into the kitchen, shaking his head slowly.

The doors of the kitchen swung open and a man dressed in a black suit came through. Giovanni got up, holding his hat in his hand. "Don Beppe?"

"Yes? What can I do for you?"

"Don Beppe, my name is Giovanni Falcone, the son of Mastro Paolo from Giovinazzo. Don Emmanuele told me about you and your business here in Brindisi, and he suggested that I visit you, hoping that you might have some work for me." Then Giovanni looked at Don Beppe, a man of medium height with very florid complexion.

"You are the son of Mastro Paolo?"

"Yes, I'm one of his sons."

"Where are your brothers?"

"They went to America."

"And you, didn't you go too?"

"Well, Don Beppe, it's a long story. But Don Emmanuele told me that you have a thriving business here in Brindisi. I need work and I have experience working in a restaurant and hotel near Rome. I wonder if you can help me. I also have a wife and child to support."

"And your father, Mastro Paolo, how does he fit into this puzzle?"

"Don Beppe, that too is a long story.

"What can you do, precisely?"

"At a restaurant near Rome I worked mainly as a waiter and busboy. When things were slow in the kitchen and dining room I helped out in the hotel. I know how to set up a dining room." He looked at the dining room and with his hand he circled the room. "I did this while I was waiting for you."

Don Beppe looked around. "I don't think that the waiters are going to like that," he said.

"I was waiting here with nothing to do, so I thought, let me set things up, at least to show you that I can do this kind of work and also because I wanted you to see that I am not afraid to work."

Don Beppe remained silent.

"Don Beppe, I wouldn't be here unless I was desperate."

"When did you get married?" Don Beppe asked.

"Not too long ago. I met my wife when we were both working at that restaurant in Rome. She was the director of the hotel operation. She's a very capable person, and, if I may say so, if you need someone to run the hotel, believe me, she's the person you would want."

Don Beppe said, "I have known your father for a long time. I can't imagine him not taking you and your family in."

"Don Beppe, there was a problem," Giovanni answered. He paused for a while and then went on. "The woman I married has a child, but not from another marriage. My father would not bless our marriage. That is why I am living at the house of Don Emmanuele until I find a job."

Giovanni stopped there. Don Beppe had listened carefully. He said, "Young man, I know your father. He is a man of principle, so I can understand his feelings. But also I admire your will in this matter, accepting this woman and her child. I have great respect for your father, so I will give you a job. Now, about your wife. I'll see if there's work for her. Where are you going to live?" he asked.

"I really don't know. I came here just to see if I could get work. Now you have given me a new life. I suppose I can find rooms for us. We don't need too much. Ada can take care of little Andrea and I shall work as much as you need me and in whatever capacity you say—washing dishes, setting and serving tables, whatever."

Giovanni's spirits were buoyed. He saw his temporary salvation. Now he could return to Giovinazzo and prepare for his move here. He got up and hugged Don Beppe, who smiled, his florid face lit up.

"You can tell your father that I am helping you out of respect for him and our friendship. Now the salary is no great thing, you understand, but it is something." Giovanni reached for Don Beppe's hand and kissed it.

"Come now. There's no need for that," he said. "I have a small apartment behind the restaurant which I use for different things. You can clean it up and then move in. It is better than the street and besides I won't charge you for the use of the apartment."

Giovanni was very moved by what Don Beppe had done. His own father would not even let him into his house, but this man, a *paesano*, took him in, gave him a job and now a place to live. He couldn't express his thanks to Don Beppe enough.

"Go back to Giovinazzo, get your family and come back today. Tomorrow I'll go over your tasks with you in both the restaurant and the hotel."

Giovanni's feelings were a combination of joy and sadness. He felt that he had found a new father in Don Beppe but there would always be an ache in him for his father's love. Giovanni had adored Mastro Paolo and to have fallen out of favor with him was difficult. But now Giovanni had new responsibilities. Throughout the train ride, he mulled these things over. He thought that before he left that day to return to Brindisi, he might try one more time to see his father. He truly wanted his father's blessing. Upon arriving in Giovinazzo,

Giovanni went directly to Don Emmanuele's house. Ada ran to the door when she heard the bell ring. Fear was written all over her face.

"Get ready to go, I have found a job in Brindisi and Don Beppe is giving us a small apartment to live in," he said.

Ada gave a sigh of relief.

PART VII

They arrived in Brindisi at night. A few porters were sitting around smoking and talking.

"I need help here," Giovanni said. "I have a trunk and some bags."

"What hotel?"

"The Bella Napoli," he answered again.

"Ah, Don Beppe's hotel! Yes, I'll take you," one of them said.

"Don Beppe" the porter said "he knows everybody, and everybody knows him. Are you going to Greece or Albania?"

"No, he has given me a job there to work as a waiter and to help in his hotel."

The porter thought to himself, he's no better than me, just a waiter. "I'll load the dolly and you can follow me. It's a bit of a walk, but with a little patience we can get there in about twenty minutes."

The apartment, when they entered, was a few rooms, not particularly well-lit, with a window in the kitchen. Giovanni was in no position to complain. It was a place to drop all their bags, get some sleep and then the next day start working. Ada could clean up the place and make it fit for human habitation.

When they woke, Giovanni jumped when he saw the time. He meant to be there at work very early. What would Don Beppe think of him? He dressed quickly. He didn't even have time to shave.

At the restaurant, the others were working, setting tables, putting out kitchen utensils, cleaning them, and shining the silver. Don Beppe even had special dishes with the picture of Mount Vesuvius on it, and around the picture were the words "Bella Napoli." Giovanni was to find out that Don Beppe was better than the people that he had worked for before. He was strict but understanding. He treated his people with respect but he demanded that they do their day's work.

One of the waiters told him that they had expected him to be there early, just like the rest.

"I understand how you feel. I would feel the same way," Giovanni said. "I came here to see Don Beppe in the morning, went back home to Giovinazzo, then got my family and our goods and came back here. When we got here last night late, I was exhausted. I hope that Don Beppe doesn't get mad at me."

"Don Beppe gets mad when you don't do the work right. He gives us a certain amount of liberty, but if you make a mess of things he'll dump you," the waiter said.

"I hope not to do that." Giovanni said. "Where should I begin?"

"The first thing is to go and get a shave."

At ten in the morning a tall, thin man came in to the restaurant. People greeted him in the manner of slaves to masters. In profile he had a long nose and an angular face. This was Don Beppe's son, Domenico, called Mimì. He usually dressed formally in a black suit and vest. The restaurant staff paid careful attention to him even though everybody knew that Don Beppe was the boss. Mimì didn't help with the dining room or with the kitchen staff. He stood around looking officious.

One of the waiters told Giovanni that Mimì was living with a Roman woman, something that Donna Maria Antonietta disapproved of. Don Beppe's other son Ciccio had a wife, Memena, who was very religious. That a woman would live with a man who was not her husband was upsetting to her. Furthermore, Mimì was a Freemason, and he wore his anti-Catholicism openly.

Since Don Beppe was known to support a mistress he could not very well chide his son about his way of life. Mimì was less ostentatious about his sexual affairs but his liaison with Sara, his lover, was something that he did not hide. His mother, Donna Maria Antonietta was resigned to the fact that her husband and now her son were sinners. "That's what men are like," she sighed to Memena.

Mimì stepped out into the street to look at the passersby. He saw sailors from merchant ships with their in-port uniforms. There were sailors from India who had dark skin and wore gowns and turbans. Others from exotic places wore rings in their ears and painted their faces in different colors. Mimì was wondering what their lives could be like back in their countries when he heard his mother call him from her room.

"Yes, Mamma?"

"Don't forget to tell Sara that I am here waiting. She told me that we were going shopping."

"Mamma, how many things can she do? She's got to do all these other things, doesn't she?"

"Why must I be made to wait? Who does she think she is, the Queen of Italy?"

"She knows that she promised you, and you can be sure that she'll bring you shopping."

His mother made a gesture of impatience with her hand. Mimì was her boy, and he knew that he could get away with a lot.

That first day Giovanni was very much at ease because he knew all that he had to do. He tried to distance himself from the other workers, because he knew how petty and envious they could be. The cook was from Tuscany but the other workers were from Brindisi. Giovanni and the cook were the outsiders. Don Beppe was in his chair reading the morning newspaper when the head of the Fascist brigades of Brindisi came in. Don Beppe shook his hand and led him to a table.

"Gino, bring the Captain a cup of the best coffee we have," Don Beppe ordered.

"My dear Don Beppe, how are you doing?" The Captain asked.

"You know, dear Captain, we live when we have customers. In this season we have the usual customers who come for a few days."

"I have come to talk to you about your son Mimì," the Captain said.

"What? Again?"

"Don Beppe, I am here because you are a man of respect." The Captain stopped, stirred his cup of black coffee and sipped it. "The head of the Fascist Party is tired of seeing Mimì's name in reports. I have spoken to you once about his political activity. Either you don't believe me or you don't believe that the Party will severely punish anyone involved in subversive activity."

"Captain," Don Beppe implored, "I guarantee you that there will be no next time. I will take him by the ears and shake him. There will be no next time," he insisted.

Don Beppe accompanied the Captain to the door and even a few steps down the street. They shook hands and separated. Don Beppe came in the restaurant. Giovanni had been eavesdropping the conversation while he cleaned silver. He remembered having seen the biggest bigwigs of the Party in Rome, especially Mussolini.

Don Beppe called Mimì over. "I just had a visit from the Captain of the Fascio."

"Again?" Mimi asked.

"Yes, the Party knows that you go and meet with those troublemakers. Don't you understand? My dear son, to the Fascist party officials it doesn't mean anything that you were not a member as you say. The fact is that you were there."

"Oh." Mimì said, waving his hand in the air. "I am not a member of that group and that is all I am going to say."

"I'll tell you what you are going to say," Don Beppe said. "You will stay away from them. I do not want to find your body floating in the harbor or anything like that," Beppe said.

The next week Mimì went for his evening walk. Suddenly, a blanket was thrown over his head. He panicked as strong arms wrestled him to the ground. Wrapped in a blanket, unable to move, he was carried to a car. He couldn't see. No one spoke, the only sound was that of the car motor running. He struggled to breathe. The car came to a stop and he was carried out. He heard a door shut and the blanket was removed but a blindfold was immediately put on him. He could breathe now but saw nothing, except feet in black shiny leather.

"All right, my dear intellectual. You were the one who once shut down the railroad and gave out flyers against the government. Now we are going to give you a little of our intellectual life," a voice said and others laughed. Some hands loosened his trousers and pulled down his underwear. Mimì had heard that the Squadristi could be very mean people but he never thought that they would fool with him. His father was, after all, their friend. They came to eat in his restaurant and occasionally when one of them needed a room for an afternoon his father accommodated them. Mimì felt a tube entering his anus and with it a pressure of liquid into his insides. Mimì began to squirm. If it didn't hurt at first it now began to hurt, and the pressure inside him grew and grew. He needed to void immediately, but a hand held the tube in place as the liquid rushed into him. Mimì thought his stomach was going to burst. After what seemed like hours Mimì was brought into a metal tank and the tube pulled out quickly. He began to defecate with the filth going onto his clothing and all over him. Mimì had heard about these cod liver oil enemas. When he was finished he was raised out of the tank, turned over and the tube inserted again with the liquid rushing again into his body. This happened several times until Mimì could no longer exert any control over his body. He was left in his filth. The strong hands picked him up and carried him to the street and dropped him there on the sidewalk. He never saw a face and could never recognize a voice. All he could do was lift himself up, revolted by his own stink, and walk. He needed to stop frequently for the liquid and filth to come rushing out of his body. For every five steps forward, he would stop and defecate again.

It seemed like miles until he could see the lights on the ships in the port and he knew that he was getting close to home. His stomach churned and burned. He felt all his insides tied in a knot, welling up until his body expelled yet another rush of filthy water.

By the time Mimì got home he smelled like a sewer and felt pain all over his body. He tried knocking at the door but was ashamed of having Sara see him in these circumstances, so he took off his clothes outside on the street, bundled them up and threw them into a refuse barrel on the street. He knocked quietly at the door of his rooms. When Sara answered all sleepy-eyed and saw Mimì naked and reeking of filth, she let out a gasp. Mimì started to cry. She put him in the tub and ran water over him holding her nose.

"It's that group you meet with, that's what it is. Your father is right. You must stop seeing them at all costs," she said as she scrubbed him. "Let's see now what your father and all his boasting will do for you," she said.

"Leave my father out of this. When you think of the free dinners he gave them, all the drinks, the coffees." He began throwing up from the smell.

When Don Beppe heard of this the next morning, he went to Mimì's rooms to see how he was. Mimì was in bed, covered up to his neck in sheets and blankets. His pale face emerged to see his father. Never was the contrast greater between them. Mimì white and weak, Don Beppe, red-faced and energetic. His father sat down, his hand on Mimì's chest, murmuring "I told you to stop going there. I told you to stop going there, and you will never go there again."

Later, Don Beppe sat at one of the tables in the restaurant nursing a coffee. Preventing Mimi from going back to that group of dissidents was the first order of business. Don Beppe thought of his son lying inertly and vowed that Mimì would never, ever again put himself in danger.

Word soon got out about what happened to Mimì. The gossip traveled fast and got as far as Giovinazzo. Don Beppe's brother, Tommasino, heard about it and came immediately to see Beppe and Mimì. When he arrived, he and Beppe sat over coffee as Beppe told him all that had happened.

"Shouldn't you be thinking of getting Mimì out of here before he disappears for good? He should get out of here and not come back until this has been forgotten," Zi' Tommasino said.

"I don't think that is the solution. They have made their point, and if Mimì doesn't get it, I think that he deserves all that they give him. I am hoping that he will follow my advice and stay away from those Freethinkers and Masons he calls his friends. His mother is distraught over this. While the Fascists are in power, it is not going to be forgotten. He is on someone's blacklist. I think that they used Mimì to show the others what they could expect from the Party if anybody got out of line," Beppe said.

For the next few weeks no one from the Fascist Party came to the restaurant. Tourists came and went, staying the night before they left for Patras the next morning. Don Beppe lost some of his verve and temporarily lost his wish for amours with every pretty woman he saw. He was so affected by Mimì's experience that he often sat quietly, lost in his thought, a cup of coffee in front of him.

One week, other dissidents were taken and jailed. No one heard anything further about them. Don Beppe had decided to lie low on the Mimì affair. He didn't go to the Fascist officials to protest but waited there for them to come to him. If they ever did, he didn't know what he was going to do. If he protested, they might even invent a case against him.

Mimì and Sara assumed a low-key role around the restaurant. It was better to forget what the Squadristi had done to Mimì, but Sara was angry at him for having been with that gang of Socialists. She knew that Mimì had leftist leanings. He joined the Masons as a protest against the role that the church played in Italian life, of this Sara was sure. Mimì hated the church and would do anything he could to insult it. He was appalled that his father often went whoring with a priest, Don Blasi. That hypocrisy offended Mimì's sense of what was right.

Every now and then Ciccio, Beppe's other son, would come back from America where he worked as a granite cutter. It was his savings that helped establish the restaurant and hotel. He would send money to his father who in turn would spend it on the business, thus making Ciccio a partner in the enterprise. This time he came home, gathered up his wife and two children, and went to Brindisi to oversee the business directly. Things in America were not that great, he reminded his father and brother. In America, due to the depression there was an atmosphere of helplessness and people often went hungry.

Ciccio had the same type personality as his father and knew how to deal with people. He had observed his father and seen how he extended credit to powerful people and who then became beholden to him. Ciccio even interested himself in the kitchen and by watching the cooks, he learned to cook in the event there were a need. His specialty was to do the shopping for the day's menu. He loved doing this. He got up early and brought with him a scullion who carried whatever he bought. Ciccio knew how to pick fruit and vegetables and had a silent pact with the butcher who made sure to give him only the best cuts of meat. For Ciccio shopping was an art. He was a hands-on person, digging into the work of the kitchen and going to the market. Mimì on the other hand was all appearance. He walked around the restaurant with his hands in the pockets of a tailored suit and greeted people in a cursory way. After his episode with the cod liver oil enema he was even less sociable.

Ada and Sara began a friendship when both had jobs in the hotel. There were women that cleaned the rooms and did the menial work, but Ada and Sara had higher status.

They spent much time telling each other their stories. Ada told Sara how she had been duped by a rich, older man who left her pregnant. It was Giovanni who saved her and gave her a new life. She told all of this with deep feeling. She formed a bond with Sara who had similar experiences to relate. She had met Mimì when she worked in a small restaurant in Rome. Mimì assumed that since she was a waitress she was an easy woman. In time they became lovers, but Mimì never thought of marriage. For him that was a middle class custom.

Mimì's mother prayed and said the rosary. Mostly she asked to have her husband be faithful to her and for Mimì to marry. When Sara became pregnant, Donna Maria Antonietta kept after Mimì to marry Sara so that the child could be born legitimately. Mimì was opposed, though Sara was willing. Sara believed like Donna Maria Antonietta that legitimacy was the uppermost concern. Donna Maria Antonietta seemed like the obedient wife but she plotted to get her way. Secretly, she brought the parish priest to the hotel to talk to Sara and to convince her that she should press for marriage and ultimately for the baptism of the child when it came.

When it was born, it was a boy and named after Don Beppe. Sara started in on Mimì to baptize him. She thought that she would start with the baby and then get to marriage. Mimì demurred, but with Sara and his mother both working on him, he finally acceded. On the same day that he was married, they turned around and baptized the baby. Mimì went through the ceremonies coldly, but Memena, Sara and her new mother-in-law were ecstatic. Ada felt great sympathy for Sara when she heard her story.

The baby became the center of Don Beppe's life. When Ciccio came with his family there were two little Beppes, his grandsons. Ciccio also had a daughter, named after her grandmother Maria Antonietta. While Don Beppe loved her, the two boys were foremost in his thoughts.

The atmosphere in Brindisi and in the rest of Italy was one of war. Soldiers were on the streets either alone or in squads. Every shop and office had a picture of Mussolini. The newspapers showed photos of an Italian attack on Ethiopia. Jokes were made about how the Lion of Judah's camels could not find their way back to Addis Ababa because the Italians built asphalt roads. There were parades to celebrate the Italian invasion of Greece and Croatia. Children wore miniature army uniforms and waved banners at political meetings. In Africa, Italian troops had overtaken the local militias. There was a newspaper photo of an Italian general standing with his foot on a dead Libyan. People went around with a new sense of purpose that Don Beppe did not particularly like. It was a form of hysteria, he thought, with people gladly receiving the propaganda. Newsreels had Italian troops assaulting a gun post in Greece or collecting prisoners of war in Ethiopia. Mimì never commented on any of this because he remembered all too well what the Fascists did to him. The Captain that came to see Don Beppe issuing a warning to Mimì had not come back to the restaurant. It was just as well. Don Beppe didn't want to see him.

Giovanni tried to ignore what was happening. He wanted to work, provide for his family and do his job. In the back of his mind, was the picture of his father who had closed him out of the family. Only he and his father could solve that problem.

His life with Ada and Andrea could not have been better. Andrea referred to Giovanni as "Pappa," and this made Giovanni love him more. Giovanni and Ada had a rich, personal life. They were close and tender lovers and the bond between them grew. They made no reference to Don Andrea and Carlo. That was all in the past.

With respect to his two daughters-in-law Don Beppe showed a distinct favoritism for Ciccio's wife, Memena. She had all the attributes that he admired in women. She was a good cook, a person that kept a clean house, a fine mother and a very respectful daughter-in-law. He also liked that she spoke up when speaking up was needed. Sara was quiet and gave in easily when Don Beppe fussed. He detected her weaknesses and exploited them in his dealings with her.

One day the Fascist Captain showed up at the restaurant. Don Beppe received him coldly. He didn't rush to give him a cup of coffee and treated him like a traveling salesman whom he would see only rarely. Dressed in his best Fascist uniform, the Captain sat down with Don Beppe and talked about Mimì.

"I have not seen Mimì lately, Don Beppe, where is he?"

Coolly, Don Beppe answered, "He's here as always."

"I don't see him," the Captain said.

"My dear Captain," Don Beppe said tersely, "he's here every day. Why do you ask? Isn't it enough that you gave him the treatment for dissenters? So, what do you want now?"

"That was an unfortunate incident, but at times it takes something like that to warn a person who is not doing his duty toward the regime."

"After the way I treated you, he didn't deserve that. You should save that for the riff-raff. He was sick for a week."

"Don Beppe, I regard your friendship highly, and that is why I am here today. I think that we need a gesture of sympathy from Mimì."

"What are you talking about? I don't understand you."

"Let me be brief and to the point," the Captain said. "Your son once promoted a strike at the railroad. We let that slide, we let it go. But then he kept attending the meetings where Socialists and worse had discussions against Il Duce. We had to act. Now for his sake," he paused, "we think that he must make a gesture of faith in the party. He needs to show that he is with us."

"My son has always had his own mind and I never interfered with that. What you did with that enema treatment was horrible." The Captain did not show any concern. "He could have died, you know that?" Still no response from the Captain.

"If he came with his son--or perhaps both your grandsons that you claim to love so much," the Captain paused, "and signed them up as *Balille*, Fascist Boy Scouts, for the regime. You know what I mean. Buy them the children's uniform and teach them to raise their arm, to salute Il Duce."

Don Beppe got up signaling the Captain that the meeting was over.

"I have to think about it and talk to Mimì, but in the meantime I want you to know how offended I am by what you did to him—and to me as a friend," Don Beppe said and walked into the kitchen. The Captain left the restaurant, tucking his swagger stick under his arm.

Don Beppe called Mimì to his room. At first, Mimì was reluctant. But Don Beppe convinced him. Mimì went to a store in the center of town and bought two uniforms of the Balille and returned home. Each mother dressed her child. A photographer was called in to photograph both of them standing with their right arm raised in the Fascist salute. Then Mimì took them downtown to sign them up.

At Fascist headquarters the hangers-on looked at him as he entered with the two children. He went to the central desk and said "I want to sign these children up as Fascist Boy Scouts."

The desk sergeant called for an official, who shortly appeared in uniform.

"Yes, what can I do for you?" he said.

"I am here to sign up my son and nephew as Boy Scouts of the Fascist party." Mimi looked at him, wondering if he or the desk sergeant had a hand in the enema treatment he received.

The official took out a sheet of paper. "Do you love and respect the regime of the Duce?" The children looked wide-eyed.

"Yes," Mimì said.

"Will you defend the cause of Fascism?"

"Yes," Mimì said.

"I officially pronounce you both Fascist Boy Scouts this day and for every day onward in the name of our beloved leader, Il Duce, Benito Mussolini."

News came filtering back to Brindisi that things were not going well for Italy in Africa. The local population would see boats filled with Italian soldiers leave from Brindisi headed for North Africa. This was helpful for the economy of Brindisi because the businessmen, the hotels, the restaurants and even the whores made a great deal of money. Occasionally a soldier would appear on the streets in crutches or bandages. People listened when such a soldier went for a coffee or sat in the park and told stories about how things were really going. These stories told of the death of soldiers because they were not adequately prepared for war. They told of supply breakdowns and downright failures like sending soldiers to Croatia and Greece in summer uniforms during early winter. In the newsreels and newspapers, people saw Italian forces fighting bravely and receiving medals. There were even pictures of Mussolini meeting with Hitler. Seeing Mussolini in the presence of Hitler, who they were led to believe was the most powerful man in the world, gave credence to the notion that Mussolini was a great man himself and therefore the Italian people had to follow him. But the stories told by wounded and maimed young men who returned were also believed. The Fascist party needed to dispel the skepticism so they held regular parades where soldiers marched in full regalia and speeches were made. They forced people to leave work and bring their children as Fascist Boy Scouts to the parades to show their dedication to the cause.

Don Beppe had an ominous feeling about the war. After the enema treatment the Fascists gave his son, his interest in Party affairs became more and more desultory. Without the party bigwigs who no longer patronized his restaurant, Don Beppe had to depend for his living on the travelers who came and went.

Don Beppe's son Ciccio held American citizenship because he served in the American army in the First World War. All the immigrants that served were given this privilege. Ciccio watched the situation in Italy change and realized that he had the possibility of returning to America. Feeling very bad, he gathered up the family, his wife and two children, and took the trip to Naples. They were able to leave Italy. He promised Don Beppe and his brother Mimì that he would do what he could to help them but he felt that it was no longer safe for him and his family to stay in Brindisi. Don Beppe accepted Ciccio's decision.

─────────────────────────

There was official propaganda but the real news of the war was passed from person to person. Don Beppe heard that Allied forces had reached Sicily and were making progress cleaning out the Germans there. Everyone knew that the Germans would not walk away quietly.

They would fight to the end. For Don Beppe this spelled the beginning of the end for the Italians. There were serious things to be taken into consideration. The war would be all around them with civilian casualties, property destroyed and lives broken.

One morning there was a terrific noise. People jumped out of their beds to see what it was. Overhead were planes and not Italian planes. Bombs were dropped in the port destroying the breakers and ships that were docked there. People ran out into the streets over broken glass and saw ships sinking into the bay. Overhead British bombers dived and circled to bomb again. In the aftermath, houses were smoking and debris blocked the streets. The once-quiet town was reduced to chaos.

During the day, Fascist officials and civilian authorities came and went from their headquarters. Now instead of their imperious walk, they ran. Inside, the Captain in his black uniform and high boots shouted orders.

The mayor of Brindisi was there. Why was there no defense of the city when the British bombers came? they asked. Where were the cannons and the planes? The Mayor demanded to know.

"They were on a different front," the Captain answered. The Mayor did not appreciate the Captain's answers because there was death and destruction all over his city. The Captain personally escorted the Mayor from the building. He claimed that his authority exceeded the Mayor's and shut the door behind him.

Two nights later the Fascists fled in cars, trucks and on motorcycles. Suddenly their headquarters was an empty building littered with papers and overturned chairs for the children of Brindisi to wander in and gape at.

News seeped out that the Germans were having a difficult time defending themselves against the allies in Sicily and Salerno. The American troops had landed there and were headed for Rome. Shortly after the attack on Brindisi, a ship arrived carrying British soldiers and they were unloaded on the main dock. The airport at Brindisi was of strategic importance to them. It would give the British a stepping stone in all directions, Northern Italy, North Africa, Albania and Yugoslavia.

At the word that soldiers had arrived, the ladies of the night gathered at the gangplank on the pier. As the British filed out the girls yelled their names, Cristina or Gina, at them, hoping to be remembered and cash in on the new source of income.

During the day a British major arrived at Don Beppe's hotel. Don Beppe had been to America many years ago, and knew a bit of English, but not enough to deal with him. No one else knew any English either. The major walked around the hotel, a swagger stick tucked under his arm turning and pointing to things. Don Beppe didn't know what he wanted. By means of signs and gestures, it became obvious to Don Beppe that the major was requisitioning the hotel for his officers. The enlisted men would be in tents on the outskirts of town. The British took over Fascist headquarters and tore down every sign of the Fascist party in the building.

During the day British officers came and went from the hotel, as Don Beppe watched their every move. Things that were dear to him were pushed around with no regard to their value. The British wanted to convert the hotel into officer's quarters and wanted to do it in a fashion that they were accustomed to. But Don Beppe cherished many items that he had in the hotel and the restaurant. There was dishware from Ginori, flatware from Krupp in Germany, painted scrolls on the walls from China. He would pay sailors going to Asia to bring back rare birds. They had to buy at least five with the hope that one survived. Don Beppe was a man of parts and had always insisted that everything in the hotel and restaurant be of quality. He watched as the British arranged and rearranged things. When he protested, the British waved him away. Don Beppe regretted not hiding some of the more valuable things.

The next two days were spent in sheer consternation with Don Beppe upset over what was happening in his beloved Bella Napoli. Soldiers walked out of the buildings carrying things out that never reappeared.

One day a British officer arrived who spoke some Italian. He was a finicky sort, well dressed in his uniform and with gloves placed carefully in his cap when he was indoors. He walked around the hotel as if he were its owner. Don Beppe and Mimì stood silently as the Captain explained in careful Italian that the hotel was requisitioned for the officer corps. The officers that would be billeted there were to come and go as they wished, with no interference from Don Beppe or anyone else, under pain of being jailed by the British military police.

Don Beppe sat in a velvet chair that was his favorite, the one he would sit in to have a snooze in mid-afternoon. He wondered what would happen next. Rumors circulated that the Germans were on their way out of Italy and the Italian army had capitulated in North Africa, Ethiopia and Abyssinia. In fact, the whole edifice of Fascism had fallen. Mussolini was taken away to Switzerland where he was protected by the Germans. There was, in effect, no Italian government, except one general who became the spokesman for the fallen Italian government. The King was hustled away for his own protection. In the north, the partisans, who resisted Fascism from 1929 on, were going from city to city capturing the local Fascist administrators. Any fool knew that it was all over for Italy.

Giovanni watched the developments in Brindisi. The Fascists once all-powerful were now in hiding. He remembered the Captain of the Fascist party in Brindisi, how he walked around, like a peacock, a Beretta pistol in a sleek leather case tapping lightly against his side, his boots so shiny that you could see your face in them. Where was the Captain now? Called to Rome on urgent party business, someone said.

Work slacked off at the restaurant since the usual customers were gone. Don Beppe had constantly to deal with the British mess sergeant. They wanted meat, lots of it, but there was no meat to be had. Actually, Don Beppe knew a fellow who was a purser on a ship. He stole the meat from the requisitions and sold it on the black market. When Don Beppe could get meat on the black market he did so for his own family. In this, he included Giovanni and his family. The meat had to be cooked elsewhere otherwise the army cook could smell it. Giovanni was sent with a special box to return it to the hotel.

Giovanni did his work, watching the English with great curiosity. One night Ada was approached by a drunken English officer. He bellowed at her door that he only wanted to talk to her. He was married and had left his wife and children and gone into the army. He talked until he cried. Ada remained quiet behind the door, Andrea was sleeping and she was otherwise alone. She did not mention it to Giovanni because she thought it might lead to trouble.

The news that came back from different sources was that the war was going well for the Allies and the Axis forces were taking a beating. On the Eastern front the Russians advanced headed for Berlin. The Germans were completely bottled up in various places, but refused to surrender. The camps in North Africa were filled with Italian soldiers that had surrendered, seeing the military cause completely lost. For the Italians at home the realization grew. A little at a time the photos of Mussolini disappeared from households. Some took photos of Mussolini and the king and hung them in public toilets.

During these years of the war, Giovanni rarely heard from his brothers. Of his father, mother and aunt, he heard nothing. Mastro Paolo had not forgotten the offense that his son caused him. Giovanni occasionally sent a letter to his brother which went unanswered. Giovanni dreamed that after the war he would try to emigrate again. This time he would be armed with evidence that he was not tubercular and anti-fascism would no longer be a barrier. He too would go to America and make a life for himself, just like his brothers.

As the war continued, the British kept hold of Brindisi and its valuable airport. At night one could hear the planes roaring over the town as they took off. Giovanni lay in bed and envied the pilots who went free and unfettered into the night.

He survived during this time because Don Beppe was kind to him and his family. If he didn't receive a salary sometimes, he didn't grouse about it. At least he had a roof over his head and a dish of food in front of him. Don Beppe even paid for Andrea's schooling at the nuns. Giovanni was sensitive about money since he was totally dependent on Don Beppe. He scrounged for things the English discarded, soap, shoes, anything he could sell on the black market.

The British geared up for an advance on Naples. Their airplanes flew them to Naples and then they fanned out into the countryside where the Germans had fled but were still fighting the war. A skeleton force in Brindisi maintained the planes and other equipment. Mussolini's men were routed everywhere. The partisans in Northern Italy found them and killed them unceremoniously, lining them up against a wall and shooting them.

It was Mimì's wish to find the Captain that ordered the enema that the Squadristi gave him. It became an obsession. He would walk around town looking for him but the Captain, just like all the other Fascists was not to be found.

Ada continued her work in the hotel, and given her experience, had reorganized the tasks of the maids. Her good looks and efficiency won over Don Beppe who never met a beautiful woman he didn't like. This created some jealousy between her and Sara. Since she was married to the owner's son, Sara claimed some privilege over Ada. The fact was that Don Beppe for all his whoring looked down upon Sara as a cocotte. Her experiences were not too different from Ada's, but to Don Beppe's eye, Ada was superior. He gave her special tasks that made her look like the favorite. Mimì had spoken to his father about this, but Don Beppe was not someone to be ordered around by anybody, including his son.

When his nameday, San Giuseppe's came, March nineteenth, Don Beppe put out a table of pastries and liqueurs and invited friends to come by and drink to his good health and do homage to San Giuseppe. Don Beppe put on his black suit, a shirt and tie and stood at the door. Everyone from the mayor to the next door neighbor came by.

Donna Maria Antonietta sat nearby and everyone greeted her. She often felt that this was her best day of the year. It was a day when she was also acknowledged. She was brought out of her room where she spent most of her time sewing, crocheting or reading. Don Beppe's personality saved him from the usual depression that beset persons who had to sit through a war. He bargained, he cajoled, he joked, he told dirty jokes to his friends and he tried to take it all in stride. The English finally learned that he was someone to be respected.

With the war winding down, Don Beppe started thinking about what would happen afterwards. Property, he thought, could be purchased at a bargain price, and he was already thinking of buying a larger building which would house a bigger restaurant and hotel. The main problem was that no one yet knew what money was going to prevail. The currency of the Fascist regime was worthless, as was the money that the King had circulated. And so, Don Beppe, in spare moments thought about how he was going to make it big once the war was over and the British left his hotel. In Brindisi one could see the beginning of the end. Shopkeepers and fisherman could no longer count on the British to purchase their wares. Brindisi had to adapt itself to a new economy.

———————————————

News came that Mussolini was captured by the partisans, dragged back to Milan and killed. He was hung by his heels in the main square along with his mistress and some cronies. Giovanni mused about how it all went up in smoke, the uniforms, the saluting, the titles and the parades.

With the news of Mussolini's death came the information that the King and his entire entourage were taken prisoners. A general was authorized to come to terms with the Allies, which he did. The Allies demanded unconditional surrender, with no privileges or advantages given to him or his people. Throughout Italy there was celebration, especially where Allied troops were stationed.

There was new commercial activity in black market items, medicine, sugar, and coffee. Mess sergeants who had control of important items did well. The peace was a joy only to those who could profit from it.

The families whose loved ones had perished in North Africa, Greece, and Croatia had to assess their bitter losses. Mussolini had even sent troops to Spain to help Francisco Franco and other soldiers to Russia to fight the Communists. Some returned and some were buried there. Families did what they could to find out about their missing, loved ones.

Giovanni stood in front of the restaurant watching the new animation of the people. Don Beppe went running around town trying to make deals to get food for his restaurant but with meager results. Pasta was scarce because there was very little flour to be had. Don Beppe negotiated with the officer assigned to his hotel and restaurant to obtain flour.

Even those that had supported Fascism felt better that fascists were out of power. The next question was when, how and what would be the new government. Shopkeepers stood outside their stores to greet people and pass the time talking. Giovanni sensed the yoke was removed and that many people had shown attachment to Fascism because it was the easiest way out of a difficult situation. What the opportunists' fate was to be when a new government was in place no one knew. Some put American or British flags in their shop windows, but everyone knew who the fascist supporters had been.

Don Beppe, who was as opportunistic as anyone else looked forward to developing his business. He didn't give a damn if the new regime was Fascist or democratic. Meat was difficult to get and was not the highest quality. He featured fish on his menu in order to stay open.

One day the British got up very early and began to clear out of their hotel billets. Don Beppe's wife woke him to tell him. He dressed quickly and went to see what was happening. The British were moving out, taking their equipment, their radios, their duffle bags. Don Beppe watched as some of his precious belongings were carted away. He saw these being put into the personal duffle bags of the soldiers. In four hours all that Don Beppe had worked for and had obtained with great pride disappeared in boxes and duffle bags thrown in the rear of trucks. The restaurant, which was his first love, was denuded. He pushed a chair aside and sat on it, crying. Mimì appeared and was astonished at what had happened. His father pointed to the wall where a painting of the port of Brindisi had hung, now just a bare wall.

"They took everything," Don Beppe muttered bitterly.

"Pappa, Pappa, don't worry. We can start again. When the tourists come again, we can start just like we started in the beginning."

Don Beppe was inconsolable. His wife and several employees tried to comfort him, but his heart had been broken.

"At my age, how can there be a beginning?" he asked. "Some of them seemed so civilized, how could they do something like this?" he cried.

———————

A new government was formed and life began anew. In Brindisi port activity increased. Ships began coming from faraway places like Sumatra and the Philippines. Instead of the cold, hard faces of the English there were Indians, Koreans and Africans. A bit at a time the city became a bustling center again. Don Beppe had to indulge in various balancing acts to get food and pay for it and the daily struggle took his mind off his sorrow.

Giovanni began to think about going to America. He discussed the matter with Ada, who, although uneasy over leaving Italy, was willing to go along. She had adjusted to change in her life before.

Giovanni began writing to his brothers to see if they could help him get to America. The memory of the episode in Naples haunted him. He had bad dreams about it, remembering the cold-hearted doctor who declared him to be sick.

Now communication became easier and letters crossed the ocean in a relatively short time, approximately a month. During the post-war recovery people of Brindisi received packages from their relatives in America. The Americans sent them coffee, sugar, blankets, woolen socks, anything they thought would help them and make their lives more comfortable. Giovanni waited for a letter to come inviting him to America. They are my brothers, why don't I hear from them? he asked himself.

The end of the war was not marked by any great parades. Italy was the loser and the Americans and English the victors. Mussolini had told Italy to hold its head high, but now he was dead, hunted down and hung.

One day a letter arrived from his brothers and Giovanni rushed to open it. The letter spoke about what had been happening in America during the final phases of the war. They did not speak of Italy as being beaten. They merely spoke of the fact that the war was over, thank God. As for Giovanni's hope to go to America with his family, nothing was said, which disappointed him very much.

Don Beppe was in better spirits because now food stuffs, which previously went to the war effort, were becoming available in the markets. He could on occasion write lamb or pork on the large blackboard that served as his menu. For vegetables he had to go out into to the country and buy from farmers who now had the best market they ever had. Prices began to rise, not just for foodstuffs, but for everything. Medicine was practically unavailable. In some cases sulfa drugs and penicillin which were recently discovered could not be found even on the black market. Ada became the director of the hotel with Sara at her side feeling envious. Up to that time, Ada and Sara got along because they were the outsiders. But that was Don Beppe's will and he didn't care if Sara felt jealous.

Mimì and Sara had to live with the fact that their only child and Don Beppe's namesake died of meningitis, something for which there was no cure. The hurt was stamped indelibly on Sara's spirit more than that of Mimì, who, certainly sad about his loss, was able to shake off the lethargy that grief brought.

As Mimì walked back from the market, he sighted the former Captain of the Fascist guards sitting in a café. He was stunned to see him so soon after the war. This time he was not dressed in his black outfit but in a dull, ill-fitting suit, blending in with the other people in the café. Coldness came over Mimì when he saw him and his mind began to churn. Later at the restaurant, he made some discreet inquiries about the Captain, but no one really knew anything about him, other than the fact that after the war he had returned to Brindisi which was his hometown. Mimì made a mental note to keep his eyes on him, honing the edge of his hatred.

The next day Mimì returned to the café. There he found the Captain again, reading a newspaper. Mimì stood at the bar watching him out of the corner of his eye. The Captain stood up, paid for his coffee and started out the door. Mimì followed him as carefully as he could. After walking several blocks the Captain entered a building. Mimì waited a few moments and then went to the same door and looked at the names on the bell plate. Now Mimì knew where he lived.

At the hotel Ada kept careful track of all they had as far as bed sheets and blankets which were in short supply. Don Beppe was trying to replace bed linens that had been looted but every hotelier tried to do the same thing. Don Beppe with his usual acuity kept track of old people that died. Then he would visit the family and make an offer to buy household things from them. He was good at horse-trading and even if he had to buy many small items that he really didn't need, he did so in order to get the big things he wanted.

In the evenings, Mimì would return to the café where he saw the Captain. One night Mimì found him playing cards with some people. Mimì waited but he got so bored he went home before the Captain did. Another night Mimì waited until the Captain got up and went home. Once again, Mimì followed him noting the route. Another night he took a knife from the kitchen, a cook's knife with a strong, sharp blade. He put it in the inside pocket of his jacket and headed for the café. The Captain was there playing cards and joking. Mimì stayed in the shadows. When the card game broke up, the Captain took his hat off the wall rack and started walking home at a leisurely pace. Mimì kept his distance. The Captain smoked a cigarette and walked as if he didn't have a care in the world. To get to his house, he had to turn down a small, dark alley. As he made the turn, Mimì took out the knife and held it close to his body. He looked around to make sure that there was no one else on the street and then he rushed up behind the Captain. He put his arm around his neck and pushed the knife into his heart, at the same time giving the knife a turn. A dull moan emerged from the Captain's mouth. Mimì held him up until he knew that the knife had gone right through the flesh. When he thought that he had done the job, he pulled out the knife and let the Captain slide down to the sidewalk. Mimì walked to the port. It was late and there were not many people walking the streets. A few Indian sailors walked by. Mimì looked down to hide his face. After they passed, he threw the knife far out into the water. He went home, made love to his wife, and fell into a deep sleep.

Giovanni's heart gave a leap when another letter from America arrived. This time his brothers said that as soon as immigration was allowed he could come to America and his brothers would help him get settled. They also voiced a wish that he try to make peace with their father, because at his age, and not knowing what fortune held in store for any one, he might be seeing him for the last time. Giovanni mulled over that remembering the reception he got the last time he went home. His brothers gave him some papers they obtained from the government office in New York with which to apply for immigration; one copy for the American government and one for the Italian government. The top page of the sheaf of papers was a medical form. A shiver went down Giovanni's spine at the mere thought of a health examination.

He knew he must go to his father's house to ask for forgiveness and for his blessing to go to America. He summoned up his courage and went to Giovinazzo.

It was not easy for Giovanni to knock on the door of his house. He had too many bad memories to deal with. His aunt answered the door and gave a sigh when she saw who was at the door. Giovanni said nothing. She began to cry because she wanted to hug and kiss him.

"Don't worry, Zia, don't worry," Giovanni said.

"Your father said that he would never see you again."

Giovanni opened the door wider and went inside, leaving his aunt behind him.

His father was sitting in the living room and gave a start when he saw Giovanni standing there.

"Father, I have come to say good-bye to you. I am going to America to join my brothers."

His father said nothing.

"I shall always love you, my mother and my aunt."

His father was silent.

"Father, I know that I have disappointed you, but my wife, Ada, and her son are now mine to love and look after. She is a good woman who loves me and who looks after me. If you got to know her you would love her too."

His father looked away.

Giovanni could no longer stand to be in the room. He turned to his mother and aunt and kissed both of them. Then, Giovanni left the house, shutting the door behind him.

━━━━━━━━━━

In Brindisi he packed his goods. It was important to see Don Beppe one last time.

"Don Beppe, I can't tell you how much I owe you for taking me in and giving me work and a home."

Don Beppe waved the statement away. "You needed help, and I was ready to give it to you. I only regret that it could not be more. Did you see your father?"

Giovanni closed his eyes for a second. "He wouldn't say a word to me."

"Giovanni, your father is a proud and stubborn man, like a mule. When he fixes his mind on something, he will not budge from it. Try to move forward. In America you will have a new life."

Giovanni could not hold back his tears. Don Beppe wrapped his arms around him and gave him a kiss on each cheek.

―――――――――

When the train arrived in Naples, Giovanni's heart was thumping so loud he thought it would burst out of his chest. He set out to the Health office, papers carefully kept in a folder in his luggage. When they arrived, Andrea was cross because he was roused out of sleep.

In ten minutes Giovanni returned with a beaming smile waving his signed papers at Ada.

The dock was as busy as an ant hill with workers yelling, talking, smoking and cursing.

The passengers were a mixture of people, some well-dressed, some artisans whose hands betrayed their trades and then there were the *contadini*. Giovanni could tell something about them just by listening to their accents, usually dialects from various parts of Italy. There were Neapolitans, Venetians and Piedmontese.

Ada was seasick for the two weeks of the journey. She stayed in the large room that was for women. Ada managed to get Andrea to be with her in a smaller bed, but the room was small and unventilated. Giovanni slept in a similar room, where he was kept awake by men making their way to the bed after a night of playing cards or talking politics.

The days went slowly on their voyage. Giovanni liked to look at the sea. He wondered how Columbus and the early explorers made the trip in small ships.

He had always had a love for the water. When he was a boy in Giovinazzo he liked to go to the port and see the fishermen repair their nets. Their boats rocked lazily at the shoreline, to be pushed out to the sea at the first hour of morning. When the fishing boats returned the women came to see the catch of the day. Giovanni saw fish that were still squirming, fighting for the water that was their breath, redfish, mullet, prawns, occasionally a small shark that got caught in the nets and was hauled in.

For years Giovanni wanted to be a fisherman or a sailor. Of great curiosity to Giovanni were the tattooed arms of the sailors depicting everything from the crucifixion of Christ to pictures of dancing girls. He remembered once in Brindisi in a café a sailor said he could make the girl in his tattoo dance and he squeezed his muscle to make her hula-skirt move to the howling laughter of the children. Someone in the crowd usually bought him a coffee for this show.

As a fisherman he would be able to see all that the sea held, and suggested to his father that he be sent to be a fisherman, but Mastro Paolo shook his head saying, "Some are made for fishing and others are made to cut stone. You belong to the latter."

On the ship at mealtime people gathered at the entrance of the dining room, unless they were seasick. Ada was one who never left her bed and Giovanni brought her some bread to put in her stomach. An attendant went from bed to bed with a pitcher of chamomile tea. Ada prayed that the ordeal would end soon. Each day Giovanni would tell her how many days were left and she would roll over in her bed and moan.

It was Giovanni's job to look after Andrea. The boy had found a companion his age and together they explored the ship. By now Andrea had grown into a strong, sturdy boy, handsome and with a winning personality. In Brindisi he had won over the heart of Don Beppe. After school he would sit with Don Beppe and tell him everything that happened with his teachers, the nuns and their foibles. He imitated them, their manner of speaking, walking, and gesturing to Don Beppe's amusement. Andrea impressed everyone with his intelligence. Whether he remembered some of the events surrounding his adoption by Giovanni, Ada couldn't tell and didn't want to approach the subject. From now on, Ada wished he would only know Giovanni as his father.

Together with his friend, Andrea went down to the depths of the ship and watched the sailors work in the boiler room with long spouted oil cans going from one machine to the other. Andrea was fascinated by hearing the engine pistons pound. The two boys slipped into the kitchen and watched the cooks work. One chopped onions and another made a soup in a gigantic cauldron. On the last day of the voyage,

Ada, still feeling that all her insides were emptied out, struggled to get dressed. Teams of men in dark uniforms sat at tables set up for the occasion. There was another section of medical people. Giovanni's heart gave a jump. "Again," he thought. "Again."

All the passengers were on deck for the entrance into New York harbor. Mothers made sure that their children were dressed in their best, in spite of the obvious poverty of some of the passengers. They wanted to start their lives in America in a clean and orderly fashion.

The passengers had been alerted the night before to gather their belongings and place them all together for they had to go through a disembarking process. For this the adults, also dressed in their best, had to wait in line for hours.

At one point a mother was led away crying loudly, holding a child. The doctors would not admit the child for a medical reason. That chilled Giovanni's blood. As he advanced in the line, he could feel the blood draining from his head and felt faint.

The personnel at the medical station worked quickly and briskly. A tall man with a white smock walked around with authority. He commanded with gestures, and everyone obeyed.

One of his secretaries held a batch of papers and one by one she called names. There were people who wore long frock coats, beards and curls down their cheeks. Sometimes he watched them standing together speaking a language that he had never heard before. He had noticed that when they prayed they bowed continuously, their cheek curls bouncing against their faces

When his name was called Giovanni got up fearing the worst. He followed the nurse, along with three other men. He was examined, questioned and then the interpreter said, "You're all right, you can go." He had been so preoccupied that he did not see the Statue of Liberty when they entered the port of New York.

Now Giovanni and his family stayed together with their belongings. They reached the edge of the gangplank. A man in a uniform looked over the papers of each immigrant and then waved them down the gangplank. Again, that uneasy feeling overcame Giovanni when he arrived where the man in the uniform stood. He looked through Giovanni's papers, then with a sweep of the hand, sent him on to America.

Ada and Andrea were dressed carefully for the arrival. She also had the worry that she would not be accepted by Giovanni's brothers because as it had been said many times she had a "history." She muttered to herself, "that's my business and no one else's in this world."

Giovanni looked everywhere for his brothers but could not see them. He had their address written on a crumpled piece of paper in his pocket. He wondered if he would remember them, they had probably changed. A lot of years had passed, would they know him?

"America," Giovanni mumbled to himself. He had finally made it to America. He looked around and saw the streets alive with activity. Is this what was meant by America, he wondered? It was the intense degree of movement that caught his attention, cars, trucks, people, traffic and noise. Is this the America that I had dreamed about?" Giovanni remembered his first arrival in Rome, a lesson that he had never forgotten. He told Ada and Andrea to stand by their goods and not to let anyone touch them. "Sit on them," he said.

Then he walked around the area, hoping to find his brothers. His faith in them began to falter. He remembered his father saying that no one in the family was ever to have anything to do with him. Would they turn their backs on him? he wondered. Then he heard a yell, "Giovanni, Giovanni." He looked up and there were Francesco and Paolo standing in their coats and battered hats. He looked at them and recognized them by their fine features. They grasped hold of each other and cried. They tried to tell all the things that happened to them in those years. It all came out and at the end as they wiped their tears with the backs of their hands. When he introduced Ada to them, they both nodded courteously and kissed her. He introduced Andrea as "my son." They kissed him too. Then each brother took hold of some bags and they left the dock, leaving Italy behind them, perhaps forever. After several noisy starts the driver put the truck in gear and it began to move, slowly at first then it picked up speed. Giovanni, his wife and son looked out the windows at the biggest city they had ever seen. "America, America," Giovanni murmured.

PART VIII

What Giovanni wanted to do was to earn his living working as a stone cutter. His brothers had continued at their trade, but they thought that since Giovanni had worked in the hotel and restaurant trade that was where he wanted to go. Giovanni itched to get his hands around a chisel, grab a mallet, start hammering and cutting letters.

Another reason the brothers did not want Giovanni to go into the stone trade was because Silvio had died of pneumonia, complicated by silicosis. Every stone cutter's family knew that sooner or later the stone cutter would develop silicosis, which in many instances became tuberculosis.

Francesco knew a man who had a grocery store. He suggested to his brother that he take up the grocery business, then they wouldn't have to worry about him getting tuberculosis. Giovanni met with him and worked out a salary. He would begin work in a week.

Francesco found them an apartment not far from his house. For the first two weeks they were in America they lived with Francesco and Paolo's families.

Both Giovanni and Ada knew that there would be a difficult adaptation. There was the question of knowing English. Here they could not even say "thank you" because they did not know the language. People's speech sounded so harsh to their ears and reminded them of the English in Brindisi. The first day Giovanni stopped a fellow on the street and asked him directions in Italian. The man just looked at Giovanni and said something that Giovanni did not understand.

Andrea was put in a school but did not understand a single word. He felt lost and each day he went home and complained. He said to his mother, "Mamma, why don't we go home to Italy?" *"Figlio mio bello, adesso siamo in America,"* Lovely child, we're in America now. This did not satisfy Andrea, who dreaded going to school. He recognized that several students in his class had Italian names. When he spoke to them, they did not answer him in Italian. One or two of them answered in English but they understood Andrea. Still he could not manage to join in because he did not understand. When he went home, his parents calmed him, saying that in due time he too would understand English and have a better time. It was at times like these that Giovanni's love went out to Andrea. He wanted to protect him always and cushion his falls.

Ada felt unwanted by her sisters-in-law. They did speak Italian and Ada enjoyed telling them about the trip to America. They had never been anywhere, except to Staten Island where they went once or twice a year to have a picnic. Ada felt no warmth from them and she figured that her husband's father must have poisoned them with his anger. But in spite of what Mastro Paolo had said, Giovanni's brothers were close to him. Ada regretted their departure from Italy and at first refused to unpack her trunk.

Giovanni went to work in the Italian grocery store. He knew the kinds of cheeses and cold cuts that the owner sold. He also knew all the pastas and the dried beans, everything that was to be found in an Italian grocery store. Giovanni liked the job because the customers were mostly Italians and he could speak to them just like he spoke to people in Italy. There were customers of all ages that came in. The owner, Filippo, was a man in his sixties and had owned the store for more than forty years. He was well known in the neighborhood because he sold quality products, cheeses and salamis, mozzarellas and ricotta that he made downstairs in the cellar. He had a sense of humor that extended to customers and employees alike. One time he sent Giovanni to the hardware store and had him ask, in his poor English, for a left-handed monkey wrench. The request was written on a piece of paper in case he forgot how to say it in English. The owner of the hardware store sensed Filippo's humor and went along, sending Giovanni to a fruit store and to a plumbing supply store. When Giovanni returned empty-handed Filippo laughed along with the others in the store. Although Giovanni did not like to be the butt of their jokes, he took it and shrugged his shoulders. There were several incidents like this, but Giovanni learned to cope and to answer in kind. The second time with the same joke, Giovanni understood what Filippo was doing and returned with a monkey wrench and handed it to him with the handle turned to the left side. Now it was Giovanni's time to laugh and the owner took it in a good-natured way.

There was a feature of his job that he loved, and that was to walk in the store in the morning and smell the cheeses and meats. It seemed like he was in Italy again. One of his jobs was to grind up good cheese for sprinkling. People were too lazy, he presumed, to grind their own cheese, so they bought it already ground up and that was one of Giovanni's jobs. On certain days he would watch Enzo who was from near Bari make mozzarella. At the counter he helped lower the giant-size provolone and cut it in half with a large knife. He never knew that it too had liquid. He also learned to stock shelves and wait on customers. It was a world that he knew from a distance but he had now become a part of it.

Filippo, the owner of the store, was from a small town in Calabria. When he came to America he came without a trade and a friend brought him to work on a coal truck. He worked there for a winter. Each day he had to go with a fellow that drove the coal truck. They started when it was dark in the morning and worked until late at night. In the morning they filled their truck with coal. They drove their truck under a large chute and at a signal from the foreman a rush of coal came down. There were jokes here too. Sometimes the operators would get an unsuspecting fellow to stand nearby and press the button to release the coal. The fellow would be covered with coal dust but worst, he was made to look like a fool. This happened once to Filippo, and he never forgot it. At night he would come home looking black, he and his clothes covered with coal dust. He knew that this was not the work for him even though he was paid well for it. After his first winter things slowed down in the warm weather and knowing he would be laid off, he looked for another job.

A *paesano* of his, a certain Gatto, was working in a large Italian grocery store. At least, Filippo thought, I don't have to get my hands filthy with coal. There he filled shelves with cans and boxes, but he hoped to get a job at the counter where he would meet people. Filippo possessed a *favella*, a quick wit that made him liked by customers and the boss as well.

Filippo worked there for two years before he got to be a counter man. Then the boss began to pay particular attention to him. The boss had two daughters, Marina and Elena and he kept a good eye open for an eventual suitor for them. Filippo was doing well and drove a sleek car, a Dodge that he kept meticulously clean. If business got slow, he would send the delivery boy to clean and even wax it. If the delivery boy complained he found himself without a job. The Dodge was one of Filippo's loves. In fact, the other people on the job called it *La carrozzella,* the little carriage.

The boss was having a family party and Filippo was supposed to bring all the food to the boss's house in his car. The occasion was an important one, when the younger daughter, Elena, had her First Communion. The boss warned the workers that if anyone slipped up, they would be out on the street.

That day Filippo dressed in better than just workingman's clothing. The boss's house was luxurious in a way that Filippo had never seen before. The house had high columns at the entrance giving it a Grecian look. The kitchen was the biggest room in the house. People were busy cleaning, chopping, and cooking.

Filippo arranged the salami, provolone and mortadella. Mozzarella had been made fresh that morning for the party and Filippo made a display of it. There was going to be food on every table of the house in all the rooms. The boss shouted orders to everyone, including Filippo who was sent to get the floral arrangements and put them on the tables.

After several busy hours Filippo stood back to admire his work. The boss retreated to his room and then emerged in an attractive, dark blue suit. None of the employees had ever seen the boss in anything other than an apron and every-day clothes, but this was his baby daughter's First Communion and he was going to be dressed in his best.

Before leaving for the church, a photographer got the whole family together and took a picture. The boss's older daughter, now a plump eighteen year old, stood at her father's side. He held her hand and put a great, spreading smile on his face for the picture.

Filippo took a liking to the boss's daughter, Marina, so nice with an olive complexion and a broad, pretty face. This was no ordinary girl, he thought and he wanted to get himself into her thoughts and head.

The First Communion over, everyone returned to the house to enjoy the food. The wine was plentiful, made by a *paesano* of the boss from Canarsie. It was thick and the darkest red Filippo had ever seen. Guests went to the child and gave her a kiss and an envelope with a money gift inside. She put these in a large, decorated silken purse, made specifically for this purpose. The gesture was called giving "*la busta.*" There were friends that came from Manhattan, Queens and some from New Jersey. One *compare* came the farthest from Connecticut to Brooklyn. Filippo watched all of this. When Marina was walking across the room, with Filippo's eyes fixed on her, a corsage fell from her dress. Filippo rushed to pick it up. "*Ecco, signorina,*" he said as he handed it to her. She blushed as she took it in her hand. "Thank you," she said. They exchanged looks and Filippo thought that he had gotten what he wanted. She would recognize him.

At the end of the evening people began to leave. There was ample food left on the tables in spite of the fact that people ate heartily. After the last guests left, the boss summoned all his workers and had them collect the unused food to return it to the store.

He said, "Filippo, here is the key to the store. I want you to supervise getting it all back there. When I come there tomorrow morning, I want to see that everything is in place, do you understand?"

Filippo was surprised that the boss would trust him so much. Once all the food was in the truck off they went, with Filippo feeling rather grand to be holding the key to the store. The other workers, some of whom had been there more time than Filippo, were envious. "U boss," as they called him in dialect, had favored Filippo. Filippo said to himself, "If they don't like it, they can go to hell."

The boss came in late the next day, something no one had ever seen before. First to arrive and last to leave was his motto. He was always there with the store in full swing when the others arrived.

"Filippo," the boss said slowly, "I was very happy with the way that you did your job yesterday at my daughter's First Communion. I liked how you took over the job and got everything done right." One of the countermen turned his head the other way, as if he didn't hear what the boss said. From that moment on, Filippo noticed that the other workers never spoke about the boss to him. They never shared any more confidences about the job, fearful that he would tell the boss. Filippo said nothing and went about his business.

A few days later the boss had to go to do some business downtown and told Filippo that he was in charge, especially ringing up the sales. The boss had never done this before. He, and only he, touched the cash register even if it meant that the customer had to wait in line. Now, his man of confidence would be Filippo.

Filippo thought about his situation with the boss. First, his role in the party at the boss's house, trusted with the key to the store and working the cash register when the boss went out. What would be next, he wondered. His mind was on Marina, the boss's daughter. How could he get to talk to her, to have some kind of contact that made him less of a worker in the store and more of an individual to her

Two of the workers decided to destroy Filippo's newly found status in the eyes of the boss. Before Filippo's arrival, they were the favorites, but with Filippo's energy and initiative, he had gained ground on them and they resented him.

One day when the boss had to go downtown, he told Filippo to take over the store. Everybody knew that before he went out the boss always counted the money in the register. While Filippo was in the basement doing an inventory, two of the clerks took half the money in the register. When the boss returned from his errand downtown, he went to the register and counted the money noticing that half of it was missing. He looked up at the clerks, "Did you do any business while I was out?" One of them said, "No, boss, we had no business," and kept working.

The boss spent the whole day wondering about this. It poisoned his day. He had come to really like and trust Filippo. He decided to play a game of watchful waiting.

The next time, before he left he said in a loud voice, "Filippo, I'm going to the bank, so you take over the register, okay?"

"Fine, Boss. I take care."

On his return from the bank the boss went and counted the money and again there was half gone. The boss was beginning to get very upset.

"Filippo, did we have much business while I was away?" the boss asked.

"Not really, we had a few small purchases, nothing big," Filippo answered innocently.

The boss took Filippo aside in the basement. "Filippo, I have trusted you completely in the running of the store in my absence. I have looked upon you as a son in dealing with you. But I have to tell you that two times now that I have gone away I have come back to find that half the money was missing from the register."

Filippo blanched. "How can that be?" he asked incredulously. "How can that be? I am the only one who is supposed to use the register when you are away."

"Filippo, either you are a liar or..." the boss said.

"*Signore,* I swear on my mother's grave that I have not touched any of that money for myself. I always appreciated that you trusted me enough to have me handle the register in your absence, and I am proud of it. But steal from you?" his voice trailed away.

"Close to a hundred dollars was stolen," the boss told him.

Filippo answered, "I would kill whoever it was that took the money." Filippo's cheeks were flushed red with anger. He thought of the two countermen alone up in the store when he was downstairs in the basement. It had to be one or both of them. They were no longer friendly with him and he sensed that the truth lay somewhere in the area of envy.

"Mr. Boss, I believe that the clerks up there did it because they are jealous that you trust me. They think that since they have been here longer than me they should be the trusted ones. My heart tells me that they are doing this only to get me fired by you and then one of them would take my place."

"What should we do?" he asked Filippo.

"Look, Mr. Boss, there is a small crawlspace above the store where I can see what is happening in the store through a vent. You tell me that you are going to do business downtown and then I will say that I am going to the basement and then from the basement I can get up to the attic and the crawlspace and see what happens when you leave."

They planned their game for the next day. The boss, said, "I'm going downtown to the bank, so Filippo you take over, okay?"

"Fine, Mr. Boss, I take over."

Once the Boss left, Filippo went to the cellar and from there he climbed up to the attic and crawled on his stomach to the vent. There he was able to see the two countermen. After a few minutes, one of them said to the other, "Check to see if the boss is gone." He came in and nodded to the other.

The first fellow went to the register and rang no sale and the drawer came open with a ring. He immediately counted the money and took half of it and put it into his pocket. Now Filippo saw how they did it. He crawled back to the basement and cleaned himself, took two large cans of tomatoes and went back to the store.

The next time both Filippo and the boss watched it all. The boss was livid. If he could have jumped down from the attic directly on to the men he would have done it. Instead they returned to the store. One of the clerks noticed that the boss was dirty and disheveled. The boss walked up to the main thief and socked him in the jaw. The other fellow turned pale as the boss turned to him.

"Boss, I didn't do nothing. I didn't do nothing. It was his idea."

The boss unleashed a slap across his face.

"*Disgraziati, tutt'e due.* Dirty bastards. Get out of here before I kill both of you."

Feeling well satisfied, Filippo and the boss put on their aprons and went back to work.

It wasn't long before Filippo was invited to the boss's house. The first time was an anniversary, then a Confirmation, then other occasions, until it became obvious that he was slowly becoming a member of the family. This pleased him because Filippo liked Marina and Marina liked him. Then Filippo took the final step of inviting Marina on a date to a movie. It was gut-wrenching for him to ask her out. What if the boss didn't like the idea of one of his workers dating his daughter? But since he was slowly becoming a member of the family he decided to take a chance. How relieved he was when she said that it would be a nice idea for them to go on a date. He urged her to ask her father if he approved. She quickly said he did.

From one date, to a regular date and finally to the time Filippo had the courage to ask the boss for his daughter's hand in marriage. The boss gave him a long talk on the virtues of marriage, how marriage was forever and for the making of children. Then he went into a long talk about how he came to America and started out delivering coal and after much hard work opened his store. He had to put up with thieving clerks, finicky customers and unreliable suppliers. Filippo sat through it all not saying a word. At the end, Filippo said that he hoped that the boss would give him his daughter's hand in marriage. The boss said yes, hugged and kissed Filippo, then said, "You will be the son that God did not give me."

There was a prolonged courtship and then in the second year of their courtship a date was set. Filippo married Marina and eventually became the new boss.

———————————————

Slowly Ada was getting used to America with its strange ways. People ate sandwiches for dinner, and ate supper at six in the evening. One day a beggar came to the house. Having little money to give the beggar she decided to give him a box of the cereal she had bought because Andrea had heard about it in school. They didn't like it, so she gave the beggar the box of oatmeal. Later in the day when she opened the door she found the box of cereal there. Even the beggar didn't want it. Shaking her head she threw the cereal in the trash.

Her relations with her sisters-in-law remained civil but not warm. The brothers had married into a staid traditional family. Coming from Rome, Ada was an outsider, someone they didn't trust completely. They were shocked that Ada made no efforts at being religious. Ada was cynical about the church and its ministers because of the poor treatment she received at the time of Andrea's birth and her marriage. In spite of any slights that she received, Ada tried to have a good family relationship with her sisters-in-law, although at times it seemed hopeless.

Every Sunday was spent at dinner at the house of one of the brothers. There was good food and wine to wash down the food, and pastries from the Sicilian's shop. The children all ate at a smaller table in the kitchen. After dinner the brothers sat down to play a few hands of *Tresette*. This is what Giovanni's life had become in America. Work all week, six days a week with "U' boss," and then on Sunday, dinner with his brothers.

In idle moments he wondered if coming to America was all it was put up to be. In Italy, even during the dark days of the war he ate and had a roof over his head at Don Beppe's. But in America he missed the old towns along the Adriatic in Puglia and the Romanesque churches. Each town had built the fortifications to ward off conquerors. There was none of this, but he knew that he could not return to Italy, not now after he had tasted the openness of America. God bless *l'America*, his brother used to say whenever he won at cards. He would throw the cards down face up and say, "God Bless *l'America*."

Giovanni had listened to Filippo's story and watched him work. Giovanni got the itch to own his own store. He had learned a great deal. He became a connoisseur of cheeses and meats and knew how to deal with customers to Filippo's satisfaction. Giovanni realized early on that if you worked for someone, you made that person rich. If you worked for yourself, you made yourself rich. Where could he get the money to start his own delicatessen business? He discussed the idea with his brothers who told him that a stone cutter's salary put them in no position to lend him money. Ada volunteered to go to work, provided that someone could be found to take care of Andrea. This idea did not set well with Giovanni.

One day while working, Giovanni approached Filippo. "*Caro boss*, I have an idea, but I need some advice from you who have become a very successful businessman." Giovanni skipped over the fact that Filippo married the boss's daughter and inherited the business.

"What is it?"

"Filippo, you were kind enough to take me in and give me a job with which I support my family, but I would like to have my own business."

"And?" Filippo interrupted.

"I don't have enough money to start the business. I went to the bank and they told me that I have no credit, no collateral, so they won't lend me the money to start."

"You must remember that I made an investment when I hired you. You knew nothing about the business, and I taught you everything," Filippo said.

"That's true, Filippo, but I would like to be like you, to have my own business, and I think that I can do it on my own, but I don't have the capital to start."

"I don't know," Filippo said, "I don't know. Where am I going to find somebody like you that I can trust? I can go away now for a vacation and know that I won't get stolen blind by crooks that I hired. That is not easy to come by."

Giovanni listened intently, nodding his head.

After waiting a while, Filippo said, "Let's be thinking about it for a while, then we'll see," and that ended the discussion for the moment.

Giovanni's brothers kept asking him if Filippo was going to help, but Giovanni said that Filippo was thinking about it. Filippo didn't commit himself to helping him, so Giovanni continued working as best he could.

The brothers in the meanwhile continued at their trade. People died everyday and everyday they were given granite stones to carve and embellish for a tombstone. Paolo's son, Lino, had told his father that he was interested in becoming a stone cutter like his father, but Paolo said everything he could to discourage him. Paolo was beginning to have trouble breathing. He started having trouble going up stairs and after any exertion, he could hear his own heavy breathing. No one had to tell him what that meant.

Lino brought his father to the doctor. The doctor said that since Paolo had been around granite it meant that he might have silicosis, and they should be on the lookout for tuberculosis. He urged Paolo to make an appointment with a specialist that the doctor recommended.

Giovanni could remember the words silicosis and tuberculosis were words that no one uttered in the past. They used euphemisms like "the chest" or "the wheezing," but never silicosis or tuberculosis. There was no cure for either.

For years, each Saturday afternoon Paolo sat and listened to the opera on the radio. No one could make any noise during those hours. For Paolo, opera was the greatest art of all and the only thing that could take his mind off his health. During his years in Italy and his time in America, Paolo had heard or seen some of the greatest opera singers in the world. He prided himself on the fact that he knew all the words to the arias and often asked people to test him. He always was right.

During the day, Paolo could feel a light fever, another sign that he had a pulmonary illness. This left him with fatigue. He tramped across the city to go to his job. At the end of the day he returned on the subway, and slept a good part of the trip.

Since Baldy was the delegate to the union, Paolo went to see him at the union hall. There was Baldy, his hat pushed back on his head, his necktie askew, talking excitedly with someone. When he finished, he greeted Paolo as he would a *paesano*, with a great big hug.

"Paolo, what are you doing here? You lose your job or something?" Baldy asked.

"Baldy, I have the dust in the lungs."

Baldy became serious. "Paolo, maybe the doctor is not sure. Did you get a second opinion?" Baldy asked.

"The doctor sent me to the specialist. He said that I had silicosis and that they had to be sure that I didn't get tuberculosis. What does this mean for me?"

"Paolo," Baldy said, "I'm no doctor. He's the one who has to tell you what to do."

"The doctor said that I had to stop working or I would get tuberculosis," Paolo said.

"Look, Paolo, if you have to retire from the job, you have to put in a claim for workmen's compensation. Then you have to wait for them to have a hearing. Then they make their decision as to whether or not you are disabled. If they find you disabled, then you will receive a modest," and he stressed the word modest, "a very modest payment each month."

"What can I do, Baldy, what can I do?"

Paolo kept going over the procedure that Baldy had laid out for him: go to the doctor, go to the workman's compensation board, fill out an application for workmen's compensation and then sit and wait for the hearing.

"Nicoletta, I spoke to the doctor and he said that I have silicosis. Then I went to see Baldy for advice, he said that if I had silicosis, then I would have to stop working because it would be too hard on my lungs."

Nicoletta brought a handkerchief to her lips.

"How are we going to get along on our savings and whatever pension we get?" Paolo said.

"I don't know, but God always provides," Nicoletta said.

Paolo made a gesture of futility with his hands, "God will provide! My dear wife, please tell me how He is going to provide?"

"I don't know. We always look to God when our load gets too heavy for us here on earth," she answered.

"I have worked and sweated all these years and now I have a sickness. If I don't watch out, the doctor said, I might get tuberculosis and then I will die. Die." he reiterated, and the sound of his voice resonated all over the house.

"Paolo, we are not alone. We have your brothers. Maybe they can help you.

"My brother Francesco has his own worries. Someday he too will be told he has silicosis, so don't expect any help from him, but Lord knows that if I needed it, he would take the shirt off his back to help me."

"What about Giovanni?"

"Are you kidding?"

"He is an *avaro,* a cheapskate. I've said that all the time," Nicoletta said.

"No, he's not stingy. He too has had a tough life."

"How can you say that he has had a tough life? He has a nice house. You've seen it. That *puttana* of a wife lives like a *signora,* and their son goes to a private school run by priests while ours go to the public school where they are teased and called guineas and wops by the Irish kids."

"I don't bear him any hate. He is my brother," Paolo said.

"You don't bear him any hate? Don't you think I saw your face when he was showing us around his house?" she threw back at him.

"Stop this terrible talk. True, he has had some good luck but from the beginning he was the outsider of the family. Although we treated him like a brother, we all knew in our hearts that he wasn't. He was the son of our father's wife. I have no rancor toward him. He had to live the war years in Italy while we were safe here in America," Paolo answered.

"Nonsense! You worked very hard," she said.

Not knowing what to answer Paolo shook his head with fatigue. "Let's not go over this again."

The next day he went upstairs to his brother's apartment, and told Dora, "Tell Francesco when he comes home to come downstairs. I have to talk to him. It's important, tell him," Paolo said and left.

Paolo had the address of the workmen's compensation office and looked for the building among the maze of concrete buildings. He asked a few people where the building was, but no one was sure. He saw a policeman and asked him.

"What do you want to do there," the policeman asked.

"I gotta go and see the workmen's compensation people," and he pointed to his chest, hoping the policeman would understand.

"I'm sick and I gotta go there to get a pension," Paolo answered timidly looking at the tall Irishman with a pink face and steely blue eyes.

"Well, the best I can do is to send you to 100 Montague Street. That's where it may be, but you better ask them if that's the right office." He turned away to look at traffic.

"Sonamabitch," Paolo uttered to himself.

He started looking for 100 Montague Street. Finally after combing through the whole downtown area he found it. It was a short building with no sign on the door. Once he went inside he saw in golden letters, "Workmen's Compensation Board."

At the desk he explained to a woman that he was there to get a pension. The woman gave a sly smile. "Mister, we don't give pensions here. You have to apply for one, that's what we do," she said smugly. She gathered some papers and handed them to him. "Here are all the papers you have to fill out. You get a letter from your doctor and a letter from your current boss and then bring them here and we will file them. Do you understand?" As Paolo turned away and looked at the number of sheets, he could hear her murmur, "These guineas, when the hell are they ever gonna learn. They're here for years and still can't talk English. I wish to hell that somebody would put them all on a ship and sent them back to Sicily."

"Italy," Paolo shot back. "I am from Italy, Bari, not Sicily."

Paolo filled out all the papers with the help of his brother. He didn't want to make any mistakes, because as Baldy said, "Paolo, sometimes these things take time, a lot of time, so you don't want to make any mistakes that's gonna make it take longer."

Lino, Paolo's son, was a good student with a quick mind. Everything he heard he absorbed. He read newspapers at first for the funnies, and then later for articles on sports, then articles of general interest. "Pappa, I want to be a lawyer," he would say. And his father answered, "Lino, you are too kind a person to be a lawyer. You have a soft heart."

"That's okay, Pappa, I can still be a good lawyer."

Growing up in a home where only Italian was spoken, Lino learned to speak not only standard Italian but also Barese dialect. Lino loved going to the movies where he saw how "*gli americani*" lived. Their lives were different from his own, and many times he wished that he was an "*Americano.*" Then he would not have to be embarrassed by his parents who did not speak English well. His father turned the English language around and upside-down as he tried to explain himself to someone. He always ended by saying, "*Lino, spiega quello che sto dicendo,*" explain what I am saying. And then Lino would translate all that his father had said. People listened more intently to Lino than to his father. But it still gave Lino a twinge of embarrassment to hear his parents speak English. His father dragged him everywhere and translating was the biggest job that Lino did for his parents. He did it much less for his mother. Her English was better than his father's. Besides, they really didn't need English. When they went to the store to buy food or clothing all those merchants were Italians.

It was tough for Paolo to go to his boss to explain that he was sick and had to stop working. Paolo had worked for him more than twenty years and felt that he could talk to the owner--who was part Italian--in a way that did not cause him any embarrassment.

"Tony," he started. "I have bad lungs. The doctor said that I can't work no more because of the dust in my lungs, and if I continue to work, then I might get tuberculosis."

"Paolo, I've have had several workers that got silicosis. It's not easy for them to work. They got winded fast, couldn't lift things, and then they started to cough and cough. Then you know they got silicosis. Then I seen them go home and slowly die, either from tuberculosis or heartbreak. Life ain't no party. It never was meant to be. And how do you think I feel when one of my workers come to me, like you are doing now, to tell me that they can't work no more? I feel bad, very bad, but that's what it's all about. Life ain't no party."

Just think, Paolo said to himself, I don't have to go to work no more. Too bad it had to be for a sickness! he thought.

The owner wrote a letter saying that Paolo had worked for him for twenty three years, and was a good worker, smart, reliable, no Monday morning blues from drinking too much. On the way home on the subway, Paolo read and re-read the letter several times. It sounded like he was dead.

Day after day he waited for the mailman to see if he brought the letter about a hearing and every now and then he would call Baldy, who told him to be patient. These things took time. There were a lot of other stone cutters who had applied for compensation and were still waiting for a hearing. He did tell Paolo that he would be setting up an appointment with the union lawyer who would take his case. Once again, his father took Lino with him to the lawyer to translate.

The day of the appointment with the lawyer, Lino did not go to school. Lino told his parents that he had to be in school. His father said, "I need you now. School can wait a day." The boy hadn't wanted to miss playing punch ball in the schoolyard with his friends.

"But Pop. The teacher told me that they were going to start something new. I can't miss that!"

"Yes, you can," Paolo answered sharply. "You want your father to go there and understand nothing? Is that what you want?" Lino felt guilty that he would be letting his father down and quietly acquiesced.

Every night Lino had heard his pappa winding his alarm clock for work the next morning. This time, as he lay in his bed listening through the wall to that familiar sound, he realized something in his life was coming to an end.

The day of the meeting with the lawyer, Paolo put on a suit and tie and took out his best hat. He had a hat for the working day and another one for holidays and important things like this.

They left the house early so as not to be late for this meeting. Paolo's future depended on it. After a long haul on the subway they got off and wandered around the streets looking for the building. When they finally found it Paolo noticed that it was made of granite and he ran his hand affectionately across it, feeling the coarse stone.

They entered the door with trepidation. Paolo did not know what to expect, and his son wondered what good he could do in this situation, other than translating for his father.

The receptionist ushered them into an office where they found a man sitting surrounded by papers. He rose up almost scaring them.

"Yes? What can I do for you?" he asked brusquely.

They didn't know what to do. Paolo pulled at his son's sleeve urging him to say something.

"This is my father," Lino said. "He is a granite cutter and the doctor says that he's sick. The shop steward sent us here to talk to you."

The man nodded.

"And what am I to do for you?" he asked Paolo.

Lino answered, "My father was told that he's sick with silicosis and he's supposed to stop working. At least, that is what the doctor said." And he waited. His father said nothing and left it all up to Lino.

"Young fellow," the lawyer said, "there is a process to this, and I am currently doing about thirteen of these cases."

Lino wasn't sure what to say. "We were told by the shop steward that you could help my father get a pension," Paolo said.

"We are going to do everything we can to help your father, and the first thing to do is to get a letter from the doctor and a letter from his job."

Lino pulled them out of an envelope he held in his hand.

The lawyer looked the letters over. "I see you did your homework, son. Who told you to get these?"

"The shop steward did," Lino promptly answered.

"I see," and he continued reading. When he was finished, he looked up and stared at the two of them for what seemed to them to be forever.

"I am glad that you got these letters. That's the beginning of the file," and he put them down and he called the secretary,

"Mary, start a file on this case." The secretary came in took the papers, and returned to her desk. Paolo felt naked when she took the letters. They were his passport to a pension.

The lawyer leaned back in his leather chair and looked at them. He didn't wear a jacket and had his shirt open at the neck with his tie askew. To Lino he didn't look like a lawyer should.

"Right now we are at the beginning of things. It's going to take time to see this to the end. If you think that this is something that will be done in a day, or a month, or a year, you're mistaken," he said with finality. "These things take time. Do you have savings that you can live off?"

Paolo was offended by the question. He thought that it was none of his business if he had or didn't have money to get along.

"I have some," he said wondering why the lawyer asked that question, other than to find out how long he could hold out before he was down to zero on his money.

"Well, you are going to have to live and these things, as I said, take time, and you have to think about how you are going to live."

"Why can't you get me the disability right away? The doctor says that I am sick, and that is what is important, isn't it?" Paolo said and then immediately felt bad. He thought maybe he was being too gruff with the lawyer. He, Paolo, needed the lawyer, the lawyer did not need him.

"I have just finished telling you," and he stopped and turned to Lino. "Tell your father that these things take time. He's going to have to learn to wait."

Looking at the lawyer, Paolo knew in his heart that the man wasn't Italian. He was an American and that meant that he did not know how Paolo and his brothers and the many others that were granite cutters thought. The lawyer was balding, with a white neatly clipped moustache.

"He will continue to get sicker, and we need to do something to prevent that from happening," Lino said.

"Look Sonny, I am the lawyer here. I know what's best for your father as far as the law is concerned. Do you know that the union hired me to take care of all these cases? Do you know that we are going to have to study your father's case carefully, because the state isn't going to give him money if they think that he can continue working?" There was a pause. "You don't seem to know that the state will do anything it can to avoid paying your father."

Lino felt ashamed that he didn't know these things.

"Now, this is the last time I am going to tell you this, so please pay attention," the lawyer said. "I have your letters. That constitutes an application for disability benefits. We have now made a file on your father. Tomorrow, my secretary will bring the information to the State of New York Workmen's Compensation office and file it officially," he hit his desk lightly at each syllable of officially. "Then we wait for them to contact us about the hearing, and it will be a first hearing. Sometimes there are several hearings. Is that understood?" He looked first to Paolo and then to his son. "If that is understood, you will be hearing from me, and good day to you both." He looked down at his papers and kept his head down. Paolo and his son got up from their chairs and walked away.

The next few days, Paolo would go every day to the mailbox to see if anything from the lawyer or the state was there. It never was. He did this each day, every day, at eleven in the morning. The rest of the day he sat in his chair and listened to his breathing, hearing how labored it sounded. When would the end come?

On Saturdays he listened to the opera on the radio. He remembered the days spent waiting in the cold to get into the Metropolitan Opera House to hear the great singers. He and his brothers always managed to get enough money together to attend the operas. And he listened as arias passed through his head, one by one, all the great ones. At times he was so overcome by the sheer power of the music that he would stand and sing the arias aloud. And still no letter.

His wife began to worry about him, because all he could think about was a letter from the state or from the lawyer. His every thought was: "Will they recognize my disability or not? Will they see that I am sick and can't work any more?" Those thoughts went through his head night and day.

His brother Francesco tried telling him that everything would be all right. He would get his disability. But all the reassurances from his brother were not enough to quiet Paolo's mind. He would hum and sing aria after aria. He then stood outside the gate of his house right by the sidewalk and sang arias. People walking by thought it was strange.

Filippo had agreed to give Giovanni the money to start his own store. Giovanni stood on the sidewalk watching the painter finish his work. "Giovanni's Italian Delicatessen." Giovanni was in an apron. The painter gave an old English twist to the letters and they shone like gold. For all the things that Giovanni knew how to do he didn't know how the painter managed to get the gold letters done in that fashion to look three dimensional.

When the painter finished, Giovanni paid him and went behind the counter and cleaned and wiped the slicer for the fourth time that morning, in spite of the fact that he had only made one sale involving it—a half pound of salami. "That's all right," he said to himself, "more will be coming."

In time more did come, and Giovanni did a good business at lunchtime when workers would come in for a sandwich. At the end of the day he had made his minimum and that was enough to pay the rent for the month. At first, the store seemed small because he was used to Filippo's store which was bigger.

He kept the place meticulously clean. There would be no sign of dust or dirt anywhere, and he threw handfuls of sawdust on the floor. He had learned the trade from Filippo, who was proud to have lent Giovanni the stake to open his store. He prayed that Giovanni would have what it took to keep the place going. Giovanni assured Filippo that he would never lose the store and that he would make it a success. "I hope so. *Dio sa*," Filippo said.

When he first opened the store, Giovanni thought that customers would be coming in droves and he asked Ada to help him by being the cashier. She agreed. Now that Giovanni was running his own store Ada would have felt disloyal not to help out. In Italy lots of wives helped their husbands in their stores. Andrea would come to work there after school, making deliveries, helping his father at the counter and fetching cans. Andrea proved to be an apt pupil although there were times he wished he were on the street playing with his friends.

Giovanni liked to kibitz with his customers. He had learned some phrases from Filippo, and tried them out on customers.

"You like this mozzarella? I just make this morning," Giovanni said, knowing it was a lie. "Here, *Signora*, try this piece of cheese. It will melt in your mouth. Try it, please, no charge," and he cut a small wedge of cheese for the customer to taste. The customer always bought a pound of the cheese after that. When he went home at night Ada would have supper ready for him and Andrea.

The customers of his store were almost all Italians. Sometimes a Jew would come in for the good bread that Giovanni sold. He found them strange, with their Germanic language, their long black coats and curls. A customer called Solomon would occasionally come by and talk to Andrea. An old Jewish woman came when the store opened and bought a bread roll for a nickel. Each day she trudged up the street to get her roll.

In time Giovanni had built up a nice clientele. He was able to pay off the loan to Filippo much earlier than he expected and then he felt even greater freedom since he had no debts. He became established in the neighborhood and even took an ad in the newsletter of the local Catholic Church.

One day, Giovanni was late in coming home and Ada fretted. Giovanni was so regular that it was not like him to come home late. When he finally came in, she asked, "Why didn't you let me know that you would come home late?"

Giovanni didn't answer, and Ada noted that he had an odd smile on his face as if he was hiding something from her.

"Ya, ya, ya," he said.

"What do you mean, 'ya, ya, ya'?"

"I was on an important errand. You see, *mia cara*, I had to go pick up a car," and he screamed the last four words.

"A car? Whose car?" she wondered.

"Our car," he said and jingled the keys in front of her face. She broke out into a big smile.

"Our car? You mean that we have our own car? I don't believe it," Ada said.

"Oh, you don't believe it? Then, what's these keys for?" and he gave an extra jingling of them.

They went outside and there was a tan Dodge. It was used, but the fellow who sold Giovanni the car said that it was in mint condition and Giovanni bought it on the spot.

"Okay, you bought a car, now who's going to drive it?

"Me, that's who," Giovanni answered with mock offense.

"Where did you learn? You can't drive a car," she said.

"For the last three Sundays, Mauro, the plumber, taught me. I drove his car around the streets until I could do it blind."

"It's true? We have a car?"

"It's ours and it's all paid for. Come on," Giovanni said proudly.

The car started with a loud noise, then the engine calmed down. With a sudden lurch they took off. Andrea sat in the back seat as full of pride as his father was. Giovanni drove around several blocks. Ada saw all the stores that she walked by each day. She remembered her life, how her father worked so hard and they just barely got by. She recalled her great error and then quickly got rid of the thought as one would erase words from a blackboard. None of that, she said to herself. If only her father, not to mention Don Andrea could see her. "Now who is *La Signora*?" she asked herself. She sat back in the seat and let the stores and houses flash by her. "Now who is *La Signora*?" she repeated out loud to Giovanni and Andrea. Giovanni could only smile at her. He knew in his heart what she said and to whom it was directed.

At first, Giovanni's brothers would come by the store and help, although Giovanni was uncomfortable about it. After all, this was his business, his, Giovanni's, and he didn't want anyone else thinking that they could come in and act like the boss.

Giovanni spent many a time at night before falling asleep thinking about his brothers. How wonderful it was when they received him in New York on their arrival. He thought that everything would be like that day, but it wasn't. He knew that his sisters-in-law didn't like Ada. Dora had said, "You can't go through the life she had and not have some dirt on you." Giovanni let that go by and didn't pay any attention to his sisters-in-law. He saw them once a week and that was enough for him.

Giovanni also remembered how much it hurt him to charge his brothers for things that they bought from his store. At first Giovanni wanted to say to them, "Go, go, take whatever you want. You are my brothers. You can take what you want," but he knew that would not work. He couldn't do that. The look on their faces when he charged them the exact price that he charged his customers pained Giovanni. He looked away when they put the money on the counter and only later put it in the register. They stopped coming to help out after that. And when he got his car, they thought he took a long time to come by and show them the car and take them for a ride. Francesco said to him, "Giovanni, next summer, when you take a vacation, let's go to Vermont and visit the grave of our dead brother Silvio."

"Yes, yes, of course," he mumbled. But Giovanni had no hankerings for a vacation. Business was good. The money kept flowing in. He even toyed with the idea of buying the store next to him, the remnants shop that an old Jewish man ran. If he could buy that store, he could fix it up and then he would have more space and more goods to sell to more customers.

How strange it was, Giovanni thought. His brothers were here in America, where there was money to be made, yet they still lived in four rooms. While he, Giovanni, who spent the war years in Brindisi barely eking out a living, came to New York and now he owned a store, a house and a car. Why couldn't they see how easy, yes, easy, it was to make money? Granted, I had the help of Filippo, he argued to himself, but they could have given up cutting stone for another business. They were good workers. They could have made it too.

Paolo kept waiting for the arrival of his disability letter. When it finally came, he ran in the house waving the letter.

"It came, it came," he yelled. His wife had tears in her eyes. Finally, he would get a pension, she thought.

The day of the hearing, Paolo needed Lino's help again. Paolo and his son sat down on the third row of the court room. Paolo tried to figure out if the others there were stone cutters with the same lung disease, but he couldn't tell.

An elderly lady dressed in black sat with a younger woman who held her hand. The judge came in, and everyone rose.

The bailiff called a name, "Simonetta Grimaldi, please stand."

"Your honor, Dante J. Marino, Attorney-at-Law, representing Mrs. Grimaldi," and he pointed toward the elderly lady in black.

"Please proceed, Mr. Marino," the judge said sternly.

"Your honor, Mrs. Grimaldi's husband, Antonio Grimaldi, was killed in a workplace accident, and Mrs. Grimaldi is asking for disability rights that her husband would normally get. He was killed when a truck carrying cement overturned, as is stated in the autopsy report." He reached into his briefcase and pulled out a piece of paper and waved it at the judge, "the cause of death was compression. It is our contention that the accident was due to the cement driver's carelessness and incompetence."

The judge turned to a table where two men sat amidst reams of paper.

"Does the State have a copy of this document?" the judge asked.

"Yes sir, Your Honor, it does," and he sat down.

"What is the basis of the plaintiff's claim?" the judge asked.

Paolo studied the face of the judge. He couldn't tell what his background was. His father always told him that you should study a man's face to see what his character was like. Paolo trusted his feelings in things like this.

The judge asked Mrs. Grimaldi to take the stand.

"Mr. Marino, please proceed."

"Thank you, Your Honor," and he paused. "Mrs. Grimaldi, when did your husband die, on what day?"

Mrs. Grimaldi fumbled with a handkerchief in her hand and had a lost look on her face. "I don't remember the date," she said in a low voice.

"A little louder, please, Mrs. Grimaldi, a little louder," the judge said.

She looked up at the judge and said, "I don't remember the date exactly," in her heavily accented speech.

"Surely, you must remember the day that he was killed or died?" the judge said matter-of-factly.

"I don't remember exactly, the twentieth of May or some time around then," she said. The lawyer stood up and said, "Your Honor, Mrs. Grimaldi is still in mourning over her husband's death. I know the date of the accident, and the State knows the date of the accident, so there is no question there, or is there?" he said turning to the two lawyers at the opposite table.

"No question, Your Honor," one of the lawyers answered crisply.

"Your Honor," Mr. Marino said, "May twenty-first."

"Please proceed," the judge said and sat back.

"Let it please the court, that on the said date of 21 May while Mr. Grimaldi was working for the Lemore Cement Company as a cement worker, a truck owned by the Lemore Company while executing a turn in a constricted area overturned coming down on Mr. Grimaldi and thereby crushing him and killing him."

As the lawyer went over the facts of the case Mrs. Grimaldi began to sob quietly and continued to cry as the lawyer went from one fact to the other.

"We contend, Your Honor," the lawyer Marino said, "that the cement truck, which weighed over four thousand pounds, overturned because the driver had miscalculated how much space he had available to him in that closed area and this caused the accident that killed Mr. Grimaldi."

"Mr. Marino," the judge purred, "Besides his wife, how many young children did the late Mr. Grimaldi leave?"

"Four, Your Honor," Marino answered tersely.

The judge then turned to the lawyers for the State, "Gentlemen, do you have any questions of either Mrs. Grimaldi or Mr. Marino?"

"Yes sir, Your Honor," the shorter of the two got up and walked slowly to the dock were Mrs. Grimaldi sat sobbing. "Mrs. Grimaldi, what exactly did your husband do in the course of his work?"

She looked up lost and turned to the lawyer and the judge and said, "I don't know. He was a cement worker, that's all I know," she answered.

"Your Honor, I can't hear the witness, can you please instruct her to speak louder?"

"Mrs. Grimaldi," the judge said slowly, "could you please raise your voice so that the State's lawyers can hear you?"

"I don't know. He say that he make cement and do cement work, that's all I know."

"Your Honor, if it please the court, Mrs. Grimaldi is a housewife who knows nothing about cement making. It's unfair for the State's counsel to ask such questions. If he has any technical questions, he should address them to me or a representative of the Lemore Company, not to Mrs. Grimaldi, who is still grieving her husband's loss," Marino said and sat down.

"Grieving? It's been six months since he was killed. It is the position of the State that Mr. Grimaldi was killed not in the execution of his work but rather through his own fault, through his incompetence. He had no business being in that area when the accident occurred. According to representatives of the Lemore Company, Grimaldi's job was spreading and finishing cement once it was poured on a flat surface. What was he doing in the truck area? He had no business there. If the accident had occurred in his own particular work area, then the State could be more compassionate, but he went totally out of the area of his skill and was killed there. It is not the fault of the Lemore Company or the State Compensation Board that he was killed in that manner. Your Honor, the position of the State is that Mrs. Grimaldi be awarded the minimum payment for the accident, $32.50 a month for seventy two weeks, and that is all."

Mr. Marino leaped up, "Your Honor, 'being out of the area of his expertise?' Who is kidding who here? When you work in cement and concrete you often have to go around the whole work site, getting water to mix the cement, carrying bags of dry cement to the mixer, and a dozen other steps in the procedure of mixing and pouring cement. Mr. Grimaldi had every right in the world to be where he was. The State says nothing about the driver, whose incompetence caused the accident that killed Mr. Grimaldi. The Lemore Cement Company is liable for the results of the accident."

A noise shattered the quiet between the dueling lawyers. A rosary which Mrs. Grimaldi held in her hand fell to the ground. They looked and then went back to their arguing.

"Your Honor," the State lawyer said, "the State cannot be held responsible for matters of chance happening where a worker was not supposed to be. This is a matter of pure chance, not 'carrying out his work', as the plaintiff says."

The judge sat up straight and said, "Are there any other concluding arguments before I render a decision?"

Quiet ensued. "All right then. Mr. Grimaldi was certainly in the wrong place and the wrong time. He wasn't spreading cement on a sidewalk or any other place. This is unfortunate, but had he been elsewhere he would be alive today. He does leave behind, however, a wife and four children, so the award to his family is seventy five weeks at fifty dollars. Case closed.

Mrs. Grimaldi got up and left with the lawyer holding her arm whispering to her, "This is a gross miscarriage of justice, *Signora*, and I am going to appeal this case to the highest court." Paolo could hear the lawyer Marino saying to her, "It's an absolute outrage. They could have given you more and for a longer time," and they walked out.

A policeman stood up and called out "Paolo, Paolo," and he began to stutter, "Falcone," and barely got it out. "Here," Paolo said and stood up. "Here."

"Come forth and sit at this table," the policeman said.

"Falcone," Paolo said.

"Yes, Falcone," the policeman repeated.

The judge looked over his glasses and asked, "Where is your lawyer?"

"I don't know, Mr. Judge, he supposed to be here, but I don't see him. He say something like preliminary hearing, so he say he no need to be here."

"It is in your best interests for him to be here, preliminary or not."

"I don't know."

The judge paused a minute. "All right, let's move along and he'd better be here for the final hearing.

The judge continued. "Mr. Fal, Mr. Fal…."

"Falcone," Paolo said.

"Ah yes, Falcone. This hearing is to examine your claim that you were injured, or, in this case, made ill due to an exposure to stone dust, is that true?"

"Yes, Mr. Judge, I don't have good lungs because I be stone cutter for long time. I can't breathe good," Paolo stated.

"Mr. Falcone, how long have you been a stone cutter?"

"Long time. I begin when I was twelve years old in Italy. Yes, twelve years. My father, he got a stone yard, and I didn't want to go to school to be somebody else, so I be a stone cutter like him and like my brothers, we all begin at ten or twelve years old."

"Mr. Falcone, Do you have any evidence that you began working at twelve years old?" The judge asked him.

"No, I don't got no evidence. My brothers can tell you," Paolo answered.

"Unfortunately, your brothers do not constitute credible witnesses," the judge answered.

Paolo had no idea what the judge meant.

"Judge, my father he die a long time ago. Because of bad times he lose his stone yard. My brothers and me we go first to *Egitto....*"

"Where?" The judge queried.

"*Egitto,*" Paolo said with some confusion.

His son got up.

"Your Honor, *Egitto* is Italian for Egypt."

The judge looked up at Lino over his glasses.

"And who might you be, young man?" the judge said.

"Your Honor, I am Paolo Falcone's son, Lino. I know Italian and English. And Egypt is the English word for the Italian '*Egitto*'," and he sat down.

"Thank you, son. Are you a licensed translator?"

"No sir, I am just a student."

"Let the record read that the plaintiff's son, a boy of," and he looked at Lino, "how old are you?"

"Your Honor, I am twelve years old," Paolo said.

The judge had an amused look on his face. "Gentlemen of the State, do you accept this translation?"

The short man got up and said, "Your Honor, we accept it. It is not crucial to our case."

"If you want, sir," the judge said to the short lawyer, "we can call a recess and have a court appointed translator come here and translate whatever Mr. Falcone says."

"That won't be necessary, Your Honor, we accept that translation."

"Fine, let us continue."

"Mr. Falcone, you were saying that your father's stone yard business failed and you went to Egypt, is that so?"

"Yes, You' Honor," Paolo said.

"Please continue," the judge said.

"We go to *Egitto* and we can't work good because they don't like Italians there. So we come home and we come to *L'America*, and we work."

"What year did you come to America, sir," the judge asked.

"I think it was 1925."

"You think?" the judge asked incredulously.

"Yes, it was 1925. We begin to work in a stone yard in the Bronx for a man, his name is Mr. Berlin, or something like that. We work there for five year, about five year."

The judge looked over some papers, "And where did you work after that?"

"I work lots of places. I cut stone for the buildings in New York a lot. Lots o' buildings."

"And who was your boss?"

"He name Mr. Louis, something like that."

"Mr. Falcone, do you have wage receipts for the various jobs you had?"

"I don't know. They give us money at the end of the week, cash. We got no receipt but I got the letter from my boss. He say I work for him twenty three years. But I don't got no receipts."

"In other words, there is no way we can prove that you worked on these jobs. Did you file income tax?"

Paolo was stunned. He never knew of anyone filing income tax. The union delegate told them that since they were day workers, they didn't have to pay income tax. The delegate told Paolo and the others, "Don't worry, do you think the government worries about you? Forget it," but Paolo didn't want to say that in the courtroom.

"Mr. Judge, nobody tell me file income tax, so I didn't do it."

Even Lino sensed that his father was in trouble.

———————————

At home, Paolo moped around. He tried calling the union delegate, but the secretary told him the delegate was out of town but Paolo could call him again. Then he called the union lawyer, the man with the fine, grey moustache that he saw in his office once. When he finally got on the line he told Paolo, "Mr. Falcone, you did not have a strong case, that's why they passed you over this time. Now you have to wait until we can get a second hearing so your case can be heard more fully. Now, bear in mind, Mr. Falcone, this does not mean that you have lost. It means that you needed more solid evidence that you worked all those years. The letter from the boss only covered a relatively short period of time. The judge didn't have enough evidence to sustain a claim that you are medically impaired."

Such language went over Paolo's head. The only thing he could think of was, "Why you didn't come to the judge?"

"I know that this is a hard pill for you to swallow. You have, Lord knows, worked a long time and do have a medical disability, but you didn't have the kind of evidence to show that you worked all those years."

"But the boss say I do okay, and he pay me cash all the time. I take my money and that's it."

"I understand what you are saying, but that is not the way the law works," the lawyer answered.

"The law, she crazy," was all Paolo could say.

"Mr. Falcone, at some point there will be a second hearing, and at that time we shall get the union doctor there and a few other medical specialists, lung specialists, more evidence, and then we can prepare a good case.

"And why you no prepare a gooder case the other day?"

"Mr. Falcone, you must understand that I have dozens of cases like yours to do. It takes a great deal of time to prepare the case, don't you see?"

"I don't see nuthin'. You didn't help me," and in a rage Paolo slammed down the telephone. He could feel the rage well up in his eyes. "You no help me, *disgraziato, figlio di puttana,* miserable sonomabitch."

He kept repeating these words to himself throughout the day. Listlessly going from room to room hoping to find some peace. He put on the radio, hoping to find the opera program but that was only on Saturday. All he could find were soap operas, of which he understood next to nothing.

Finally, he resigned himself to going back to work at least until he could get another hearing. He picked up his bag of tools and took the subway to the Bronx to where he thought he would never return. He had forgotten for the two months he was at home just how far the Bronx was and how long the trip on the subway took. It was interminable, station after station until he reached his stop and climbed the stairs of the subway to the light. He took that long walk alongside the cemetery, past the florist shops where the painfully sweet smell of flowers attacked his senses for two blocks, just as it always had. He went in the boss's office and looked up at him. "I can work," he said sadly.

"All right, Paolo, you can come back to work. Too bad it didn't work out for you, but you're a good worker and I'll always have work for you. Let's pray that it will continue this way."

Paolo picked up his bag of tools and went to his usual workbench. One by one he took out chisels of all sizes for different kinds of work. They slid from his hand to the bench making a dull sound. Then he looked for the foreman. He put Paolo to work on a large piece of granite that was going to be used in a government building downtown. And so he began again.

———————————

Lino did not have a settled mind, settled enough to go to school. He wondered how long his father would have to wait before he got his full pension for silicosis. He remembered every detail of that hearing, from Mrs. Grimaldi's black dress to her tears. He remembered her look of exasperation when the little state lawyer whittled her testimony down as far as he could. "A widow with four children," Lino said. "What a rotten deal she got." He wondered if he should become a doctor instead of a lawyer, then maybe he could help his own kind in a different way. Not like that union lawyer who used words like "obfuscate," "preternatural," words Lino felt he was using only to confuse him. But Lino would not be sidetracked, he went home and looked up each word that the lawyer used, vowing to use them in the lawyer's presence in the future. His hate was also reserved for the little State lawyer, a non-descript man, short, wearing a blue suit, with a big wave in his hair. On him, it looked silly, but he certainly had bit hard when he started in on Lino's father.

At school instead of playing punch ball with his friends at recess, Lino sat in the shadows thinking about his father. Is this what's waiting for him at the end of the line? All those years of work and then a pint-sized lawyer with a tricky way of using words just erased it. Years that his father breathed in fine granite powder until it filled the tiny sacs in his lungs so that when he climbed stairs he had to stop every three steps to catch his breath. His father's color had started going from a florid red to a slight grey, something Lino was troubled to see.

Monday to Friday, Paolo made the long trip to the Bronx and back. As he chiseled, he hummed operatic arias to himself. Once he raised his voice so high in a rendition from Aida that all the work stopped and the workers stared at him. The foreman, who was working at his own workplace, looked at him. "Paolo, you all right?"

"Of course I all right," Paolo said, but he was embarrassed at the same time. To break the tension, the foreman said smiling, "Hey, guys, we got a star here," and everyone went back to work.

Everyday that Paolo went to work he hummed the opera tunes that he knew. Sometimes he would take an entire opera and go through it under his breath, humming and occasionally waving his hands as if he were conducting the opera. In the subway car, people noticed and made comments. They had seen everything on the subway. Out on the street Paolo would continue but he usually ended his operatic recital as he walked into the stone yard.

Saturdays, Paolo sat by the radio listening to the opera as he had done for years. The music transported him to faraway places like Africa, Paris, Rome. He knew the scores from German and Russian operas, though he didn't know how to speak the languages he remembered some of the words. At night, he dreamed that he was in a concert hall and when the curtain came down at the end, he bowed just like the great singers. He awoke refreshed, having dreamed that he was a tenor in an opera. Over the years, he and his brothers had gone to the Metropolitan Opera House to see the stars, including Caruso, Galli Curci, Rosa Ponselle and many others. He woke feeling like a great singer, and went to work with a willingness he had never felt before. One day as he sat in the subway car humming an aria, a fellow near him called out, "Hey, why don't you sing louder so we can enjoy your voice." At first, Paolo refused shaking his head. After a few more requests he stood up, his work clothes not yet dirty and the workday hat he carried clasped in his hands. "I sing first 'Recondita armonia,' from Tosca." He stood up in the swaying subway car and with a cracked voice, nothing like the voice he heard in his head, sang the aria from beginning to end. By the time he got to the end his voice had broadened into a full-blown sound. At the end people clapped and he sat down, feeling like he had been on the stage.

Some of the people on the subway did not look fondly at him. A fellow at the far end of the car whispered to someone near him, "Some guinea singing songs at this hour of the morning! He must be crazy." Other days, when he got on the subway car, he looked around and if he saw someone smile at him, he'd say, "You want mo' music? I sing, *La Traviata*." He would stand and sing until he arrived at his stop in the Bronx. His life had become all music and opera. Everywhere he went he sang and people even threw money at him for his performance. He rejected it saying, "I no sing fo' money, I sing fo' love."

One Saturday morning when Paolo and his son went to downtown Manhattan, Paolo began his singing act. Lino sat in the subway car humiliated and stunned. He knew that his father loved music but it never went beyond humming tunes at home. Paolo got up and asked, "What opera you wanna hear? You tell me, an' I sing." Lino tugged at his father's sleeve. "Pop, what are you doing?

"What I'm doin'? I sing fo' the people."

People threw coins around Paolo's feet but he ignored the money. Lino accompanied his father as he went from store to store downtown singing an aria in each place. That night Lino took his uncle aside. "*Zio*, I think that Pop's gone crazy."

"What you mean?"

"Do you know that everywhere he goes he sings opera? When I was with him today, we went to downtown Manhattan to buy work shirts. The minute he got on the subway car he began to sing opera. I don't know. I am afraid that all that stuff with the union and the compensation has made him a little crazy."

"Don't talk like that," his uncle snapped. "Remember, he's your father."

"I know that, *Zio*, but at the same time he's in the subway car singing at the top of his lungs, and what's worse is that he can't really sing. He has no voice and what he doesn't know is that the people there are laughing at him, not applauding him for having a good voice. Some of them even say outright that he's crazy. I know because I heard them. And you should see how they throw pennies at him when he sings. It was killing me."

Even Francesco had to acknowledge that the singing had gotten out of hand. He sat down to discuss it with his brother. "What the hell are you doing going around singing your head off everywhere you go?" Francesco asked him.

"I love opera and I love to sing opera," Paolo answered.

"But you are singing every minute of the day! You go to the store and you sing opera, you go to work and you sing opera. Why do you have to sing opera all the time?"

Paolo got up and sang a lovely aria from La Bohème, off key, but the essence of it came through.

"Let me tell you something. Everybody is saying that Paolo Falcone has gone crazy. Now I am beginning to think the same thing. At work I hear that you stand there singing opera. You go to the chicken market and you sing opera. When is it going to stop?" Francesco asked.

There was only one thing for Francesco to do. He would go see Dr. Crocetto, whose wisdom he trusted and accepted unreservedly.

"I think he's crazy, and I just don't know what to do," Francesco told Dr. Crocetto.

The doctor thought a minute. "I'll talk to him."

Paolo was in the waiting room, and he sang the whole time. The secretary did not know what to do. The doctor peered out of his room and asked Paolo to come in. Humming, he walked in the door, inhaling the antiseptic smell of the room.

"Paolo, dear friend, how are you, how have you been?" the doctor asked.

"I am fine and I am waiting for the letter to say I'm disabled and cannot work no more, so I pass the time singing. Now everybody starting to think that I go crazy. How can you be crazy when you sing the arias of Giuseppe Verdi and Giacomo Puccini? That's what I tell them when they look at me funny."

"When did you have that hearing?"

"Oh, must be a couple months ago, I think," Paolo answered.

"Paolo, do you have any complaints about the body, I mean do you have headaches, fever, anything like that?"

"No, doctor, I don't have no fever, I feel all right."

That night, Francesco talked with his wife and sister-in-law about Paolo. Going to Dr. Crocetto hadn't done anything special, except that the doctor said that if this continued for the next month, Francesco should come again to see him to take special measures. Francesco thought that the next thing to do was to contact the union lawyer to see if they could get another hearing.

In his office the lawyer told Francesco that these things take time, that there was no way to move his case up on the calendar, that they had to have a hearing in which they called in doctors—for both sides, he noted—and other testimony so that they could try to get a better decision. Leaving the office, Francesco did not think that anything was going to get done. Francesco told Paolo's wife, who sat down and cried.

"Never, never in my whole life" she said, "did I ever think that something like this would ever happen. I went to see the priest," she said, "and he said that we should go to the doctor."

"I think that we gotta go back and see Dr. Crocetto," Francesco said.

Once again they trudged to Manhattan and Francesco sat next to his brother who sang his arias all the way. He was embarrassed by Paolo's behavior but knew that he should be loyal, so he acted as though nothing was happening. All around them the people smiled or laughed outright.

Dr. Crocetto examined Paolo for any physical ailment that he might have.

"Sometimes a physical illness can trigger this kind of behavior," he said as he tapped at Paolo's chest. "Nothing. I see nothing here as a cause for this behavior," Dr. Crocetto said tersely. "I am afraid that he should see a psychiatrist."

"Does that mean that he is crazy?" Francesco asked.

"No, it does not have to mean that. It can mean that he is going through a difficult period, a situational thing, and this is the manifestation of it."

"Doctor, will this psy…psy.…"

"A psychiatrist is a doctor of the mind. He can help your brother," and he made an appointment for him to bring his brother to this mind doctor.

The psychiatrist had an Italian name, Grosso, and that reassured Francesco. Dr. Grosso, a middle aged man with graying hair, called Paolo in, and indicated with his hand that Francesco should wait in the waiting room. His brother was in the office with this doctor for a long time. After about an hour both emerged. The doctor asked Paolo to wait while he talked with Francesco.

"Mr. Falcone, I am afraid that your brother is mentally ill," he said flatly.

"You mean he's crazy?"

"Well, the word 'crazy' can mean a lot of things, and it can mean nothing. You mentioned on the phone that he had been turned down for worker compensation for a pulmonary disease, didn't you? Well, that disappointment may have triggered this behavior. It's not what I would call normal behavior."

"Is there some medicine that he can take for this that would set him right?"

"Not really. This behavior is a form of depression," the doctor said.

Francesco did not know what he meant by depression or how this applied to his brother.

"Mr. Falcone, I am going to suggest that he be placed in a psychiatric hospital for observation and for any further treatment that he might need."

"You want me to send my brother to the crazy house?" Francesco asked.

"We don't call it that. It is a hospital that treats people with mental illnesses or disorders. I am saying," and he stopped for a moment, "I am saying that it would be best for him to go there and be under observation so that he is not exposed to any harm from his condition."

Francesco was completely flustered. The thought of his brother being put in mental hospital, or, as he knew it the crazy house, was more than he could stand. How could he go home and tell Paolo's wife and son that their father is now going to the crazy house?

That night Francesco could not sleep because of this situation. First of all, Paolo would not have any income. But he quickly reassured himself that so long as he, Francesco, had an income, he would share it with his brother's family. They would not go begging. He called Giovanni. He was doing well with his store but he often had excuses to not go to his brothers' home for dinner. Giovanni said that he would also help his sister-in-law if Paolo had to go to the psychiatric hospital.

A letter arrived from Doctor Grosso which Francesco opened quickly. He read it and thought he had gotten the gist of it, but called young Lino to make sure that he understood it completely.

"My dear Mr. Falcone: It has become necessary for your brother, Paolo Falcone, to be temporarily hospitalized for a mental disorder. Please take this letter to the hospital at Kappewan, Long Island, and present it to the department of incoming patients. The personnel there will then become responsible for Paolo Falcone's stay. I am hoping that this time at the hospital can give your brother the much needed care which his condition calls for. Respectfully yours, William Grosso, M.D."

Francesco read it over and over again until he understood what it meant. He and Lino discussed the contents of the letter and then sat down with Paolo's wife to see when they were going to take his brother to the hospital. From the other side of the house they could hear Paolo singing "Che gelida manina" from La Bohème. Francesco could not hold back any more. He broke down crying and babbling in his tears. He felt that he would be committing a sin of treachery in not telling Paolo the truth about what they were doing with him. Francesco did not know what he was going to do about this. Lino looked at his uncle and said,

"*Zio*, he's my father, and I am old enough to take him to the hospital. I can do that, you know. I'll take him."

"I better call Giovanni and see if he can drive him to the hospital," Francesco said. But Giovanni said he was too busy, that they had better call a cab or simply bring him there on the train. Francesco was terribly disappointed. Now when he needed help, his own brother, Giovanni, could not find the time from his money-making to bring his brother to the hospital.

"That's all right, *Zio*, I'll take him," Lino said.

During the week, Francesco and Lino talked again and again about how they would take his father to the hospital.

On the day that Paolo was to go to the hospital his wife laid out his clothing. His underwear was impeccably clean, and his clothing was the clothing that he wore on feast days and for the occasional mass that he attended. Francesco and Paolo's family decided that they would not tell him where he was going because they did not think that he truly understood what was happening. Francesco, with tears rolling down his cheeks, kissed his brother good-bye. Paolo's wife was in the other room crying. Lino and his father headed for the subway. Singing as always, Paolo walked with Lino holding his hand. Lino looked straight ahead. The people on the Long Island Railroad apparently had never had someone sing to them as they rode along. Paolo was in better voice than usual. He was well-dressed and still a handsome man. On and on Paolo's voice accompanied the wheezing and puffing of the train. The conductor called out the station, Kappewan.

It was a long walk uphill to the hospital. Surrounded by a wrought iron fence, it could be a big hotel, Lino thought. He led his father to the big entrance doors. He saw nurses and doctors inside, all of them holding clip-boards. What kind of a place are they sending my father to? he wondered. Lino approached "Incoming Patients" desk. He produced Dr. Crocetto's letter.

"All right, I see. What is your relation to the patient?" the clerk asked?

"He's my father," Lino said.

"Are you authorized to sign papers in his name?"

Lino wasn't sure but said yes.

Lino went to a bench, sat down with his father and began to fill out the admission papers. There were some questions he did not understand but continued to fill out what he did know. He went from question to question and at the end he signed his name in his schoolboy's handwriting.

Lino handed it back to the woman at the desk, who looked it over, line by line occasionally asking Lino a question. At the end, she signed it and said, "Now we are going to take your father to the ward where he will be staying. You can go home."

This was the part that Lino was dreading. He didn't want to cry because it might upset his father. "Pappa, these people are going to help you," he said. "Mamma and me and Uncle Francesco will come and see you lots." He could barely finish the sentence as the tears started. "Good-bye, Pappa."

An attendant led Paolo away through the door. Lino heard his father sing "Recondita armonia" in the distance. Lino walked out of the hospital, down the hill and to the train station.

That was to be the last he would hear of his father's voice. Two weeks later, Lino and his mother were informed that Paolo had died. They said, "all of a sudden he stopped singing, sat back, and died."

Giovanni's business prospered. He hired more workers to do the jobs that he had insisted on doing himself. Things could not have been better for him.

Andrea was approximately the same age as Paolo's son, Lino. They used to see each other at holidays but in the last few years Giovanni had claimed that he didn't have the time or that they had been invited elsewhere. When Paolo was alive, both brothers had felt hurt that Giovanni found other things more important than being with his family on Christmas or Easter. The brothers' wives had never liked Ada so they were not disappointed but the brothers were. Giovanni had helped with Paolo's medical expenses and continued to help his widow by sending over a bag of groceries every now and then. Gone was the warmth that came with being together on important holidays and sitting down after a big dinner to play cards or tell stories over coffee and fruit.

The model for Giovanni's success was Filippo. By now Filippo was succeeded by his daughter and her husband, an American who had no clear idea of what it took to run a business. Whenever Giovanni had a business question, he always went to see Filippo in his luxurious house. There, accompanied by a good bottle of wine, they discussed business affairs. By now Giovanni had acquired a very nice house, bought a new car each year and paid for private schooling for Andrea. Giovanni would on occasion complain about what it cost to send Andrea to these

Catholic schools but never failed to bring it up publicly, proud that he could afford the expense.

With his business flourishing, Giovanni started taking things a little easier. He let a trusted employee deposit the daily cash in the bank or go to the market to purchase the cheeses, salamis and other items. Down the street from where his store was located was the widow, Minerva, a buxom, jolly lady of obscure origin. Sometimes she said she was from Italy, around Venice and Trieste, sometimes from Austria, Switzerland or even Yugoslavia. Having been widowed for some time now, she fastened her attention on Giovanni because he was such a charming man with a quick wit. She tittered at his jokes. She would call in an order of groceries and then ask if he could have it delivered.

"Have it delivered? But of course, my dear lady, I personally will deliver it to you," he said. He would take the car and then park at least a block and a half away from her house and walk there.

The first time he did this she was so happy to see him she invited him in and offered him cookies. "These must be from Alexander's grocery store, they are so stale," she said and then they both laughed. This became a weekly ritual and each time he managed to stay longer, until he could be counted on to be away at least an hour before he returned to the store. He grumbled that the help must have robbed him blind by now, but still, each week he went to visit her. The visits became more intimate.

One day, as she offered him pastries she leaned over him, and he could see her ample bosom. Giovanni wondered each time whether he should be a little bolder. This time as she leaned over, he reached for a pastry and grazed her breast, which sent an electric shiver down his back. She acted as though nothing had happened. Giovanni could no longer stop himself and when she leaned forward a bit more he kissed her on the ear lobe. She giggled and blushed. Giovanni kissed her on the lips. Her breasts were heaving and her eyes were closed as Giovanni, by now completely excited, put his arms around her and led her into the bedroom. One piece at a time Giovanni removed her clothing. He was still in his work apron. He undressed as fast as he could until he was next to her completely naked. He looked at her body which was round and smooth and offered no resistance to his advances. After that, the visits became more frequent. Sometimes, at night, he told his wife that he had to work on the books at the store. He would go to Minerva's place and they would make love.

His dalliances with the widow Minerva were only a small part of the new Giovanni. He was invited to go to the track with another grocer, the Neapolitan, Rizzo, and from then on at least once a week he went to the track and bet on the horses. For Giovanni, this was truly a luxury to be able to be a bit careless with his money. The two would dress up and drive out to the track in Long Island and spend the day analyzing racing forms. They bet on each race. Sometimes Giovanni lost as much as a hundred dollars but this didn't bother him. He made one hundred dollars in an hour working in his store. At home Ada would see him all dressed up and asked where he had been. "Doing business in Long Island," he would answer.

Andrea, now teen-aged, had developed into a strong and handsome boy. He had proven to be an adept pupil at Our Lady of Hope High School. Giovanni would puff out his chest and talk about "my boy, Andrea" who had won a prize for mathematics and was an athlete of promise.

One summer, Ada asked Giovanni if she could go to Italy. Thinking of the widow Minerva, he agreed that the summer was the best time. Maybe he could even join her for a short vacation. "But you know my help. No matter how much I like and trust them, they would probably rob me blind."

"Then, you better stay here. Andrea and I could go for a few weeks, months maybe, and we will see everybody," she answered.

"For me my parents and my aunt are dead. My little sister Filomena has married a union bigwig in Giovinazzo. Besides her, who else is there for me to see?"

"Make up your mind," Ada said. "because I have to make the arrangements. I was thinking, it would be nice for Andrea to have a friend with him."

"A friend?"

"Yes, he's a grown boy, and the things that interest me no longer interest him. Why don't we take his cousin Lino with us? After all, they are poor and this will be a treat for him." Giovanni thought this over. It was true and he acknowledged it. He didn't do very much for his brother's wife and family since Paolo died. He continued sending her a bagful of groceries once a week, but he never gave her any money. "Lino is a fine boy and our Andrea would feel good about having his cousin with him," Ada said.

"Let's think about it. We don't want to do anything that might turn out to be a precedent, you know what I mean?"

"Giovanni, why are you so tight with money when it comes to your family?"

"Listen, during the war, they were here in the United States and we were in Europe going through a lot of suffering. Why didn't they take care of themselves? When we came to America, look what we did." He waved his hand around the house to show his wealth and accomplishments. "We worked and made something of ourselves."

"This is a stupid comparison. They had their trade and they worked at it as best as they could. Then your brother got sick in the lungs and died. What can they do now?"

Giovanni thought about it and said to her, "You, Andrea and Lino can go for a month, and I will join you for a two-week vacation. After all, how much can they steal from me in two weeks?"

———————

The day of their departure arrived. When they were all inside the terminal and their bags and passports and tickets had been checked, they sat silently. It was there at this moment that Giovanni regretted not going with his family, but he reminded himself that he would be meeting them in Rome for two weeks toward the end of their stay.

Looking around, he noticed others speaking Italian. He wondered how they had made out in America. He recalled that just a few days ago he had the old store sign taken down and a new one, a neon one, put in its place. The salesman had convinced him that a neon sign could be on all night, and anyone driving or walking by would see it at any hour. "Giovanni's Dairy and Delicatessen." From the front window you could see the cheeses hung from the ceiling like columns, hams and salamis circling the perimeter. The strong smell of meats and cheeses attacked the senses of the customers the second they stepped in through the door. Behind the counter the clerks wore sparkling white aprons with the name "Giovanni's Dairy" embroidered on the pocket. All of this flashed before his eyes as he looked at the other passengers.

When the departure was announced, Giovanni got up, kissed Ada and the children. Lino whispered in his uncle's ear, "*Grazie, Zio, grazie,*" to which Giovanni waved his hand away. "*Niente, niente, figlio bello.*"

Back at the parking lot he got in the car and drove home, first stopping to visit the widow Minerva.

In Rome, it was a pleasure for Ada to hear people speaking Italian, not like in New York where all she heard were Southern Italian dialects and other foreign languages. Her sisters-in-law thought her proud and haughty. They thought she looked down on everything Italian in New York. "Let her go back to her own city and country if she doesn't like it here," Francesco's wife used to say. Ada did feel different and superior. Even Giovanni saw how she maintained a distance from her sisters-in-law.

Although Ada's parents had died some time ago she went back to her town outside of Rome. She saw that what had been a lovely small town deriving its income from grapes, figs, and almonds was now filled with tall apartment houses. She did not recognize any of the people.

In the back of her mind, she thought of Don Andrea and the Lentino hotel and restaurant nearby. She was dressed like a *signora*, not a country woman. Now she had gold bracelets and a large, diamond ring. She could have gone there and told them all to go to hell because she, Ada, who had been wronged by Don Andrea and by that clown, Carlo, had made good. She was Ada Falcone. The temptation to return and gloat was great.

When Giovanni comes, then we shall see if we go there or not, just to show them, she said to herself. But then, let the past be the past, it's all over, she said to herself.

Right now she and the boys were going all over Rome driven by a paid chauffeur. Andrea didn't remember Italy very well, since he was just eight years old when they left. It was a novelty to him, too. Lino felt slightly guilty, since his mother at home had to skimp and save and they were staying in a fine hotel, eating in expensive restaurants and seeing museums. It was very generous of his uncle to include him in this trip. It was going to make it more difficult listening to his mother talk against his aunt, the outsider, *la forestiera*.

When Ada was resting, the boys prowled around Rome. They'd get coffee and ice cream and stroll around Trastevere and over the bridge into the center of Rome.

On the main street, they saw three women who were made-up and flashily dressed. Their sleek clothes outlined their bosom and hips. The boys were taken by such beauty. One of the women looked Lino and Andrea over and gave a wink. "*Ciao, belli, che fate?*" Hey, boys, what are you doing?

"*Dove andate?*" Where are you going? the brunette asked. "*Volete fare un po' di musica?*" How about making a little 'music'? and they all laughed at this.

Andrea and Lino were excited to be with such cosmopolitan women. The girls they knew at school and in the neighborhood were just that, girls. These were women.

"*Venite, ragazzi, venite con noi,*" Come on, boys, come with us, they said. The two women took the boys by the arms. They went down the street into an old building, through a dark courtyard and up a floor. One of the women fumbled with her keys, cursing as she dropped them and then picked them up. They entered a dingy room.

"*Wey, ragazzi, eccoci qua,*" Here we are, the brunette said. "*Che vi pare, facciamo un po' d'amore?* What do you think? Want to make a little love? They went into different rooms. When they finished, the woman caressed Andrea's cheek. "*Beh, finito, eh?* Finished? "*Okay, bambino dammi due mila lire.*" Okay, kid, give me two thousand lire.

Andrea reached into his pocket and handed her some bills. He was truly in another world. She peeled off a few bills and returned the rest to him. "*Beh, finito. Bye-bye, come dicono a Hollywood. Bye-bye,*" "All through. Bye-bye, as they say in Hollywood. Bye-bye" she said and ushered him out of the room. At the same time Lino came out with the other woman.

Ada counted the days until Giovanni would come to meet them. She had grown used to being taken care of and felt at a loss without Giovanni to manage things. She waited for a letter, a telegram, anything that indicated when her husband would come.

While Ada rested in the hotel room one day she received a call. Through the crackling and static of the line she could hear her husband speak;

"*Ada, sono io.* It's me. Yes, everything is all right. Business is good, as usual. The usual things, you know."

Ada waited to hear what he was going to say about the visit.

"All right, now listen. Next Friday I am leaving from New York on the airplane and I arrive in Rome early the next day. Okay? Can you meet me at the airport? How are they doing?"

"They are having a great time. There is not a part of Rome that they have not explored. Frankly, I only see them supper time. But I know that they are enjoying themselves."

"Good. Listen, so next Friday, okay? Bye-bye now. I love you."

"I love you too. I miss you very much. Ciao."

On the day of Giovanni's arrival from New York, Ada told the boys that they had to be with her at the airport to receive Giovanni. "No disappearing for the day, understand?" she said.

"*Zio. Qui, qui.*" Uncle, here we are. Giovanni smiled as he saw them at the airport. They all embraced. Ada had tears in her eyes. They huddled together.

Giovanni looked out the window of the taxi, as the cab wove swiftly among cars and trucks on the autostrada.

"Where are the old buildings you used to see along this street?" he asked the driver. "Time passes. The old ways are no longer any good because in the old days, who had a car? Today everybody has a car," he said.

The Rome Giovanni remembered was plain, beautiful and uncomplicated. He remembered his walks here with Fabio and how each person they met looked into their faces with a shock of vitality. All that had changed. Back then he had very little money in his pocket. Now he had only to put his hand in his pocket to find as much money as he needed. Years ago with Fabio they were poor and it didn't cost anything to walk so they went from the station to the Forum and all over Rome on foot. Now when he walked, people spoke English to him and tried to sell him things. He answered, "*Ma, io sono italiano,*" But, I am Italian.

After seeing Rome, Giovanni was curious to return and to see Don Andrea's hotel and restaurant, the Lentino This was the wish that he had savored over and over at night when he couldn't fall asleep. Would those people recognize him? What had happened to Don Andrea and that pig, Carlo?

Giovanni hired a driver to take them to the Lentino. Giovanni remembered what it was like in the old days when you had to take a cart or if you were lucky you got one of the slow buses. It was bittersweet for Giovanni to come to this place that he had known during an important time of his life. The events here had brought about his break with his family and caused him to lose the love and the blessing of his father.

Giovanni began to feel uncomfortable. He was sweating and felt the sudden urge to get out of the confines of the car. The road curved, and he recognized it with a lurch in his stomach. The red poppies beside the road and the view of distant hills now made Giovanni breathe more heavily than usual. The Albergo e Ristorante Lentino looked smaller than he remembered.

Inside, the restaurant was now gaudy and velvet draped. They were led to a table and a man appeared. He was rotund, balding and wore a suit. Holding large menus, he came to the table with a false smile on his face. At the table he bowed to all, especially to Ada. When he referred to her as "*Signora,*" her face tightened.

"*Buon giorno, signori,*" he said. "How are we today?"

Giovanni recognized Carlo.

"*Buon giorno,*" Giovanni answered for them all.

"The *Signori* are from America?" he asked.

"Why do you say that?" Giovanni asked, as he felt his anger starting to rise. "We are from the South."

"The South!" Carlo exclaimed. "What a beautiful place. Once a year I go to the South, Bari, Brindisi and Taranto, just to get the sense of the place, of the sea and the countryside." He handed them menus. "And, of course, what wonderful people they have there! Country people are the salt of the earth."

Giovanni remembered how Carlo used to call him a *cafone,* a clod.

"Yes, country people are the salt of the earth," he repeated mechanically, studying Carlo's face. The mock uniform with the epaulets and gold buttons had been replaced by a neat and sedate business suit.

"Tell me," Giovanni said, "there was a fellow—the owner—his name was Don Andrea." That name made Ada blush.

"You knew Don Andrea?" Carlo said with astonishment. "You knew him? How?"

"My father had some business dealings with him. Is Don Andrea still here?" Giovanni asked.

"No, he died a little after the war. He had a daughter who is now my wife," Carlo said. "Yes, and we have three children. It was at the end of the war that we married. The government had fallen and all the politicians that Don Andrea knew, senators and generals they all disappeared. We married and I wished to continue the tradition of this business in spite of hard times. Food and supplies were hard to get. We barely scraped by. You see," and here he turned and pointed to the room with its faux Roman décor, "we have restored its old grandeur...So you knew Don Andrea?"

"Yes, I did," Giovanni answered.

"Those were the good old days," Carlo said with quiet melancholy. "In those days this place was one of the most popular in Rome. Nothing could compare to our kitchen."

"What ever happened to Mesiù?" Giovanni asked.

Carlo looked at him, his eyes squinting. "You knew Mesiù?" he asked. "Mesiù was from the time before the war, during the time of Mussolini. In fact, Mussolini used to come here with his friends and ministers."

Throughout this conversation Giovanni kept a straight face. "Mesiù was a tyrant in the kitchen, as I recall it," Giovanni said.

"But who are you that you knew Don Andrea, and Mesiù? I was here in those years," he burst out.

Throughout the conversation Ada recalled the pain that Don Andrea and Carlo had caused her. She looked at Carlo with icy eyes. The two boys were completely bored by the conversation. Giovanni stood up. Ada walked slowly around the table to Carlo and slapped him hard on the cheek. Carlo staggered for a second, tears in his eyes, looking at her for an explanation. The waiters watched the scene from their stations.

"That is for everything, you pig!" Ada said and they all walked out.

Andrea could not understand why his mother had done that. He turned to her and asked, "Why?

Ada looked straight ahead. "Someday I shall tell you," and then she paused and said, "or maybe I won't."

━━━━━━━━

They revisited Brindisi and everything Giovanni saw reminded him of some past experience. Don Beppe had given Giovanni a lot of chores to do and so he had seen the whole city. The city had its old port with ancient statues and buildings. Romans had once traveled the Via Appia and down to the sea on these wide steps at Brindisi. The Normans had used this port as a jumping-off point to the Holy Land for the Crusades. The buildings maintained a muted dignity from the grey of their granite. Even then, Giovanni thought, they must have needed granite workers to cut the stones and put them in place. He got an eerie feeling from this old part of town. The restaurant Bella Napoli had closed they found out.

The tourist role did not fit Giovanni. He found himself handing out money all the time for gifts, taxis and waiters. He began getting edgy. He wanted to get back to work. They left soon after for New York.

━━━━━━━━

At the store he found things all in their places; nothing seemed out of order. He sat down with his accountant and for a day they went over the figures of sales, receipts, inventory. The business had grown and Giovanni had the feeling that he had achieved the height of his success.

Andrea told him that Uncle Francesco was not feeling well. He was complaining of a pressure in his chest, and he had a lot of trouble climbing stairs. He went to Doctor Crocetto who reminded him that forty some years of cutting granite was now beginning to show its full effects on him. Just like his brother, Francesco started to slip. He had to stop working and was waiting for his own hearings. Unlike his brother, he didn't go around singing. Francesco stayed home and read the newspaper or listened to the radio. He heard that the Americans went to the Far East to fight a war. He couldn't imagine what war there was to fight out there. But he did worry because his nephews Andrea and Lino were reaching the age where they could be called to the army. With a war going on in a place called Korea, there was enough to worry about.

Giovanni received an urgent phone call from Lino. "Uncle, come quickly. Uncle Francesco was brought to the hospital last night. He couldn't breathe and we called the ambulance. His wife is worried sick."

"Where is he now?" Giovanni asked.

"He's at the hospital near here, the Mount Sinai hospital," Lino answered.

"Lino, right now I am very busy, but I shall get to the hospital as soon as I can," Giovanni said.

"My mother is worried sick. She doesn't know what to do. Her sister is no help since her husband died. Could you please get there right away?"

"I'll do my very, very best," Giovanni answered.

He waited until the noon rush ended, and then he hung up his apron and started for the hospital. He thought about how both brothers were felled by silicosis and he was glad that he had given up the stone trade. He wove through traffic. At the hospital, he parked his car and went in. He noted the clean smell of the hospital, but for him it was also the smell of death. Every time he had gone to a hospital, someone died shortly after.

When he got to the room his brother was in, he knocked lightly. Francesco's wife opened the door.

"I thought you'd never get here," she said, her voice full of worry.

"I got here as soon as I could," Giovanni answered.

"I am afraid he is going to die," she said and began to sob.

"What do you mean, die? He's as healthy as a horse. He was always strong, stronger than our brother who died. Francesco's going to end his days relaxing around the house and tending to his garden in the summer," Giovanni answered but without conviction. "What has the doctor said?"

"He says that all the years he spent as a granite cutter have taken their toll. The stone dust has accumulated in his lungs and it prevents him from breathing well enough to live. So you see, he's going to die," she continued crying.

"I got to talk to the doctor. Maybe if he went to a place like Arizona where the air is better and dry he could regain his health in his lungs," Giovanni said.

"No, no. He said that the stone dust damage is permanent and it can't be fixed with something like going away."

"For heaven's sakes, woman, there has got to be a solution," Giovanni said.

After he left the hospital, Giovanni went to the widow's house and spent the afternoon there with her, comforting himself in her bosom. He told her about his brother's sickness, and that he would probably die. He also told her that he and a sister in Italy were the two last ones left in the family. He was beginning to feel fear. She tried to comfort him but he remained distant and lost in his thoughts.

Later in the week, Giovanni received a phone call from his nephew Lino that his uncle had died that morning. The wake would be the next day at Gallo's Funeral Home in the neighborhood.

Giovanni felt the weight of this loss come down on him. He drove over immediately to his brother's house. On the door was nailed a small wreath of flowers and on a ribbon there was written on a piece of paper, "Rest in Peace." Until then, his brother's death seemed remote, but now it hit him.

Inside, Francesco's daughters were gathered around their mother, trying to assuage her pain. Giovanni felt like a stranger in his brother's house. The windows and curtains were shut and he was closed in with the sound of sobbing.

On the day of the funeral mass, Giovanni was in the store doing inventory. He counted assiduously every item, making sure that all was accounted for. He wasn't going to be made a fool of. He knew in his heart that his helpers were stealing from him in some way. Once a worker had sliced cold cuts and then put them in wax paper and into his shirt. Giovanni found out when the worker leaned over and the wax paper started to slip out of his shirt.

They started in one corner of the storeroom where the cans of tomatoes were stacked and slowly worked their way through the canned beans and spaghetti. All in all, it took up most of his morning. It was noon when he realized that he had forgotten his brother's funeral mass at church.

Giovanni's business continued to prosper, keeping his family well housed and fed. He kept the widow Minerva happy with his frequent visits. His life remained the same, without any changes. Each day the newspapers spoke about a conflict in the Far East, a conflict that Giovanni did not understand.

"What the hell do I know about what's going on in that part of the world?" he mumbled to himself. Each day there were new happenings in something called the U.N. Here at home the law said all able-bodied citizens at the age of eighteen had to register for the draft. Andrea first, then his cousin Lino had gone to the post office for the proper papers, filled them out, and sent them in to the government. Giovanni shrugged his shoulders at it. He remembered how he was supposed to go to the Italian army, a call which he ignored and was never the worse for it. He suggested that Andrea and Lino forget about it and think about going to school. They both were headed for college and Lino reiterated his wish to become a lawyer. Andrea didn't have any particular ambition beyond high school but his father hounded him about going to school to better himself.

"You didn't go to college," Andrea said, "and you did okay."

"My situation was different. I had no opportunities so I had to move my ass to do something for you and your mother." Andrea was willing to go to college if it would please his parents that much. He thought he would end up one day with his father's store and make the same kind of good living that his father did.

Each day the news was filled with talk of war on the far side of the globe, Korea. There were reports of American forces being stationed in Korea but neither Giovanni nor Ada paid attention. All they were interested in was their store, the store that had turned out to be a gold mine. They moved to a bigger house with a bigger pool. Giovanni mused, "who ever thought that I would have a house with a pool, a pool so big that to go from one end to the other takes more breath than I have left?" As a boy, in Giovinazzo he used to go to the Tre Colonne. These were columns of Greek origin that stood in the waves at the edge of the Adriatic. There he and his brothers jumped into the water. As they swam, they'd say that the first person to reach Albania would be king of the world. Giovanni stood at the edge of his long pool and thought about how he was the only one still alive of the four brothers. No one else could remember those long-ago times.

Giovanni and Ada bought a summer home with lots of acreage in New Jersey. He began to buy horses, cows, a pig and then chickens. A hired hand looked after the animals. Summers, on weekends, Giovanni and the family would go there to get away from the terrible heat of New York City. Now that Andy, as Andrea preferred to be called, was finished with high school and was old enough to run the business, Giovanni started to take more breaks. He knew that Andy had the interests of the business at heart. In fact, he became quite possessive of it. The workers often referred to him as the Boss. They understood that when his father was not there, the son was the Boss.

For a graduation gift, Giovanni gave Andy and his cousin Lino a trip to San Francisco. They had a grand time going to restaurants, visiting dance halls and getting to know loose women. In the bars, they saw men in uniform from the nearby army camps and an aviation base. For two weeks they lived like kings, thanks to Giovanni. Back in New York City, they often talked about those days.

Six months later, Andy was drafted into the army. Mobilization had become a necessity, or so said the president, to stop communism in the Far East. Giovanni was left with an empty and anxious feeling. His son was going to the army. Giovanni's recollections about war were not good but since this was America he didn't think that there would be the empty gestures and incompetence that he saw in Italy during the Second World War. Andy after all, would be a soldier of the biggest and most powerful nation in the world.

The night before he had to report for duty, Giovanni invited his sisters-in-law and children to join his family at a dinner at a famous Italian restaurant. By now, Giovanni and his family would often eat at restaurants. They ate like kings, from soup and antipasto to pastries, accompanied by the best wines and liqueurs. Giovanni liked going to these places where the owners recognized him and the waiters welcomed them, especially since Giovanni was known as a big tipper.

The dinner went very well, lots of good food and drink. The waiters fawned over them. Never did Giovanni feel better in his whole life. This was not the case for Ada. She had a bad feeling about letting her son go. Andy tried to enjoy the evening but knew that the next day he would go down to Court Street and be in the army. The news was about armies of Chinese and Koreans running over the land in the Far East but Andy didn't pay any attention to it. After all, America was the most powerful country in the world. Who could beat America? he thought.

"Forget all that stuff and enjoy what's on the table," Giovanni said.

At the end of the evening, people went to their homes. Giovanni settled into his big leather chair in front of his television set. He felt great.

Ada, her eyes red from tears she had shed all night long, made breakfast the next morning for Giovanni and Andy.

"For heaven's sakes, woman, he's going to be okay." Giovanni said but there was no reassuring her. All the memories from Andy's birth to this moment assaulted her mind. She would stop cooking for a moment, and then stand there her sobs like muffled gulps. "I don't like it. Anything can happen," she said.

Giovanni threw down his spoon. She was making his nerves worse.

—————————

At Court Street the family went to a big, grey building. Young men came straggling in. Some were accompanied by their families and stayed outside until it was absolutely necessary to go in. Andy and Giovanni stood there not knowing what to say to each other. Now Giovanni was feeling the weight of his own worry, as well as Ada's. Finally, Andy looked at his father.

"Okay, Pop, it's time to go." He hugged and kissed Giovanni and his mother and went through the door.

Inside, there were people in military uniform. Other draftees sat waiting. One or two of them read books, others just stared into space. All had heard stories about how brutal and difficult the first days would be. Andy saw no sign of such things, everyone seemed to be efficient and to the point.

———————————

"Dear Mamma and Pappa: Today marks a week that I have been in the army. After I left you, they got us together. Then they made us fill out a bunch of papers. Incidentally, I have put your names down for the army insurance as my heirs in case I am killed for whatever reason. Then we were given a physical examination. Time moved so slowly. We went from one desk to another filling out papers. Later that day, they put us on buses and brought us to Fort Dix, New Jersey. Actually that is not too far from New York City. If we ever get to have visitors, I'll tell you. That night they woke us up at three in the morning and we had to sweep and mop the floors of the barracks. I couldn't believe that they would wake us up at three in the morning. Well, I have to go now, so stay well. I miss you both. I'll be writing every chance I get to tell you about my experiences here. My best wishes to everybody, Love, Andy."

"Dear Mamma and Pappa: In the second week that we were in basic training we had to take long marches, wearing a full pack. At night my legs ached because I wasn't used to so much walking, especially with the pack on my shoulders. The food is not bad but it isn't what I am used to. We never eat any Italian food. It's always potatoes, potatoes for breakfast, potatoes for lunch and potatoes for supper. There is always meat, but never any pasta. I see now how lucky I was to have you as my parents. We always had a lot of good food to eat, but there are people here that never ate as well as I have so now they eat like lions. One guy told me that the army is the first time he had three meals a day and I think it is true. There are a lot of colored people here. I have never been that close to colored people. They seem okay, but some people don't like being around them, especially since they have to shower and eat that close to them. Me? It doesn't bother me. Next week we are going to learn to shoot a rifle. It's called an M1. I've seen it but I have never shot one. It makes a terrible, loud noise. I gotta go now, we have a class this afternoon. It's not like regular school. Here they show movies about army things and mostly people sleep during the movie because we are up all night doing crazy things. Andy."

"Dear Mamma and Pappa: We learned how to shoot the rifle. It was noisy, but I did okay. They said that I qualified to be a rifleman. They also said that I will get to wear a medal on my uniform for it. Everyday we do the same thing. We get up early, very early, clean the barracks then we go out for inspection. After inspection we have breakfast, which is good because by then I am very hungry. Lots of eggs and bacon, which I am starting to like. We are starting to hear rumors that we'll go to Korea, but nobody knows for sure. So the sergeant said that we should count on going to Korea. Also, they gave us instructions on how to use the gas mask. I never figured what it was good for, but they brought us to a room in a special barrack. They made us put the gas mask on outside, and then when we went inside they ordered us to take it off. The room was filled with tear gas so we started crying. Tears were coming out fast and then we started coughing and spitting. Some guys got very sick, but I just cried and coughed. After, we went outside and finished crying and coughing. Later, I felt better. What an experience! Your loving son, Andy."

"Dear Mamma and Pappa: Next week basic training is over. We were told that we are going to Korea. A guy that just came back from there said that it was very cold there in the winter. We're supposed to go to a school to learn an army job, but the sergeant said that the army needed people to fight against the Korean communists. I never met a communist, so I don't really know what they are all about. But they are supposed to hate America and Americans. Since I am American, sort of, I am supposed to hate them. They taught us how to use a bayonet, and the sergeant in charge said that when we pushed the bayonet we should think that we are killing a communist. I don't know. I just want to get out alive and come home to work with Pappa in the store. Love, Andy."

"Dear Mamma and Pappa: I am on a ship and we left from Seattle, Washington. That's a far part of the United States. It's right next to Canada. After we got here on trains we were put on buses and sent to a barracks in a camp there, a really big camp, maybe bigger than Fort Dix. We wanted to go to town, but they wouldn't let us. The rumor was that since we were supposed to go to Korea a lot of American soldiers were sneaking into Canada and staying there because they didn't want to go to Korea to fight in the war. It sounds crazy to me. Love, Andy."

"Dear Mamma and Pappa: I am in Korea. A guy said that tomorrow he is going to get his camera and take pictures of us. When I get the picture I'll send it back to you. It is very cold here. We wear heavy field jackets and a hat that makes me look like a Russian. If you lose your gloves you will probably freeze your fingers off. We live in a great big tent with a heater in it so we won't freeze. Boy, does it get cold. Tomorrow we are going on a special assignment and I can't tell you about it otherwise it wouldn't be a secret. We are supposed to go see where the Koreans are. They are like the Russians except they have slanty eyes. That's what they told us. I miss you a lot. Tell Lino I will tell him everything about the army when I get back. There are lots of things to know so that it won't be hard for him. Well, I've got to go. I love you and miss you, especially those great sandwiches that Pappa makes in the store for me. What I wouldn't give for a sandwich like that. The other day they served something and said it was Italian. It's called chili. I don't know. I never had anything like that. Beans, chopped meat and they throw some macaroni into it and tomatoes. I never heard of any Italian dish called chili. Well, I gotta get my gloves, big gloves with fur inside of them. It gets very cold here, maybe even colder than New York City. Love, Andy."

———

"It is with great regret that I must send you this letter. Your son, Private First Class Andrea Falcone was killed in action on April 16th, 1953, in the battle of Pork Chop Hill. This was a major battle of the war and after he made a brave attempt to go over a hill to throw a hand grenade against the enemy he was shot and died instantly.

"Your son will also be remembered by his buddies for his good humor. They loved him a lot and they affectionately called him the Little Guinea because he was Italian. In fact, he always was talking about being Italian.

I am sure that you are proud to have such a son. He will long be remembered by all.

Regretfully yours,

Allan B. Richard, Second Lieutenant,

United States Army."

PART IX

Giovanni sat by the pool outside his house watching the play of light at sunset. A quiet breeze made slight waves in the pool. Since Andrea's death in the war, he and Ada said little to each other. Giovanni lost his ardor for the Widow Minerva who often came to the store asking for him. His mind was elsewhere. He began to close his eyes and could hear his own light snoring as his head lowered to his chest.

He was back in Giovinazzo walking through the cemetery. It was starting to get dark and he saw a figure down a row of headstones. It was a man dressed in black with a black hat who walked toward Giovanni.

"Who are you?" Giovanni called out and realized it was his father. "Pappa, is that you?" Giovanni's feelings were of doubt and puzzlement. "Is that you?"

"Yes, Giovanni, I am your father, Mastro Paolo."

"Pappa, I'm lost. I don't know where to turn or go."

"Many years ago you lost your way and couldn't find the way home. You became a different person." His father's hat spread a shadow over his face and Giovanni would have liked to kiss his face.

"Pappa, I made my own way. There was no coming back to the old way," Giovanni said.

"Yes, my son. You broke our hearts," he said.

His father stood by a stone, one that he had cut and carved. He felt the polished stone. "We all died of broken hearts," he said.

Then Giovanni saw the sea at Giovinazzo. He could hear voices, yells and happy screams. He walked in the direction of the noise. There he saw his brothers, Silvio, Francesco, and Paolo. They were at the Three Columns diving into the water and swimming out beyond the breakers, with Silvio calling out to his brothers, "Don't go too far. It can be dangerous."

Giovanni wanted to go there and join them. "Silvio, Francesco, Paolo," he yelled but they couldn't hear him. Giovanni tried calling out again but he woke with a start.

By that time it had gotten completely dark and he could only see shards of light in the pool. Giovanni got up and walked inside to comfort Ada.

THE END